continued . . .

"Sunny's fascinating story has interesting characters and a rather unusual origin. There are shape-shifters, blood drinkers, a heroine who's an unexpected unique queen, some bloody violence, and a fair amount of sex."

—*Romantic Times*

MONA LISA AWAKENING

"Darkly erotic, wickedly clever, and very original!"

—Bertrice Small,
New York Times bestselling author of *Sudden Pleasures*

"A terrific debut sure to appeal to fans of Anne Bishop or Laurell K. Hamilton . . . Sunny's characters stayed with me long after I finished the book."

—Patricia Briggs, *New York Times* bestselling author

"A spellbinding tale full of erotic sensuality and deliciously fascinating characters."

—Lori Foster, *New York Times* bestselling author

"A refreshing, contemporary urban erotic horror thriller that grips the audience." —*The Best Reviews*

"A lively writer . . . Erotica fantasy that is fresh, engaging and a damn fun read . . . sizzling sex scenes."

—*Sensual Romance Reviews*

LUCINDA, DARKLY

Book One of the Demon Princess Chronicles

"An awesome story populated with endearing and sexy characters. This unabashedly sensual gothic story will feed your need for something new and fresh. Readers will be loath to put the book down until the final page is read. . . . The ending will leave you hungry for more."

—*Romantic Times*

MONA LISA DARKENING

A NOVEL OF THE MONÈRE

SUNNY

BERKLEY BOOKS, NEW YORK

THE BERKLEY PUBLISHING GROUP
Published by the Penguin Group
Penguin Group (USA) Inc.
375 Hudson Street, New York, New York 10014, USA
Penguin Group (Canada), 90 Eglinton Avenue East, Suite 700, Toronto, Ontario M4P 2Y3, Canada
(a division of Pearson Penguin Canada Inc.)
Penguin Books Ltd., 80 Strand, London WC2R 0RL, England
Penguin Group Ireland, 25 St. Stephen's Green, Dublin 2, Ireland (a division of Penguin Books Ltd.)
Penguin Group (Australia), 250 Camberwell Road, Camberwell, Victoria 3124, Australia
(a division of Pearson Australia Group Pty. Ltd.)
Penguin Books India Pvt. Ltd., 11 Community Centre, Panchsheel Park, New Delhi—110 017, India
Penguin Group (NZ), 67 Apollo Drive, Rosedale, North Shore 0632, New Zealand
(a division of Pearson New Zealand Ltd.)
Penguin Books (South Africa) (Pty.) Ltd., 24 Sturdee Avenue, Rosebank, Johannesburg 2196,
South Africa

Penguin Books Ltd., Registered Offices: 80 Strand, London WC2R 0RL, England

This is a work of fiction. Names, characters, places, and incidents either are the product of the author's imagination or are used fictitiously, and any resemblance to actual persons, living or dead, business establishments, events, or locales is entirely coincidental. The publisher does not have any control over and does not assume any responsibility for author or third-party websites or their content.

MONA LISA DARKENING

A Berkley Book / published by arrangement with DS Studios Inc.

PRINTING HISTORY
Berkley edition / January 2009

ISBN: 978-0-425-22647-6

BERKLEY®
Berkley Books are published by The Berkley Publishing Group,
a division of Penguin Group (USA) Inc.,
375 Hudson Street, New York, New York 10014.
BERKLEY® is a registered trademark of Penguin Group (USA) Inc.
The "B" design is a trademark of Penguin Group (USA) Inc.

PRINTED IN THE UNITED STATES OF AMERICA

10 9 8 7 6 5 4 3 2 1

To Annie Vanderbilt—
wonderful friend, extraordinary author

MONA LISA DARKENING

ONE

I T WAS THE first day of spring. It was also the time to Bask, to draw down the silver rays of the moon and let its renewing light seep into us. *Us* being the Monère, the children of the moon—what I was, what my people were. Creatures descended from another planet. We were blessed with supernatural speed, strength, and beauty. As a human-Monère Mixed Blood, the first ever to be a Monère Queen, I had the first two. Missed out on the last one, though. Oh well. Better to be fast and strong, in my opinion, than beautiful. And able to Bask, to draw down our home planet's renewing light and energy and share it with my people. Oh yes, that gift was perhaps the most crucial of all, and the one I was most thankful for. Because without that renewing light, we would live only a hundred years, a human's lifespan instead of the three hundred years our lunar birthright gifted us.

If you asked my people, I think they'd take the ability to Bask over their Queen being a raving beauty any day. Or rather night. As a people descended from the moon, we were children of darkness. When the sun set, that was when our day began. Then again, maybe you shouldn't ask my people, because even though my looks were average—not hideous, but definitely not beauty queen material either—they treated me as if I *were* a raving beauty. The men, at least. The men who were my lovers.

Under the moonlit shadows of the darkened night, I glanced at two of them there by my side. Amber, my rugged Warrior Lord, who loomed a head taller than other men. Whose great strength lay not just in the heavy muscles roping his massive body, but also in the love and devotion gleaming from his dark blue eyes. That—the pull of emotions in him—weakened me more than his obvious and splendid body strength, physically swayed me toward him before I caught myself. Not yet, I thought, but soon . . . soon.

Beside him stood Dontaine, my master at arms, my other lover, blond, fair of face and body, a sumptuous feast to the eyes. Whereas Amber looked like a harsh god of war, Dontaine was like a Greek statue—a Greek god. A living Adonis with sun-kissed hair, splendid green eyes, and a body any woman would want to worship with her hands, her tongue, her mouth . . . any part of her body. He, too, looked at me with love, though I don't know why. Out of all my lovers, he was the one I rejected the most. The one I used the most. Used literally for blood.

It was an odd night, a special night—the vernal equinox, *Aequus Nox*, which meant *equal night,* when day and night were of equal length, and the sun crossed not only the Earth's equator but the celestial equator as well. Even more special, it was one of the rare times when the full moon coincided with the first day of spring, the season of renewal. Perhaps that was what was causing this strange restlessness within me—a skittishness, a feeling of something not quite right. Spring fever likely.

My people were gathered around me, and I recognized more of their faces now, recalled their names. Intricate, interweaving strings bound us all together, and I was slowly learning the many loops and circles. I'd worried over that, my lack of connection to my people, over four hundred of them. But like many things in life, names and familiarity with the people behind the names came slowly with time, and hopefully—thankfully—I would have plenty of that. Time.

I had survived to see another full moon emerge in its brilliant round glory. Quite an achievement, tainted as I was with demon darkness. If the whims of fate had swung another way, I would have been dead by now, killed by Prince Halcyon, the ruler of the demon dead realm. Instead I was his lady, his mate—the High Lady of Hell.

And where was my Demon Prince? Presiding over his people in that other distant realm, Hell, while I presided over mine here in the living realm. I was missing the festivities of *Aequus Nox*, one of the big demon holidays. At least that was how it sounded to me when Halcyon had explained it. Were it not the full moon, the time when we Basked, I would be down there with Halcyon, mixing and mingling and being introduced to his people. A daunting thought because his people had fangs and drank blood—my blood if they had the chance. But then, so did I. Have fangs and drink blood, that is.

I was a human-Monère Mixed Blood Queen with demon dead essence residing in my living being. Quite a tongue twister and mind bender. The poetic term for my condition was *Damanôen*, demon living. A rare state of being because most of my kind had been slaughtered as soon as they were made, usually by the demons whom those very unwise Monères had blood raped because, alas, that was what sparked our living dead state. Why would they do that, you might ask—drink a demon's blood? Because it gained them a demon's strength, which was even greater than a Full Blood Monère's. But, shhh, don't tell anyone that, it's a secret. A secret that demons would kill—and have killed—to protect.

The downside, and there's always one, was the physical manifestations that occurred along with that stolen power. It was pretty hard to hide what you had done—what you had *become*—when you started sprouting fangs. Now don't get me wrong. Fangs are no stranger to the Monère. Lots of us had them. But only in our animal-shifted forms. Not in our human forms. Of course, my fang flashing happened only when the niggling presence of another demon triggered the demon essence in me. Then *wham!* It was like turning into the Incredible Hulk. Only instead of growing green and muscle-bound and horrendously ugly, my teeth morphed into fangs, my nails sharpened into dagger points, and I had the uncontrollable urge to suck down blood, any which way, any damn how. Pretty hard to keep hidden a powerful urge that almost takes you completely over until you've satisfied that hunger with a sip or two of blood. By the time you've gained back your control, the jig's pretty much up.

Halcyon had come up with an even better idea. Don't try to hide it. Simply make them think it had occurred for another reason, hence my official recognition as Halcyon's mate. When I finally manifested my demon traits in front of Monère witnesses (those that tattled, which was bound to occur someday soon), they would think that I was becoming what I was becoming because I'd been contaminated by my demon lover through sex. Sex, after all, was how Monère usually shared and acquired gifts and power. And since such a relationship had never occurred before—a demon taking a Monère mate—all would blame it on that. And perhaps on the fact that I'd been down to Hell a time or two.

The real cause of this all, though, was the former Queen of this Louisiana territory, Mona Louisa. She'd swallowed down Halcyon's blood, and I in turn had sucked her light and demon-tainted essence into me. That was another secret, what I could do, Mortal Draining. It made me feel guilty that the blame would be placed on the wrong person, on Halcyon instead of me and that former bitch Queen that no longer existed, except sometimes in me. Mona Louisa was dead but not entirely gone. I felt her occasionally in my dreams.

As a vulture in her other form, she'd been able to fly, and sometimes I dreamed of soaring through the sky, of smelling death and rotting, decaying flesh down below—carrion. Even more odd, outside of dreams, in my waking state, in my *demon* awakening state, my eyes changed from my normal brown to a cool crystal blue—Mona Louisa's eyes. A creepy thing, that.

I shrugged away my morbid thoughts and concentrated on the here and now: the full moon riding like a giant beacon of light above us, and my people waiting expectantly for me to draw down its life-extending rays. There was no real science to it. I just opened myself—best way to describe it. Every child of the moon felt that distinct pull when the moon came into its full and ripe roundness. It was like an invisible, tugging rope reaching down to try to open up a door inside of you. I simply stopped resisting and let whatever was being pulled inside of me flip open and become just a conduit . . . a conduit of lunar light. It shone down on me now like a spotlight, filled me up, filled me to bursting, then overflowed out from me.

Little butterflies of light flittered down from the heavens, swooped into me and spilled out like a cresting tide, washing over my people, darting into them, bowing their backs, lighting them up like flickering candles set aflame. We shone brilliantly for a long spun-out moment in time until that lunar light was swallowed and absorbed into us. Until we no longer glowed and skin became simply skin once more, not incandescent light, incandescent energy.

The last two times I'd done this, the *only* two times I'd done this, that was it. Over. *Finis*. Not so this time. This time was different. This time something hazed my vision. Something hazed the moon, actually, because that was what I was looking at.

Like a veil being thrown across its bright surface, a shimmering darkness swept across the moon like spilling ink, blocking out the light like an eclipse, only faster, much faster. It occurred in the blink of an eye, so fast that I almost doubted what I was seeing. *Would* have doubted it had I not felt it as well—a weight like a descending hand reaching down to cover me. Not that gentle tugging sensation but something much more heavy and forceful.

My people cried out in alarm and I could do nothing to stop it or respond to them as a black power slammed into me, closed like a gripping hand about me . . . and swallowed me down into a dark and fathomless void.

Two

I DIDN'T LOSE consciousness, although that might have been kinder. Nope, I had to stay awake and aware throughout the entire experience of . . . well, I guess, dying. Because what else do you call it when your heart suddenly shudders into echoing silence and no longer beats?

The stillness of sound, the *absence* of it, was more noticeable to me because I was trapped somewhere inside my own body. I saw, I experienced sensations—the blistering heat, the gray reddening of predawn light—but they came to me filtered, through a thick and muffled layer, as if someone else was using my eyes and in control of my body and I was just along for an unwilling ride.

My taken-over body was lying on the ground. The very hard, very hot scorching ground. *Get up!* I screamed. But whoever was in charge now ignored me and just reveled for a moment in simply being back. Her thoughts. Her words.

Whoever she was, she was in no hurry to move in case it was all just a dream. I called it more of a nightmare.

She gazed up at the sky, all she allowed me to take inventory of. But it was worthy of note, actually. It was a scarlet, fractured sky, like it had been broken apart and put back together. And the impression wasn't just from the uneven layers of red firmament that transitioned one piece into another abruptly, but the twin suns themselves, shaped like the Chinese *yin* and *yang* symbols. As if a giant hand had plucked down a single sun, torn it apart, and cast the broken pieces back into the sky.

The light was abruptly blocked as a man, a mean-looking stranger, stood over us. No one I recognized. I just knew that he wasn't one of my people. The orange prison garb he wore was a really big hint.

Prison garb? I heard that other me wonder. She hadn't recognized the attire.

So he's human, flashed her thought within me, and the momentary alarm that had flared up over that rough and menacing face subsided beneath her smug superiority. Humans were inferior in strength and speed, she thought.

It was that familiar sneer in her voice that rang a bell in me. That made me think: *Mona Louisa?*

Of course. Who else did you think it was? came the contemptuous answer. Sounding exactly like that blond bitch of a Monère Queen whose essence and light I had sucked down into me.

But you're dead, I thought. Blaec, the High Lord of Hell, had killed her after I had done my unsuccessful best.

And now so are you. Her answer and the rich, malicious satisfaction she oozed in imparting that news froze me for a second. It had been my first thought, that I was dead, but still I had hoped for another answer. Hearing the words, feeling her absolute belief, totally flipped me out. I panicked completely. Started thrashing and trying to claw my way out of the thick void that surrounded me. My goal was up toward the shimmering surface so seemingly far above, glimmering with faint, sparkling light. If I could just reach that surface I knew that I would somehow be back in control.

Don't count on it, mongrel bitch, thought Mona Louisa smugly. *You're weaker than I am now.*

Which totally exasperated me. *That's what got you killed before—underestimating people. Pay attention to what's happening around you!* I told her.

Her attention snapped back on the strange human man as he crouched over her, his shaggy hair greasy and un-kempt. "Now aren't you a purty thing," he purred. "I ain't had me a real woman for years, penned up the way I was like an animal. Another man just ain't the same thing as a woman, you know." His eyes sweeping over me . . . her . . . *us* . . . glittered hard with lust.

Mona Louisa tried to move then, to sit up. But he stopped her easily with a hand on the shoulder. "No need gettin' up. I want you on your back the first time." His lips curled back in a cruel and eager smile as Mona Louisa raised a hand to push him . . . and couldn't. She—*we*—moved slowly, sluggishly. Even more alarmingly, his strength was greater than hers.

He nodded knowingly. "Took me a little while to gain back my strength. Should be a while for you, too. 'Nuff time for me to have my fill of you," he said, and began to open his pants.

"No!" she cried.

No! I screamed inside also, her fear, and mine, spiraling and echoing through our body. Without her strength, she didn't know what to do, how to stop him from raping her.

"Yes, sirree. Plenty of time to slake some of my thirst on your sweet body. Go ahead," he urged, "fight me. I like it that way better." Flipping up her long dress, he yanked her underwear off with a happy grunt and crawled on top of her. Using his weight to keep her pinned down, he roughly spread open her legs. "The others ran off. And the two other guys here are like you, still weak. No one's gonna stop me. Hell, if I'd known this was what waited for me, I'd a gone willingly to the electric chair years ago."

Both Mona Louisa and I gagged as we felt his hard male organ push against us, probing for entrance as we lay exposed there, our lower body naked, completely vulnerable to him.

I know how to fight, I screamed. *Let me out!*

With an abruptness that took me by surprise, she yielded to my demand, and I felt myself propelled up that vast syrupy distance to the shimmering surface. With a gasp, I surfaced and found myself once more in control of my body. My hands that had been futilely trying to push him off me abruptly stopped pushing and went instead for his eyes. It was a clumsy attempt, with my limbs moving slow as molasses, but my nails scraped across his face and one nail managed to poke his sensitive eye. He rolled off me with an angry yelp of pain. Then just stared at me in confusion and the beginning of fear.

"What the fuck? Your hair, eyes . . . your entire face and body . . . how the hell did you change it like that?"

"I can do many things," I said, anger—*rage*—emanating from me. "Did you think Hell was going to be so easy?" My body shook as I forced myself to stand; stand and not fall over as I spat my next words at him. "Unending pain awaits you for the crimes you have committed in life, and would have continued in this afterlife. You will not find pleasure here, only pain. An eternity of suffering."

Terror filled his eyes, and ugly guilt twisted his face. Without a word he turned and ran from me as if the demons of Hell chased after him. If only that were true. Two particular demons I would have welcomed gladly at the moment.

"Is that true? Are we dead? Are we . . . damned?"

I turned and saw a man lying a dozen yards away on the ground, turned toward me on his side. He wore a business suit and tie. A human somewhere in his fifties or sixties. A second guy, young like me in his early twenties, Hispanic, with jet-black hair slicked back in a ponytail, lay a short distance behind him. He had made further progress, pushing himself up onto his hands and knees. The sleeveless T-shirt he wore revealed muscular, tattooed arms. Everything about him screamed *gang member.*

Two men from diverse backgrounds, about as far apart on the social and economic scale as possible, and both looking to me for answers. But I had none to give them.

"I don't know," I said.

"Last thing I knew, I was in a car accident. A head-on collision," said the guy in the suit. "I think I died."

"I was shot three times in the chest," Mr. Tattoo said. He pushed up his shirt, ran a hand over his smooth brown chest. No blood, no bullet holes.

My knees wanted to buckle but I stiffened them. Stayed standing by sheer dint of will.

Can't afford to appear weak, Mona Louisa thought inside me. I agreed with her.

"What about you?" asked the older man.

"A black light came down from the moon and brought me here."

"We told you the truth," the young guy said, scowling.

"So did I," I returned evenly. Then flatly, "I don't have a pulse or a heartbeat."

Both men took a moment to assess themselves.

"Nothing here." Tattoo guy.

"Me, either," said Mr. Corporate Type. "Are we in Hell?"

Tattoo guy looked around at the bleak landscape, his disdain not quite masking the fear underneath. "Sure don't look like heaven, does it?"

I was as confused as they were. Maybe even more so, and even more shaken up inside. *Am I dead? Really dead? If so, then why am I here?*

As a *Damanôen*, a living demon, I was not supposed to have an afterlife. And humans rarely had enough psychic energy to transition to Hell. Yet here I was with three humans, two of them having obviously lived and died violently. And none of them seemed terribly upset or surprised to find themselves dead. To find themselves *here.*

"What did you do?" I asked the guy in the suit.

He took a moment to push himself onto his knees. "What do you mean, what did I do?"

"We have a death-row inmate and a gang member who died in a shoot-out, if I'm not mistaken."

Tattoo guy nodded confirmation.

"You don't seem particularly surprised to find yourself in this human version of Hell," I noted.

"Human version?" the older man said, lifting his brows.

"Just answer the question. You didn't, by any chance, happen to steal millions of dollars from your stockholders or something like that, did you?"

He stared at me with eyes that were suddenly hard and shrewd. "Something like that."

His answer made my heart sink.

Sinners. We were all sinners here.

Like an eerie reflection of my thoughts, Mr. Corporate Fraud asked, "And you? What was your sin?"

"Me?" I reflected over my life, the violence of it. "I killed three men."

"And your ability to change your body and appearance like that? Become two different women?"

"I tried to murder another woman. Ended up possessing her inside of me instead."

Making the sign of the cross, the young gang member

muttered, "*La Madre de Dios nos ayuda.*" Mother of God help us.

Unfortunately, it looked like it was too late for that.

My hand lifted to the necklace given to me by my demon mate.

Halcyon, where are you? And where in heaven or Hell am I?

THREE

As the last burgundy rays of Rubera, Hell's third moon, disappeared over the horizon and utter and complete darkness blanketed the realm, loud poppers and brilliant sparklers whistled across the sky, lighting it up with noise and festivity. It was the demons' way of celebrating *Aequus Nox,* equal night, which had a far more sinister meaning here. The display of light and noise was to scare away the cursed inhabitants of NetherHell during the time when the walls between the realms dangerously thinned. The custom was first started, no doubt, as a way to make the people feel better, safer. And as an excuse for merriment in a realm that was not often very merry.

As a device for preventing the unclean dead and their twisted creatures from crossing into Hell, it was as effective as throwing a handful of water at a raging fire and hoping to put it out. In other words, not very effective. Thankfully other means ensured their safety. But as a reason to gather and make happy, it served that purpose quite

well, though you wouldn't know it from the two dour demons standing next to him. One was among the oldest of
their kind—Blaec, his father, the High Lord of Hell whose
name meant darkness.

His father's face was almost a mirror reflection of Halcyon's own, but for the silver streaking his temples and the
darker hue of his skin, bronze instead of gold. Others
would have thought that Blaec personified his name quite
well from the somber, morose expression on his face, but
they would have been wrong. Just the fact that his father
was standing there instead of sleeping the days and nights
away indicated that he was actually quite chipper.

On Halcyon's other side stood one of their newest demons, Gryphon, whose expression of grimness matched
that of his father's. It was strange knowing someone when
they had been alive, and then knowing them as a demon
dead inhabitant, subject now to his rule in this realm,
though you would never have guessed that to be the case
with this newest citizen of Hell.

Halcyon turned to face the new demon whose milky
white skin was only just beginning to take on a light tan in
the hotter clime of Hell, marking his newly transitioned
demon state. "Aren't you glad that I insisted you come?
Almost like the Fourth of July, isn't it?"

"Bugger off," Gryphon said with no change of expression, making the demon guards attending them scowl, a
frightening sight to most. Gryphon hardly took note of it.

Halcyon smiled. "Shouldn't that be 'Bugger off, my
lord'?"

"Bugger off, my lord."

Halcyon's smile slipped away. "You've had a month to
brood and come to terms with your loss." And what a loss
it had been. Not just of life but of newfound love and the
woman he had loved and served—Mona Lisa, his Queen.

Different realms weren't the only things that separated

them. Two other things kept them apart: Gryphon's precarious control of his new demon bloodlust, and his ability to cross the portal back into the living realm. Only the older, more powerful demons risked stepping into the portals. Demons who were too weak—and you could not tell until after you had stepped inside the damn portal—were simply incinerated, extinguished, never seen again.

The latter was a barrier only in Gryphon's mind. It could have been easily overcome by simply allowing Mona Lisa to venture down into Hell. But Gryphon did not want his lady love stepping one dainty foot into Hell, even though that dainty foot had indeed done just that, twice already. The first time Mona Lisa had been dragged down against her will by a rogue demon. The second time had been by her own choice, bringing Halcyon back after he was severely injured and weakened in the living realm. That Mona Lisa was not now in Hell was only because Halcyon and his father had thought it best to give Gryphon time to adjust to his new existence as a demon, and to allow him time to gain control of his new and dangerous hunger before allowing Mona Lisa to see him again.

In that regard, Gryphon had made much progress. He had attained control of his bloodthirst, a feat that took some demons more than a year to attain instead of just one month. But then, Gryphon had been stronger, more powerful than most other warriors. He had been a Warrior Lord, one of the few ever to attain such status.

Sweat dampened Gryphon's face now as he gazed down from the balcony to the revelry of the city below. The heady scent of the blood wine that all were imbibing freely floated up to him. A nearer and even more tantalizing scent of blood came from the chalice Gryphon held in his hand with seeming ease. A chalice he had held for the last ten minutes and not yet tasted. Only when all others in the room had drunk did he finally raise the cup to his lips, not gulping it down as most new demons would have done, after having been teased so mercilessly by the scent of blood, but in carefully measured sips.

The control cost Gryphon. Was visible in the fine tremors shaking his hand. But it made a point—that he was in control of his hunger. That it did not control him. It was a point, however, that all but Gryphon had conceded over a fortnight ago. Now it was simply Gryphon's own stubbornness that kept Mona Lisa away.

When Halcyon had announced several days ago that enough time had passed to safely allow her to pay him a visit, Gryphon had replied, "I do not wish to see her ever again. I am demon dead now. My other life died when I died." He was being stupid, stubborn, and noble, of course, trying to keep her away from Hell and its bloodthirsty inhabitants, of which he was now one.

When Halcyon had tried to argue, Gryphon's calm veneer had broken, and he had lunged at his prince, sharp fangs bared. "When I was alive—beating heart, living flesh—I did not trust you, Halcyon. Did not trust a demon. Now that I have become demon dead, I know how very true my instincts were. We are dangerous. Violence is our nature. Control is learned, not natural. I do not want her *anywhere* near me—or you."

Halcyon had gently broken free of Gryphon's grip. "It is true. Our demon hunger is raw, and our nature more volatile. Violence comes more easily to us—even more to the newly dead whose rage over their loss of life is still so fresh. But that tendency can be controlled, just as you have controlled your bloodlust, especially around someone you love."

"You're wrong," Gryphon said. "My control would be even more fragile around someone I loved. I am dead, no longer a part of her life. Tell her . . . tell her to forget me." But even as he had grated out the words, his hand had lifted to the medallion necklace he wore. It wasn't just a symbol of what he once was, a Warrior Lord, it was also his last connection to Mona Lisa—what she had pressed into the High Lord's hand and had him bring back to Gryphon.

Gryphon fingered it much the way Halcyon fingered the silver ring he wore around his neck. His bonding ring. Strung on a chain, the ring was hidden beneath Halcyon's shirt, kept close to his non-beating heart. It was forged from the same silver used to craft Mona Lisa's necklace, which had his likeness engraved upon it. The symbols carved along the side denoted what she was to him, his royal consort, something he had not told Gryphon or made known to his people yet. Only his father knew.

It put Halcyon in a dilemma: How to tell Gryphon that his noble intentions were for naught. That Mona Lisa was already intricately involved with demons. Had become one, in part, herself. That she had sucked down Mona Louisa's demon-tainted essence into herself while trying to avenge Gryphon's death, and that it now dwelt in her, making her something that not many knew was possible— *Damanôen*, demon living.

Time. Halcyon had decided to grant both of them that. And he had watched Gryphon and Mona Lisa separately come to terms with their new and more volatile natures. Watched both of them exert that essential control over their new hungers, control that ensured their survival. Without it, they would have had to be destroyed. And he would have had to be the one to do so.

Halcyon watched the other demon now as he carefully sipped the blood wine. Watched barely visible, fine tremors shake Gryphon's elegant hand as he swallowed down the blood that his demon body so desperately craved. And was proud and relieved and unbearably grateful for that exhibited control.

Suddenly Halcyon felt something change, alter. As he was surrounded by the noise of his people and the loud popping display of the lightworks, he felt his bonding ring grow cold against his warm demon flesh. The ring was not only composed of silver but of rare and prized stones from their mother planet. Two precious pebbles had been crushed and mixed with the silver ore of both ring and necklace. The mystical properties of those stones linked bonded mates. That, and Halcyon's own blood that resided in Mona Lisa, strengthening their link, allowed him to sense her, to feel her living warmth in his ring even when he was down in Hell. Only now that sense of connection, that sense of *her*, was gone.

Terrible foreboding quaked through him. "Something's wrong," he said, his eyes changing to the color of churning blood, his fangs lengthening into lethal points.

Seeing their prince's response, the demon guards glanced around on heightened alert, seeking for threat, danger.

"What is it?" Blaec demanded.

Halcyon turned to his father, his gaze turned inward. "I don't feel her anymore."

"Feel who?" Gryphon asked.

"Mona Lisa," Halcyon said, and started to walk away.

Gryphon exploded, grabbing Halcyon by his shirt, his own fangs lengthening, sharpening, his own eyes burning with fury and fear. "How can you sense her, and why?" he growled.

With a mere thought, a small mental push, Halcyon sent the other demon flying away from him to slam up against the wall, held him there by his will. Tearing his shirt open, Halcyon revealed the silver ring. "We are bonded. She is my mate. Something's wrong," he said, with no time or care for finesse or tact. He whirled to face his father. "I must go."

"Then go," Blaec said. "I will oversee things here—and explain things to Gryphon."

Blaec's hand gripped Halcyon's shoulder, and the calm waves of the High Lord's control helped to steady Halcyon.

"I will return when I can," Halcyon said.

"Journey safe, journey sound. And journey home once more," Blaec said—ritual words of farewell to demon guardians before they crossed the portals. Then he uttered something more. "Be well."

Words that Halcyon could not respond to as he walked away. Because if anything had happened to his mate, he would be far from well.

FOUR

HALCYON MATERIALIZED IN the business district of New Orleans. It was quiet here, just past the midnight hour, the stroke of time that split night from day. All slept or partied elsewhere. He walked out of the alleyway, and moved with inhuman speed closer to where people gathered. As he neared the French Quarter, he slowed and became visible once more. His mental compulsion more than his lifted hand made a passing cab screech to a halt.

The hour it took to drive to Belle Vista stretched hideously long. Only now, as he journeyed by means other than his own power, did Halcyon open up his senses and cast them wide, searching for that pull of like to like, that distinct and thrilling recognition of blood. *His* blood. Always before, he had sensed it, sensed *her*—Mona Lisa. Only now there was no answering echo in return. Only emptiness. A chilling void.

Not here answered back the silence.

He searched farther, trembling as he stretched his

senses to their limits. Nothing there. Nothing that he could detect anywhere in this realm.

He arrived into chaos at Belle Vista. He sensed it, heard it in the quickened heartbeats stirring within, and quickly sent the cab driver on his way.

"Halcyon." Amber strode down the front steps, a giant of a man. Their love for the same woman bound them in harmony now in this time of crisis. Naked on Amber's normally impassive face was worry. Panic, even.

"What happened, Amber?" Technically it was "Warrior Lord Amber," as denoted by the gleaming medallion necklace he wore, identical to the one around Gryphon's neck. Gryphon and Amber, one dark and beautiful like a fallen angel, the other a massive brute of a warrior, rugged of face, powerful of body. They had been Mona Lisa's first two lovers, and were wildly distrustful of him with the natural fear of the living for the dead. All that fell away now as the big warrior rushed down to him.

"She's gone," Amber said.

Even though Halcyon knew that—knew it in his bones, in the unanswered echo of his blood—still the words chilled him.

"Is she down in Hell? Is that what you've come to tell us?" Then more ominously as the thought occurred to Amber, "Or was that black light your doing?"

"Black light?" Chilling coldness swept through Halcyon's being, must have been reflected in his face, because Amber's angry aggression collapsed. "What is it? You know what's happened to her."

He had an inkling, a dreadful one. "Tell me what occurred tonight," Halcyon commanded as Amber urged him inside where they were quickly joined by the others. Her family, Mona Lisa had called them, though only one was related to her by blood. The rest were bound to her by ties of the heart—a family in which she'd generously included Halcyon.

"Never mind," Dontaine muttered into the phone, catching sight of him. "Halcyon's here." He hung up and turned to face them, a man tall, handsomely bright. As fair as Gryphon was dark. And as equally jealous and distrustful of Halcyon as Gryphon had been—until their last encounter. Only Dontaine, among Mona Lisa's people, knew of the demon essence that had been slowly darkening her. In the order of love—of lovers—he was Mona Lisa's fourth, after Halcyon.

"My lord," Dontaine greeted now. Polite, respectful, tensely expectant.

They all looked to him, the people who loved her: her brother, Thaddeus; the other two Mixed Bloods, Jamie, and his sister, Tersa; Rosemary, their mother; and the other warriors sworn to her, Aquila, Tomas, and Chami. They all looked to him for answers. But he needed some himself first.

"Tell me what happened," Halcyon said in quiet command.

"We were Basking," answered Chami. He was boyishly lean, deceptively young in appearance. With violet eyes and curly brown hair, he looked more like a graduate student than the accomplished killer he was. "Light filled her, renewed us—all normal. Then this veil of darkness swept across the moon, covering it. Black light pulsed down, traveling through the rays of moonlight, and struck Mona Lisa. It was like this giant hand of darkness closed around her and swallowed her up. She was gone, just like that."

"We searched," said Aquila, continuing the tale. A former rogue bandit, he was a bird of prey, an eagle in his other form. "I searched with all the others who could take to the sky on wings. Dontaine and Amber searched the grounds with the other guards, shifted into their animal forms. There was no scent. No trace of her. No trail to follow."

"I called High Court and was on the phone with Lord Thorane," said Dontaine, "trying to see if there was any way of contacting you, when you showed up. How did you know to come?"

"She is my mate," Halcyon said. "We are bound together now." In more ways than many of them knew. "I came because I no longer sense her."

"Could my sister be down in Hell?" Thaddeus said, asking the question innocently without truly understanding what he asked.

"No," Halcyon said, shaking his head. "I would have sensed her if she were in my realm. She is not there, just as she is not here in this realm."

"What if she's transitioning?" asked Dontaine, and he, unlike Thaddeus, was fully aware of what he asked. "Could you have missed her while traveling through the portal?"

"If she was in Hell now, I would feel her, but I do not. If she was making the transition, it would have occurred by now."

Thaddeus's young face paled as he finally realized what they were discussing: whether Mona Lisa had died and become demon dead. "Maybe your bond, your sensing of her, changed if she . . . if she died. Maybe she's down in your realm and you just don't know it."

"I wish, I truly wish that were the case," Halcyon said gently to Thaddeus, a boy who looked years younger than his age of seventeen, with the same dark exotic eyes as his sister. "If she were a demon now, my awareness of her would be even stronger. I'm sorry, Thaddeus."

"So you think she is just no more?" Tersa asked. A quiet girl in her early twenties, she had a birdlike delicacy to her, and was normally shy and withdrawn. That she had spoken showed her deep concern. What she asked put into words what others there feared, what *he* feared. When the Monère died, those who were strong enough became demon dead and existed in Hell for as long as their psychic power sustained them. Those unable to make the transition simply faded away into the darkness. Before, Mona Lisa had more than enough mental strength to make the jump. But that was before she had become demon living. Halcyon's greatest fear coming here had been that—that she had died and was no more. Now, hearing their tale, he found himself filled with an even more horrible consideration, a possibility that hadn't even occurred to him before.

"You know something," Aquila said.

Damn his sharp eagle eyes. Halcyon could have lied—considered it for one moment—but he chose not to. "I fear something even worse than that has happened."

"What could be worse than dying and being no more?" Thaddeus asked.

"Do you know the significance of this particular day, other than it being a full moon?" Halcyon asked.

"It's the spring equinox."

Halcyon nodded. "My people call it *Aequus Nox*, equal night. When day and night are of equal length. In Hell, it is the time when the wall between the realms thins, when inhabitants of one realm can sometimes cross over into another."

"But you said she's not in Hell," Tersa said quietly.

Halcyon swung his gaze to the girl whose dark eyes were more knowing of pain than they should have been at so young an age. "There is another realm besides Hell," he said, "though not many know of it."

"What other realm?" asked Amber, his voice wary, remembering the expression that had crossed Halcyon's face outside.

"A place called NetherHell."

"Is it like Hell?" asked Thaddeus.

"No." Halcyon's heart howled inside, crying for his mate. "It is a place far worse, far more dangerous than Hell. We call it the Cursed Realm. The realm of the damned."

FIVE

THE SUN CAME up as we were trudging across the hot barren land. Or should I say suns, as in two of them, tadpole-shaped. Oddly enough, the brightness didn't affect me, though that didn't mean anything if I was a demon now. Demons could walk in the sun without feeling the bite of pain that the Monère felt. I wouldn't feel anything until my flesh became soft and tender enough to burst open at a touch, which was what had happened to Halcyon once, after prolonged exposure to the sun.

I still didn't know where the hell I was. Or if I even *was* in Hell. That should have been the most likely conclusion. Only, so many things didn't add up. Among them was my demon thirst for blood—not there. Water was what I had a hankering for, and what we were searching for. That's right, we. After our nice *What's Your Sin Versus My Sin* chat, I'd perused our bleak surroundings and fixed on a distant area where the soil appeared darker. Darker soil equating water, or at least that's what I was hoping. I'd started trekking that way, and the other two—Juan, the gang member, and Charles, the corporate fraud guy—had followed me. Since all other footprints, fresh and old, led that way, I shouldn't have been surprised. I didn't discourage the two of them or try to distance myself from them. Frankly, I was unsettled. I mean my heart wasn't beating. One moment I'm alive, Basking under the moon's rays, and then wham! A giant black hand of light smothers me and I'm whisked away to some godforsaken place with a bloodred sky and a couple of broken-into-pieces suns.

I missed the noises of my body, that ever constant drumming beat of life. Now all was silent in my body. Deathly still and quiet. The company of others, even those I didn't completely trust, was better than trudging alone in solitude. Plus they seemed frightened of me, that whole morphing into another woman thing. They weren't likely to be much of a physical threat.

For now, Mona Louisa was content to let me take the lead, staying a quiet presence within me. Wherever we were, whatever had happened to me, it had made her stronger . . . frighteningly strong. I'd only been able to surface when she had allowed it. Until then, I had been trapped inside. I don't know if it was because of that initial weakness that seemed to have affected us all; the lethargy had gradually fallen away after half an hour.

Even though the air still felt like thick syrup, a much heavier density than we were used to, the more time that passed, the stronger and more normal my body felt. Normal but for the absence of a beating heart—one crucial thing that changed everything . . . who and what I was. Which was still a mystery. For some reason, it was hard to label myself as dead. Not when I still felt so alive, and still had so much to live for, to go back to.

As the hours beneath the two yin and yang suns passed, my thirst grew into fierce, biting need and hunger began to gnaw at my empty stomach. The good news was that I had no urge to sink my teeth into my traveling companions—no urge for their blood or flesh.

I'd gained back my strength far faster than my companions had. Their strength was severely flagging now; almost back to that initial state. I heard someone stumble, fall. No other sounds. No quickened heartbeat, no labored breathing. No breathing at all except to talk—you had to draw breath for that.

"Wait, please," cried Charles, down on his knees. Juan, younger, more fit, was almost a dozen paces ahead of him. Both lagged a significant distance behind me. Juan kept walking until he reached me, his swarthy skin damp with a heavy sheen of sweat. He looked tired but still able to go on. Charles, on the other hand, had clearly reached the end of his limit.

When Juan looked as if he were going to continue walking, I said, "Charles won't be able to travel farther without rest."

Juan paused and licked his dry, parched lips. "You stopping?"

"Yeah. Were you going to leave him behind?"

"We're almost there." *There* being that darker patch of land. "A few more hours and we'll reach water."

"I'm going back," I said, and started trudging back to Charles. A moment's hesitation and Juan fell into step beside me.

"Thank you," Charles said. His face was an alarming shade of lobster red. Thick beads of perspiration dripped down his face. We were all damp and sweaty in the oppressive heat, but Charles was excessively so.

"Just a short rest and I'll be all right," he said, his voice sounding scratchy and dry.

Juan looked frankly dubious of that but refrained from any comments. He supported Charles on one side while I grabbed the other arm. Together we heaved him to his feet and dragged him over to the closest shade available, that cast by a small stunted shrub.

"Lie down and rest," I said, easing him down. There was only enough shade to cover his face. The rest of his body still baked under the two uneven suns.

"Wait here," I said to Juan.

"Where are you going?"

"To see if I can find us anything to eat or drink."

"Good luck," he muttered, dropping down beside Charles.

Hopefully luck wouldn't have anything to do with it. My sight and hearing weren't yet one hundred percent, but they were far better than my initial blunted state. And better, I believed, than those of Juan and Charles. The other two men were completely human. I wasn't. Three-quarters of me was of another species whose strength and speed were greater than any human could ever hope for.

I moved silently, careful not to make any sound, and crouched by a small thicket. Seconds passed. Minutes crawled by while I stayed completely frozen in waiting stillness. Finally, I caught a movement out of the corner of my eye. A slow slithering along the dry, brittle ground. It was a creature such as I had never seen before. The front of it was like a horny lizard while the rest of its body was that of a snake. Its scaly hide was a brown-green camouflage pattern, blending it almost perfectly into its rocky desert surroundings. But that was the only perfect thing about it. The front end walked on two stumpy forelegs while the rear part of it slithered. It was hideous enough and big enough to have me run screaming away from it had not the others' need compelled me. Not even my own hunger and thirst would have driven me to do what I did next.

I pounced on it and kept my eyes open while every girl instinct in me wanted to close my eyes and shudder as I grabbed it. It thrashed its thick, muscular body, surprisingly strong. Sharp fangs were revealed as it hissed, whipping out a long tongue. The snake part of its body was just starting to wrap around my legs when I snapped its neck. It went limp, and so did I. The shudders came as I carried the obscene lizard-snake back to the two waiting men. Juan's eyes rounded until the whites of his eyes showed. "*Dios!* What the mother is that?"

"Food and drink," I said.

Charles turned, caught sight of my offering, and jerked upright. "Jesus, what is that thing?"

"I don't know." And I didn't want to know. I dumped the body on the ground and the two men edged back away from it. I was as leery as them, but we didn't have the luxury of being squeamish. "We'd better hurry before it revives," I said.

"Isn't it dead?" Charles asked. "It looks like you broke its neck."

"I did. Doesn't mean that it won't heal or regenerate."

"Can it do that?" Juan asked.

I shrugged. "Don't know. And I don't want to wait around to find out." Next on the list was finding something sharp to cut the creature with. Picking up a small rock, I cracked it open against another rock, and presto, I wielded an instant knife. It took three repeated slices with the crude rock blade before I finally cut through the thick leathery skin. Blood dripped and I raised the snake body to my mouth and swallowed the sanguineous fluid flowing out from the cut I'd made. It wasn't as if it was the first time I'd drank down blood, but drinking it like this was different. I didn't crave it, hunger for it. Water was what my body really needed.

I swallowed two mouthfuls, enough to take the edge off my thirst, then offered it to Charles. He took it with trembling hands and choked on the first mouthful, but the next two gulps went down easier. He shuddered and passed the serpentine body to Juan.

With a muttered curse, Juan lifted it to his mouth. He'd barely taken his first swallow when the thick reptilian body suddenly twitched. Juan threw the creature away from him. "It moved! It fucking moved!"

"Are you sure?" Charles asked anxiously.

"Yeah. Look."

The head twitched, the mouth opened, and there was no mistaking the hiss, the flash of scary fangs. With a spasmodic, disjointed kind of motion, it started to slither and crawl away from us.

"Anyone wants another drink or maybe a bite of its flesh before it gets away?" I asked, not shocked or surprised. I'd been expecting it, actually.

"You joking, lady?" Juan asked, clearly freaked out.

"Far from it. Think carefully. That creature may be your last chance at food or drink for a while."

Juan gazed at the creature and shook his head. "Fuck no. I don't want nothing more to do with that thing."

Charles concurred.

I crouched down, scooped up some hot, gritty soil and rubbed it over my hands to clean them, not so much of the blood—I'd managed to be neat in my drinking—but more to rid myself of the disgusting feel of that icky lizard skin.

I stood. Asked Charles, "You ready to go?"

He nodded wildly.

I set off without another word.

"How'd you know that thing would heal itself?" Juan asked after some time and distance had passed.

"Just a damn unlucky guess," I said.

SIX

WHEN GRYPHON HAD died, life—along with his heart—had literally been torn from him. His living, beating heart. The organ with which you supposedly loved. If only that ability had been torn from him the same way his organ had been ripped from his chest, then perhaps death would have been easier. It certainly would have been more welcome. He might have drifted into his new existence with glad acceptance, maybe even peace. But his death had not come easily. He'd fought his departure from the earthly realm with every fiber of his being.

He'd been torn from life, his last breath taken in Mona Lisa's arms, and thrust into smoldering darkness. Tumbling for a countless time in an empty void of nothingness. Encased in blackness like a womb or a shroud. Then vision had slowly returned. His senses functioned once more, and he found himself in a dark realm where a giant orange moon dominated a twilight sky. He'd heard sound—his quickened breaths going in and out—and he'd breathed by habit, still imitating the signs of life. But there'd been no beating of his heart. With a fumbling hand, Gryphon had felt his chest, whole, untorn, but no pulse. No throb of life thumped against his palm or sounded within his body. He knew then that he was dead. If only his emotions were also.

In his mind's eye, he saw Mona Lisa's face again in that last moment of grief as she held him while he slowly slipped unwillingly from life. Pain such as he'd never felt before ripped through his chest, far greater even than the gruesome act that had brought about his rending death—an ache so powerful, so unrelenting, so throbbing in the empty space where his heart had once been.

"No!" he'd screamed.

Voices had shouted. Faces had peered at him, the brown faces of the demon dead. Then he'd seen a familiar face that he'd both hated and welcomed—Halcyon's golden skin, his dark eyes filled with compassion.

Weak as a kitten, or a newborn demon, Gryphon had rasped, "Send me back."

Pity had filled Halcyon's eyes. "You know that is not possible."

Rage had filled Gryphon then. Poured through him like a burning, cleansing fire, killing the last, lingering essence of his old life, the old him. His new self, his demon self, was forged into being then, washing away the weakness of love and filling him with the strength of hatred, of such blinding rage that the world changed from orange to red in the blink of an eye, and he knew that his eyes had turned bloodred. Knew that he was true demon then.

"Send me back!" he railed, the words slurring as fangs erupted painfully, filling his mouth.

Halcyon touched him, the last part of his demon birth that Gryphon remembered. "Sleep now," the High Prince of Hell had said. And Gryphon had slept.

When he next awakened, it had been in a clean chamber—soft linen, a comfortable bed, a sturdy end table, and nothing else. The room had been stripped down to bare essentials and locked. The latter, Gryphon discovered only later, when he had grown strong enough to roam beyond the bed, to seek a way out of his prison. The real prison, though, was the new world he now inhabited.

The first person he saw again was Halcyon, entering the room with a chalice of blood. One heady whiff and his eyes had fired red, his hunger growing monstrous within him. All else was wiped away—grief, rage, fear—and Gryphon became nothing more than overwhelming desire . . . overwhelming *need* for that blood.

It seemed that Halcyon was always there in those first hazy days following Gryphon's rebirth. Once the jealous contender for affections from his beloved Queen, now his ruler. Only he didn't act like a ruler; more like a brother. Someone who cared for Gryphon, bringing him the blood his new demon body craved. First lamb's blood, then over the next several days cow's blood diluted with wine, thinner, less sweet. Challo, they called the mixture. Blood wine. The normal drink of demons.

Halcyon held him when he grieved, calmed Gryphon when he raged. And he was glad then, when that unthinking madness gripped him, that he was locked up, safely contained. He destroyed the room, ripped everything into pieces. A new bed, new furniture, and new sheets were brought in.

Let me out! he raged.

When you can control yourself had been Halcyon's answer.

Emotions, though, controlled Gryphon. His rage, his grief. Railing against what had been and what was now.

Mona Lisa! He cried out her name in anguish, in love, in grief and fury. *Mona Lisa!* And knew each time he howled her name that he had lost her.

"You have not lost her," Halcyon told him, over and over again. "You will see her again when you regain control of yourself. When you can control your rage, your grief, your hunger." But he had lied.

As the days passed, and they did so slowly, relentlessly, the truth had impressed itself on Gryphon. He had lost her. Lost her to life. Was kept from her by death, by what he was now—an angry new demon whose rage was always there, constant, ever hovering.

Such a thin, fragile line separating fury from control.

When his room was finally unlocked, when Gryphon was finally allowed to venture outside its doors, a new emotion had filled him—fear of the unknown. But the unknown had only proved to be the calm order and simple luxurious surroundings of the High Prince's home.

Hell was not so bad if one thought in terms of food, clothing, and shelter—the basic necessities of life . . . and death, it seemed, too. All was provided for Gryphon by the ruler of the realm himself. By Halcyon. Were Gryphon to hazard a guess, not many other newly transitioned demons were granted the High Prince's hospitality. Probably no other demons. A very private and reserved man was his host. Yet he'd opened the doors of his home to Gryphon, taken him in, offered his calming presence, and even more important, the tranquility and order of a well-run household overseen by a small dour female demon named Jory.

Gryphon wondered how other new demons fared—where they lived, how they ate. That was one of the surprises, that demons ate food down in this realm, along with drinking the blood for which all demons thirsted. In Halcyon's house, Gryphon dined in civilized splendor as food was slowly reintroduced back into his diet—bread, fruit, meat. And ever present, always within easy reach, the blood wine of the afterlife. Challo.

SEVEN

WE FINALLY FOUND water. Not the clear pond we had envisioned, but a filthy, drying mud hole that glimmered oddly, as if bits of golden dust had been mixed into the wet soil. Whatever water source had been there had died, was dead like the rest of us.

Finding our way here had been simple. Just follow the footprints. The many footprints that had all led this way, to this illusive dark patch of land, of moist soil. Look, see, smell. None of our senses had lied. The water that we thirsted for was here, just not in any drinkable form. That didn't stop the newly dead from trying. They were fighting over it, a dozen rough men kicking, punching, shoving each other, trying to stake out their patch of mud. Our orange-clad jailbird was among them, scooping up handfuls of the wet mud and squeezing dark liquid drops into his opened mouth.

I stopped on a small rise concealed by sparse, bristly underbrush, watching the free-for-all taking place down below. Something about the whole setup raised my hackles, prickled my unease. Too pat, too convenient, too *exposed* with all of them gathered out in the open around the only water source—what was left of it.

The sight of the men fighting over the remaining water seemed too much for my companions. Juan and Charles broke cover. Started running toward the mud hole. "Wait," I called desperately out to them. "Something's not right."

"If we wait, what's left will be gone," Charles said, stumbling after Juan. They didn't even look back, just dived into the melee of desperate, thirsty men, scrambling for a handful of liquid mud. Many were down on their knees, lapping the watery sludge they had scooped up in their hands.

They still thought like humans, I realized. What they had all been. Acting on the belief that they would perish if they did not slurp down water, no matter how thick and muddy it was. Poor misguided creatures. Although pity quickly changed to disgust as I watched them fighting ferociously over their patch of mud. My would-be rapist was the most violent, viciously beating his neighbor, some big unfortunate guy. He pounded the man's head with his fists, kicked the guy's face, chest, and stomach as he lay unmoving in the mud. None of the other men tried to stop him, each desperately engrossed in his own mad scramble for something to drink.

Thirst, lack of water, would not kill them. What could, though, came quickly down over another rise. Eight men, I counted. Or rather, eight things. I wasn't really sure if I could call them men. They were humanoid, as in walking upright on two feet. But men? Perhaps once, but greatly changed now. They were huge, over seven feet tall, some carrying long wicked swords, others bearing whips. The weapons were bad, but not as bad as the things themselves. They were big, solid muscle, and ugly as sin. Not even their mothers could have loved these creatures. It wasn't so much the little horns pushing up through some of the men's heads, or even their mud-colored skin. It was the lumps and bumps on that skin, on their faces and hands. Hard, calcified, warty things. As if filthy slime had crawled out of old pipes and slithered over their skin. Like leprosy in reverse, only instead of eating away flesh, it built it up with barnaclelike deformities.

They were hideous. Repulsive.

Patches of smooth normal skin still remained on a few of the men. But most were completely covered by the ugly growth. A growth that had thickened their faces, spread out their noses, and lumpified their ears until almost all human features were lost. Malicious smiles cracked their stony faces as they approached the oblivious, fighting men.

One of them, Juan, finally caught sight of the approaching danger and shouted warning. Some men tried to run. But by then it was too late. Whips cracked, snapping around those quick enough, strong enough, with enough wit left to try to flee, bringing them down with ruthless ease.

They moved quickly for such big, grotesque creatures, and clearly enjoyed the terror of their prey. Mr. Inmate was mean enough to struggle, to try to fight them. For his trouble, he was run through with a sword. An easy slide in and out of him with the blade. He toppled to the ground, blood spilling from his back and belly. The muddy ground eagerly soaked it up.

A few other men were mercilessly cut down by swords. That was all it took, three men sliced through with swift, easy violence, and the rest became as meek as lambs. No more struggling; no more trying to escape. They allowed themselves to be herded and roped together. Even the three who had been skewered by swords were yanked to their feet and tied up with the rest—quick, efficient, very frightening. As if they had done this same sweep and rounding up of the newly dead many times before.

I was easing back away from the rise when a shadow flew over me, freezing me into stillness. Moving with careful, deliberate slowness, I turned my head until I caught sight of something even more alien than what I had just seen. A large batlike creature flew overhead, carrying something almost as big as itself.

"An imp," one of the horned soldiers said in a deep rumbling voice.

"Aye, but what does he carry?" growled another whose horns were the most prominent among them—an entire two inches of black ivory instead of tiny, sprouting nubs. The horned soldier slung the pack he carried onto the ground and reached in, pulling out a bow and quiver of arrows.

Catching sight of them, the airborne imp gave a squeak of alarm and flapped his wings faster, trying desperately to distance himself from the danger down below.

Not a word was uttered as the horned soldier pulled back the bow with beautiful form. No bated breaths, no tension. Just a quick and easy motion as he let the arrow fly. It sang through the air and struck true, burying itself through a spread wing. With a cry, both imp and prey fell from the sky and tumbled to the ground. It was quite a fall, over fifty feet, but the impact only stunned the imp. He was on his feet almost immediately.

"Crazy bull dheus," he squawked, more disgusted than fearful. "Why'd you do that?"

Somewhere in my memory, old but not forgotten, recognition stirred. I recognized the word *dheu* somehow. Knew that it meant dead.

As the imp stood up, I got my first good look at the creature. It was a thin, wiry thing just over three feet tall, with a sly and cunning face and leathery skin the color of dirt. But it was natural looking, as opposed to the unnaturally distorted bull dheus. The imp had never been human, and small though it might be, no one would mistake it for anything other than an adult of its kind.

With a snort of disgust, the imp grasped the arrow with a thin, clawed hand and yanked the barbed shaft from its wing, letting out a hiss of pain. Two drops of blood fell to the ground, and then the wing began to heal. But instead of torn tissues and broken skin knitting together naturally the way Monères healed, the broken flesh blurred and melted, formed an oozy substance that filled in the gaping hole and slowly began to reshape itself into skin and tissue.

Four of the bull dheus, the ones with horn tips, gathered around the little imp, while the four less transformed soldiers stood guard over the captured men.

"You serve one who is powerful," said the bull dheu who had shot down the imp. He spoke simply, like a child. "What have you got there?" he asked.

The imp glared up at the soldiers, then, hiding his ire, smiled cunningly and replied, "Just my youngest imp child, great master. What impressive skill you have with the bow. You must be their lord," he said fawningly.

"Pietrus, our lord? When bull dheus fly," snorted another.

Pietrus lifted a hand and casually backhanded the speaking bull dheu across the face, sending two long yellow teeth flying. The bull dheu plucked the fallen teeth up from the ground and rooted them back into his gum.

"An imp child," Pietrus grunted. "Show him to us."

"'Tis a simple winged creature like myself. Nothing to rouse the curiosity of a great one such as yourself." Reaching down, the imp stretched out a little wing from the dazed creature to show the truth of his words. The object of their curiosity roused and flapped its wing out of the imp's hold. The imp struggled to hold it down, but the other creature pushed the imp off and staggered to his feet.

Even from far away, I could see that it was indeed a

child, even though it stood nearly as tall as the imp. But it was not an imp child. What rose to his feet had smooth charcoal-gray skin, large soulful eyes, a flat pug nose, and a wide hairless head. It was adorable in a cute-ugly sort of way, like one of those kewpie dolls with their scrunched-up faces. It stood on two large feet, tipped by tiny black claws. Aside from the dark membranous wings, he looked nothing at all like the imp claiming to be his father. Whereas the imp was thin and wiry, all bones and shrunken skin, the child was plump—solid bone and mass. His face and body was round, and unlike his purported father, there were two tiny horns on the top of his head. Most startling and enchanting was the utter innocence he exuded.

A chorus of *oohs* came from the bull dheus as they caught sight of the young creature.

"Your child is lovely," rumbled Pietrus.

Ooo-kay. Reasoning and intelligence was obviously something the bull dheus lost in their transformation. Because anyone with eyes could see that no blood relation existed between the two creatures. Wings and small stature were the only things they had in common. All else was completely and distinctly different.

The little creature glanced up, startled. Fear crossed his face, the emotion clear and pure, easily seen in the large liquid eyes as he looked at the huge, towering bull dheus surrounding him. Another *ooh* sounded from the soldiers. Utterly entranced, Pietrus bent down and reached out a large hand to touch the little thing.

The imp yanked the creature behind it, shielding the child with his scrawny body. While the child did not seem overly fond of the imp, he was clearly intimidated by the bull dheus and remained still.

"You are frightening it," cried the imp, alternating between a fulminating glare and an ingratiating smile. "You are so large while we are so small. If you would kindly give us some room."

"Leave the child and you may go," said Pietrus.

"No!" squeaked the imp. "My master requires this humble child as a servant to serve in his castle, and will be greatly angered if I do not bring the boy to him."

"Whom do you serve?" demanded Pietrus.

"The great warlord Ludwick is my master. Ruler of the Green Hills."

"We serve Lord Gordane, Warlord Sovereign of the Desert Land. You trespass across our ground."

"Forgive me," said the imp obsequiously, hiding his ire. "I was not aware the spawning grounds of the newly damned belonged to anyone."

An unpleasant jolt went through me at hearing what he'd called this place.

The imp pulled out a large gold coin from God knows where—there certainly weren't any pockets I could see—and offered it up to Pietrus. "Here, Great Master Pietrus. I will pay you tribute passage."

Pietrus held out his hand, and the imp dropped the coin into his opened palm. "I will take the coin," he said, "and the child."

"But I paid!"

"And so you may go."

"Not without my child!" said the imp.

"He lies," said a younger bull dheu joining the group. He was less hideously deformed than the others and obviously smarter. "One can see that it is not his child. It has horns and claws on his feet while the imp does not, and their skins are completely different colors."

Pietrus examined the imp and child again, noting the pointed out differences. "It is as you say, Miles," he rumbled.

Miles? I started, and within me I felt Mona Louisa jerk as well. Miles was the name of one of her former guards—the one who had betrayed me on Mona Louisa's orders into the hands of Monère rogues. For his crime and treasonous act of trying to harm a Queen that he was supposed to be protecting, Miles had been found guilty by the High Queen's Council and personally executed by the Demon Prince. Could he possibly be the same man—handsome, cruel Miles who had died only a short month ago?

The color of his hair was impossible to discern beneath the filth, but it could have once been blond. Patches of his skin were still yet smooth, but enough of that hard bumpy growth covered his face and distorted his features to make it almost impossible to identify him. Only his eyes . . . his eyes were the same beautiful blue.

I swung my gaze back to study the three other bull dheus guarding the men. One had dirty matted hair, possibly red once, with green eyes. *Rupert*, a voice identified inside me, another of Mona Louisa's four betraying guards she had loaned me. And the other two, Demetrius, with the darkest hair, and Gilford, a brunette. I recognized them with a sort of vague horror. And that horror was echoed within me by Mona Louisa.

They had changed so completely and so quickly in just a month's time! They had all once been handsome men, but no longer.

The spawning grounds of the newly damned . . .

My attention was drawn back to the first group as Pietrus swatted the imp away with a wave of his big hand. It landed in a crumpled heap several yards distant.

"If it's not an imp, what is it?" Pietrus wondered. His big hand shot out and grabbed the creature.

The child screamed. Not just with fright but with pain. The high cutting sound had me on my feet and moving toward them even before I was aware of it. Inside me, Mona

Louisa screamed: *No! Run* away *from them, you fool. Not* toward *them!* But I could not run away. That innocent, painful cry would not let me.

While that shock of pain still sounded, bell-like, in the air, a giant shudder moved across Pietrus's body. Like a dark slurry stain, the ugly growth on his skin crawled off his flesh in a visible, flowing wave, and traveled down his connecting hand to the child. It was as if a giant scrub brush had magically rubbed over Pietrus, leaving behind a clear, undistorted image of the man he had once been. The immense size and bulkier build was still there, as well as the deeper, broader bone structure of his transformed face, but his skin was smooth, unblemished, his features sharp and clear.

The transference of the sludge was a clearly painful process for the young creature. The child convulsed, his round face twisting into a frightful knot of agony as the defilement rippled like an ugly wave over him and disappeared inside him.

Pietrus dropped the little creature and gaped with amazement at the smooth skin of his hands. "My skin," he said with deep wonder.

"Gargoyle," whispered another bull dheu with greed and dawning realization on his face. "It's a gargoyle child," he cried, reaching out both hands toward the little child with the full and deliberate intent of touching the gargoyle and shedding his own filthy defilement as Pietrus had done, regardless of the agonizing pain it caused the innocent creature. Eyes focused on the vulnerable child with hungry, merciless greed as they crowded in around the baby gargoyle like wolves around a young and tender lamb.

With a flurry of wings that had finally healed, the imp took to the sky, a bitter look on his wizened face as he abandoned his prize to predators far bigger than himself.

The young gargoyle raised his eyes to the sky, saw the imp flying away, and whimpered, shrinking down as the bull dheu reached for him. I slammed sideways into the big brawny soldier, sending him colliding with the other bull dheus, toppling them all. They had been so intent upon their prey, they hadn't seen me coming. I had a split second to tear off the lower half of my gown, use it to scoop up the little gargoyle, and run.

"It's okay. It's okay," I whispered to the little gargoyle, but actually the situation was pretty dire. I didn't know if I was fast enough to outrun the bull dheus who, sure enough, were in hot pursuit. One quick glance back made me aware that whatever their size, they were pretty darn fast on their feet. Five of them were racing after me and closing the distance. The little gargoyle I carried looked as big as a five-year-old toddler but was almost twice as heavy.

I looked down into those big eyes, so wide, so innocent, and told the boy, not even sure if he was able to understand me, "I'm not fast enough to outrun them. Can you fly?"

"I don't know, I've never tried," the little gargoyle answered to my complete and utter surprise, his piping voice as clear and pure as those huge liquid eyes. The shock of hearing him speak caused me to stumble. Stupid! I caught myself and put on a burst of speed, but the sound of the others was drawing frighteningly closer.

"You're going to have to try now, okay?"

The little creature nodded.

"Just tuck yourself into a ball and roll. When you come to a stop, fly. Just fly away." With those terse instructions, I sent the little gargoyle rolling from me like a big, awkward bowling ball.

Spinning around, crouching low, I tripped my closest pursuer. He went down with a jarring crash. Unfortunately, I couldn't follow up and make sure he stayed down, I had to deal with the others. I risked a quick glance to see that the little gargoyle had come to a stop and was on his feet, flapping his wings. He was trying, but he wasn't able to fly yet. Too young or perhaps too weakened. My heart sank. It wasn't looking good for us.

A warning shout came from one of the bull dheus who had stayed behind, the one with the darkest hair, Demetrius. He gestured up toward a flash of movement in the sky. At first I thought it was the imp returning. But the wings were much larger. I gaped at the creature coming toward us, feeling awe at the majestic sight—a gargoyle, a fully grown one, cutting across the sky with stunning speed and effortless ease.

That momentary inattention cost me. A bull dheu crashed into me and took me to the ground. His sword came whooshing down, glinting red in the sky's reflected light. I had a moment to pray, *Please, Goddess, lend me strength.* Then my hand latched over the hand holding the hilt, and I looked up into Miles's familiar blue eyes as we fought for control of the sword—a losing battle for me with the momentum of the downstroke already behind him.

I twisted out of the way, and the blade came slicing down right where my head had been. Miles was strong, but one solid blow to the crotch and all that bull dheu strength of his was temporarily put on hiatus. With a sneer and a shove, I pushed him off me.

A whip cut through the air and wrapped around my neck and chest. Damn, did that lash sting! Anger at being struck—at being *whipped*—filled me, adding to my strength as I grabbed the leather coil and pulled. Surprise splashed across the bull dheu's face as I yanked him off his feet. He obviously hadn't expected me to be that strong. Neither had I. I kicked him in the face, chopped the back of his neck, and down he went and stayed. No others for me to grapple with. The other two, Pietrus and the bull dheu whose teeth he had knocked out, were still chasing after the gargoyle child and about to run into bigger prey than they had expected or were even aware of.

Like silent death, the big gargoyle swooped down and gored one bull dheu with his thick horns, while delivering a powerful blow to Pietrus with a clawed hand. Both bull dheus went flying away from him like broken and bleeding dolls.

Peeling the whip off my body, I walked over to the first demon I had tripped. He was starting to rise. A kick in the face, a grinding knee into the nose, and he was down once more. A quick glance showed that Miles was still rolling on the ground, clutching his balls. The only ones standing were me, the gargoyle child, and the big scary grown-up version of him.

Wow! was all I could think as we studied each other. He—and it was definitely a he—looked like a dark, ominous thundercloud ready to rain and thunder. Wearing only simple black trousers, he stood over seven and a half feet, taller even than the bull dheus, with a stateliness to his bearing that was at odds with the casualness of his attire. He seemed a natural, if intimidating, creature of this realm. Not something twisted, distorted, changed. The horns just starting to bud on the child were fully grown on the adult male—beautiful black ivory, thicker than my wrist, impressive as hell. So was the heavily defined musculature of his tanklike build. His wings had folded up neatly on his back so that had I not seen them, I would never have guessed at their presence. The greater density and weight I had felt when carrying the child was clearly evident in the big, looming male before me. He was formidably large and savage-looking, from the broad square head, wide flat nose, thin lips, and smooth charcoal-gray skin, to his proud, intelligent black eyes. The blood smeared on his horns, dripping down his face, added the perfectly dramatic scary touch.

Bull dheus, no problem. I'd tackle one in the blink of an eye. But this huge, angry gargoyle standing before me was someone I did not want to tangle with.

Finished with his quick assessment of me and my apparent lack of threat, his claws retracted, and he turned his attention to the boy. With a happy gurgling cry, the little gargoyle tottered to the big fearsome male. He scooped the child up with a gentleness that eased the breath I'd been unconsciously holding. My body relaxed as they communicated in rolling trills, deep consonants, and quick echoing syllables that flowed together with a sliding musical cadence.

"My son, Ghemin, says that you risked yourself to help him."

It was strange to hear such a savage-looking creature speaking in so civilized a manner. What had he said? Oh yeah, something about me helping his son.

I nodded, unable to find words as I beheld these creatures of legend—gargoyle.

His gaze darted briefly behind me, and his wings snapped open like dark sails on a ship. "Come." He held a hand out to me in imperious command, his son cradled in his other arm. I went to him and almost took his hand before remembering what touch had done to the child.

"I can't," I said, snatching back my hand. "I'll hurt you."

The gargoyle looked at me with a fierce, impatient scowl. "I am full-grown. You cannot hurt me if I do not wish it. Come now, quickly."

I grabbed his hand and had a moment to marvel over the smoothness of his skin, softer than it looked. Then we were lifting into the air.

"Hang on," said the gargoyle. "Wrap your arms around my waist."

As my feet left the ground, I not only wrapped my arms around him but clamped my legs around him, too, clinging to him tighter than a monkey wrapped around a tree. And that's what he felt like, a tree—as big around as a hundred-year-old oak, and maybe even more solid. I had a moment to wonder at the great strength in those wings—none of us were lightweights, him least of all—a couple of seconds to feel the powerful flexing of his back muscles beneath my hands and realize that we were moving, but slowly, at half the speed with which he had flown in, when a warning trill sounded from Ghemin.

"Hold tight!" the gargoyle said, and tilted sharply to the right. An arrow whizzed by, dangerously close. Two more followed in quick succession. I looked down and saw Gilford, Demetrius, and Rupert shooting arrows at us. The other bull warriors whose asses we'd kicked were running back toward them, no doubt to grab their own bows from their supply sacks. The one who I was really worried about, though, was Pietrus, who had brought the imp down with one single, accurate shot. I watched Pietrus pick up his bow.

"Careful," I said. "This next arrow coming . . . his aim is very accurate. He'll go for your wings."

The arrow was unleashed and came at us with frightening speed. The gargoyle dipped sharply down, and it overshot us.

"Yup, he's aiming for your wings." And he had a target maybe three times bigger than what that scrawny imp had offered him, and at a much closer distance.

Another torrent of arrows flew up at us and the gargoyle turned to face them. Unfortunately, it exposed us, Ghemin and I. The gargoyle snatched an arrow out of the air just before it struck his son. A deft shift of his lower body, and

I felt an arrow whiz by my right leg, missing it by an inch. Another powerful twist of his body, and another arrow whistled past my ear.

When the immediate danger passed, the gargoyle dropped the arrow he'd snatched out of the air—nothing useful to be done with it, I guess—and flapped his wings, lifting us higher with concentrated effort, not so much going forward as straight up. I understood his reasoning when we hit a strong air current that caught his wings and lifted us up fast enough, powerfully enough, to drop my stomach down to my knees, the way a fast elevator going up sometimes does. We rode the strong wind, soaring up and away in a sudden sprint of speed, increasing the distance between us and our erstwhile archers down below, more and more with each passing second.

I thought we were going to make it, I really did. Then I looked down and saw that whatever Ghemin had miraculously done for Pietrus's skin had also improved his intelligence unfortunately. With a barked order, Pietrus lined up the other bull dheus in a loose circle with him in the center. On his count, they released their arrows simultaneously. The arrows came flying at us as a unit, in an evenly spaced pattern, making me curse, because one of them was *bound* to hit us. We couldn't dodge individual arrows the way we had been doing.

"Watch out!" I yelled, and then we were tumbling in the air. The big gargoyle snapped his wings shut and tucked himself around Ghemin and me, shielding us with his body. When he uncurled, there were excited shouts from down below. I opened my eyes and saw that two arrows had found their mark. One was buried in the bulky mass of his right arm. He yanked it unflinchingly out. It was the shaft sticking out of his back that told me we were in big trouble. That and the fact that his right wing was opened and flapping weakly, and his left wing was not.

"Pull the arrow out," the gargoyle said urgently. "I cannot reach it. You must do it." He hoisted me higher up his body and I shifted around until I could clearly see that the arrow had pierced his folded wing. With no other recourse—we were plummeting at a sickening speed—I grabbed ahold of the wooden shaft and gave a fierce yank. And found that the arrowhead had gone completely through the wing to anchor into the meaty part of his back. There was a stomach-churning, slurping-sucking sound and a spattering of blood as the barbed head uprooted grudgingly out of his flesh and tore back out through his wing.

The gargoyle made no sound though it had to have pained him terribly. With a powerful snap, his left wing unfurled. I dropped the bloody arrow and clutched him as our downward fall abruptly stopped. We were flying again but just barely. It was hard to grab air with a couple of holes through your wing, one through the outer tip, the other through the center. I watched as both jagged holes ripped wider under the shearing force of the wind and the combined burden of our weights.

As soon as the realization of what I had to do registered in my brain, I released him. The gargoyle growled, "No!" He tried to grab me with his hand, but I twisted out of reach.

"Get Ghemin out of here. I'll be fine," I said, meeting his eyes for a brief suspended instant. Then I was falling, plummeting, dropping like a stone.

It felt like the ground rushed up to meet me and punched me silly with a giant, bludgeoning blow. We had descended far enough that I fell no more than forty feet—like jumping from the fourth floor of an apartment building. Much better than the hundred feet up we'd originally been in the air before they'd tried to make him a porcupine with arrows. Still, the hard impact of my feet hitting the ground shot a hot wave of pain up my legs, hips, and back. I rolled and tried to assess the damage during that long tumble. My legs hurt the most, as if the devil was searing them with a hot poker. Broken? Dear God, I sure hoped not. We'd see soon enough.

I finally came to a stop and uncurled. Lying flat on my back, I had a perfect view of the sky. The gargoyle looked like a giant bat, growing smaller as he flew farther away. It wasn't the most graceful thing, his flight. More jerky, less gliding ease. But he'd regained some of his height, and without my added weight burdening him, his injured wing seemed to be holding up well enough to keep father and son aloft. If the gargoyle healed as fast as the imp did, the hole in his wing might even be gone soon. They would make it if no more arrows struck them. And the chances of that lessened with each second that passed.

With a mental sigh because I hated pain, I really did, I rose to my feet. Sure enough, hot jagged pain tore through me. Son of a bitch! The right leg was definitely broken—the ugly sound of bone grating against bone made that kind of obvious. The left leg felt as if it was broken, too. As if that wasn't bad enough, a sound drew my eyes up to the unwelcome sight of Miles and a whip-bearing demon heading my way. On the barren rocky land behind them, Pietrus and three others let fly another organized round of arrows up into the sky.

"Arrows!" I shouted, and watched with bated breath as the gargoyle angled abruptly upward, allowing the arrows to fly harmlessly past and start almost immediately to fall. The next synchronized volley, the three arrows arched up, peaked, and started to fall just as they neared their target. At Pietrus's call, another round of arrows shot forth with barely a pause in between.

"More incoming," I yelled, but needn't have even bothered. The three arrows started to fall several yards short of their target as he flew higher and higher up into the sky.

They were safe. And I was not.

I bid them a silent farewell. Even felt a sweet moment of triumph before the bull dheu's whip whistled through the air and struck me.

EIGHT

GRYPHON ROAMED THE halls of the Demon Prince's home. At first the house staff was leery of him, a new demon. But when Gryphon didn't try to jump them and tear open their necks, they gradually relaxed, leaving him alone to pace through the empty rooms like a dangerous ghost.

Blaec, the High Lord, kept an eye on Gryphon in Halcyon's absence. The High Lord had explained everything to Gryphon. Good thing Halcyon hadn't been there when he had. Gryphon would have tried to rip open his throat, and tear his head off, too, if he'd been able to. In the hours since Halcyon's abrupt departure, he'd had a chance to cool down. Now heartache more than anger ate at Gryphon like a dull, gnawing pain. Regrets . . . so many of them. And chief among them was his lady, Mona Lisa. Her face filled Gryphon's mind. Her dark eyes laughing, tender. Soft as they made love. So fierce when she fought, defending those she loved.

Mona Lisa, you were supposed to be safe, he cried inside. But safe was the furthest thing she was now. She was filled with demon essence. And no matter how small the amount, what she had within her was the same wildly savage nature that resided in him now.

From what the High Lord had told him, she was much like a new demon. It was enough to fill Gryphon with horror and heartache for her. Because what he was now frightened him—that terrible loss of control, when control had been everything to him. The strange urges, the unstable temperament was unsettling.

No matter how he still looked the same, Gryphon was different. Completely and utterly different. More unthinking beast than man. In time, Blaec had said, Gryphon would be more like himself. Never exactly the same again, but closer to what he had been in the living realm, less beset by the primitive new hunger of the dead. It would be at least two long years, and that was being optimistic, before he could be trusted unsupervised around the living.

He knew he could not be trusted around those he had once loved. He'd come to that conclusion a week after he had awakened in this realm and still found that ravenous, beastly hunger for blood undiminished within him. Even now, it had not eased in its intensity. Even though he could control it better, that control had its limits. If blood wine was there within his reach, he could go for a time without grabbing for it. But he could not deny himself that eventual sip. He had tried several times and failed. The hunger had grown and taken him over completely until he'd become mindless and incredibly dangerous. He would have attacked a maid, who had chosen an unfortunate moment to enter his room, had not Halcyon stopped him. That episode made all the house staff wary of him, for good reason. Never trust a new demon, was the saying down in Hell. It should have been branded across his forehead for all to see.

Despite Halcyon and Blaec's assurance about how well

his control had been since, Gryphon knew better. He knew how terribly fragile it really was.

Hell was not this realm. It was being without Mona Lisa. It was knowing that if he really, truly loved her, he would not let her anywhere near him for the next five years.

He had come to that resolve—to be truly dead to her—then Halcyon's revelation had come, by way of his father. And what Blaec had told Gryphon nearly unraveled all of that hard-earned control.

Blaec had thrust the chalice of blood wine at him and told him to drink when his eyes had burned red during the course of their talk. Gryphon had growled, tried to knock the drink away, disgusted with his weakness, his need, angry with the bearer of such horrific news. He had resisted until something even worse than his hunger had stirred inside of him and stretched his skin.

"Drink, you fool!" Blaec had said. It was the harsh urgency in the High Lord's voice that finally broke through to Gryphon and made him snatch up the drink and gulp it down—no careful restrained sips. Just sating that hunger, and sating it quickly, so that whatever frightening thing had moved within him quieted once more.

"Was that . . . my demon beast moving in me?" Gryphon asked, setting the empty chalice down with a trembling hand.

Blaec nodded—a short, curt gesture.

"Is there reason why you do not wish it to emerge now?" Gryphon asked.

"Only that I did not wish to explain the destruction of the room to my son, and the possible damage to you. Damage that I would have had to cause in order to control you. The first time you shift into your demon beast form, it should not be while your heated emotions rule you. I'd also strongly advise allowing more time to come to terms with your new nature before attempting to wrestle with that especially dangerous aspect of yourself."

Another near miss. He seemed to be having quite a few of those lately.

Gryphon was calm when Halcyon finally returned. The Demon Prince had only been gone for a few short hours, but it had felt like days. It was a relief to feel Halcyon's powerful presence entering the house once again. He wouldn't have returned so soon if Mona Lisa were missing, Gryphon told himself. He would have stayed to search for her. Whatever Halcyon had sensed had to be a mistake, a flaw in the bonding ring. Then Gryphon saw Halcyon's haggard face, the grief-stricken despair in his eyes.

Halcyon told them simply, "She is not there. She is no longer in the living realm."

It was suddenly hard for Gryphon to speak, to ask questions. "Do you mean that she is dead?"

A brief hesitation. Then Halcyon nodded. "I fear so."

"Is she . . . is she here?"

"No," Halcyon said. "I do not sense her in this realm."

Gone, Gryphon thought. The loss skewered him like a knife, even worse than the loss of his own life. Too many things hit him all at once—hot anger, cold despair, that first touch of raging grief. They all collided inside him, so that for a moment he only felt blessed numbness, an artificial calm before the explosion.

Then Halcyon was speaking again. "Father, a black light took her."

His words froze Blaec into immobility.

"She was Basking when a veil of darkness moved across the moon and traveled down the moon's rays into her," Halcyon said, his eyes fixed intently on his father. "Her people said the black light seemed to wrap around her, and she simply disappeared."

"NetherHell," Blaec said, looking grimly at his son.

"NetherHell?" Gryphon asked, his eyes going back and forth between the two of them. "Where is that? Is that where she is?" The wild hope that suddenly flared in his heart was muted immediately by their somber look.

"NetherHell is another separate realm. A lower realm," Halcyon explained. "And today is *Aequus Nox*, when the planets align and the sun crosses the celestial equator, allowing a short span of time when the walls between the realms thin."

"You believe this black light took her to this other realm? To this NetherHell?"

Halcyon glanced at his father, and it was Blaec who answered. "The old writings make note of such an occurrence happening once before, over five centuries ago, when the time of *Aequus Nox* coincided with a full moon. A black light traveled down and struck two Monère warriors. When the dark light vanished, they, too, were gone. They were seen a year later in the Cursed Realm, greatly changed."

"The Cursed Realm?" Gryphon said, feeling dread well up and spread inside him.

"Another name for NetherHell," Blaec said. "Not all Monère who die go to Hell. Some go to NetherHell, those who are . . . more evil. Many humans, corrupted ones, also go to that realm upon their death."

"Mona Lisa wasn't dead, though. She was alive," Gryphon said, his hands rounding into loose fists. Too tight and he would puncture himself with his demon nails. He'd found that out the hard way.

"A part of her *was* dead, though." The import of Halcyon's words sank into Gryphon, and he found himself moving. Only Blaec's hand on Gryphon's shoulder kept him from finishing the lunge he'd started toward Halcyon.

"It's not only Halcyon's demon blood in her," Blaec said, gripping him hard. "That part of her alone would not have landed her in the Nether Realm. Mona Lisa also possesses Mona Louisa's essence, which was more evil than good, if you recall."

Blaec's words—and reasoning—calmed Gryphon down enough to mutter, "You can let me go now, High Lord."

Blaec did so cautiously.

"So you are saying that Mona Lisa was transported down to NetherHell because of that tainted part of Mona Louisa's dead essence in her?"

"Yes," said the High Lord. An expression too much like sadness moved in his eyes.

"Then we go there and bring her back."

Thick, stony silence.

"Father," Halcyon said. "I need your help."

A wave of energy pulsed out from the High Lord and filled the room. Power strong enough, suffocating enough, to snatch away Gryphon's breath and squeeze a gasp from him. At the involuntary sound, the oppressive power immediately lightened as Blaec brought himself back under control.

"You cannot go there, Halcyon," Blaec said.

"I cannot *not* go, Father. Please, you have to open the gate for me."

Gryphon looked and saw something in Blaec's eyes that he could never have imagined seeing in a being so powerful and old. He saw fear—fear for his son.

"Why don't you want Halcyon to go?" Gryphon asked.

Blaec's gentle, even tone masked for a moment the dire contents of his words. "Because NetherHell is not like any place that you know of. It is the realm for the cursed, the damned. For the evil ones. And like the dead souls of the people it pulls down, the realm is twisted and evil in its own way. Those that walk the Nether Realm become altered. The damned souls that find themselves there start to change almost immediately. The corruption that is within starts to become visible on the surface of their skin after only a week's time. We know this because the gate between our two realms was once open. I closed it almost a millennia ago when a distorted Nether creature crossed into our realm and escaped into the living realm. Five demon guardians were lost and more than twenty humans were killed before we were able to stop it.

"The potential for good and evil resides in all creatures. In animals as well as humans and Monère," Blaec said. "We are all a mix of good and bad. It is the balance between the two that is important, that decides which realm one goes to for those gifted with afterlife. Those who have more good balanced in them find themselves in Hell. Those who are more evil become inhabitants of NetherHell. Unlike other realms, though, the Nether Realm continues to actively distort the physical self, mutating it. Not only does it change the outer appearance, more important, it changes what is inside you. Slowly, surely, it grows the bad part that resides in you, expresses it more fully, molds it more strongly, twisting and unbalancing the natural equilibrium. No one is safe from this effect, because no one is one hundred percent good. There is some bad in all of us. With time, and time is a crucial matter here, all who reside there change. For the worse, not the better. Even if I reopen the gate, this thinning between the realms exists only for a twenty-four-hour period. After that, the barriers between the realms solidify again, and you would be trapped in that realm for another ninety-two days until the walls thin once more at summer solstice. Ninety-two days can alter you much in body and spirit. In so changed a state, I could not allow you to return to Hell," Blaec said, looking at Gryphon. "Do you understand?"

He did. And his decision was an easy one. "Halcyon need not go. I'll find Mona Lisa and try to bring her back in that twenty-four-hour period. If I don't make it back in time, then I'll stay there in NetherHell. I'd rather become a twisted damned creature down there with her than exist here without her."

"A noble sentiment," Halcyon said. "But you are newly dead. You, alone, are not strong enough to handle this task."

"His new status will actually make it easier for him to walk the realm's thicker atmosphere," Blaec said.

"Easier to physically walk that realm, yes. But not strong enough in psychic power to survive its many dangers as I could—to have any chance of finding Mona Lisa in less than a day and bring her back. He is only just coming into his demon strength. You know as well as I do that I must go."

"I'm going with you," Gryphon said with firm resolve. "My existence here means nothing without her."

"You are young in Monère years, as well as demon years," Halcyon said, not unkindly. "You will find another to love."

"As you so obviously did," Gryphon said darkly. "In your over six hundred years of existence here, I'm sure you found dozens, *hundreds,* of other women to love before Mona Lisa."

Halcyon nodded wryly, conceding Gryphon's point. Before Mona Lisa, he had found no one. After her, there would also likely be no one. "In this, sadly, I am in agreement with our young, love-struck demon. I would rather be in that realm with her, just on the slim chance that she is there, than exist here without her. I'm sorry, Father."

Both grief and understanding were in Blaec's eyes. "You have found love. Love such as few of us ever know. It is not something to be sorry about, son. It is a treasure worth fighting to reclaim. But the thought of losing you . . ."

"It comforts me to know that you will be here if I don't return," Halcyon said, gripping his father's arms. "You have guided our people for more centuries than I have existed. In truth, I have always felt partly to blame for your withdrawal, for the apathy that gripped you for so long."

"Why would you feel guilt?" Blaec asked.

"Because had I not been here to take over the rule of our people, you would never have allowed yourself to fall into such a state."

"You are my son," Blaec said, with a fierce frown. "You and your sister, Lucinda, are the sole reasons why I still exist."

"Then you know why I must go. Please, Father. Open the gate for us."

Slowly, the High Lord nodded. "Very well. I will reopen the gate this one last time. You will have less than twenty hours to bring her back." Several hours had already passed since the clock started ticking. "If you do not return by then, the gate—and this realm—will be forever closed to you."

NINE

I was in real trouble. That knowledge was driven home stingingly sharp as the whip cut into my flesh. I wrapped my hands around the thick leather and pulled. The whip-wielder was smarter this time. He released it—not that I could do much with it. By the time I unwound it from around my neck and shoulders, Miles had reached me. His sword came slashing down, murder, mayhem, and hate filling those blue eyes.

As death faced me—final death—something shifted within me. Literally. It was like being sucked down while something else, *someone* else, rolled over me. Mona Louisa came to the fore and took control, and I felt my body shift, rearrange itself, shrinking in places, expanding in others. The bones in my face altered, taking on her distinct cast, and from deep down inside, I heard Mona Louisa speak. "Stop, Miles!"

Surprisingly, he did. He saw his old Queen, heard her command, and obeyed. The sword that would have severed my head off my shoulders stopped in midstroke. The tip of the blade dropped limply to the ground. And so did he, falling to his knees in boneless shock.

"Mona Louisa?" His voice trembled with emotion, with something that sounded almost like—*you've got to be kidding me*—joy. "Is it truly you?"

Yup. Joy quivered his voice. I was surprised because Mona Louisa was the reason for his death. His crime had simply been carrying out her orders.

He doesn't hate you, I thought.

Of course not. He loves me. And Mona Louisa, in her own way, loved him. Like a useful pet. It was weird and really creepy being able to hear her thoughts and feel her emotions while she held sway over my body. I didn't try to fight her for control. Later, perhaps. We'd see later whose will, whose strength, was greatest. For now I was more than happy to let her run the show.

As I had been with you, came back the mocking thought. *But your fighting skills are of no use now with two broken legs. My wile and cunning will serve us better.*

I certainly hoped so.

"How can this be?" Miles asked. The other bull dheu had backed away with fear in his eyes.

"Two spirits dwell in this one body," Mona Louisa told him. Or would that be bodies, I wondered? Two spirits with two bodies inhabiting the same space. It was like I was being subleased out against my will. But as long as she paid the rent—i.e., kept us from being chopped up into little pieces—I would tolerate it.

You tolerate nothing. It is only what I allow.

Oh yeah? We'd see later which one of us wore the pants of this changeable body. For now, I wanted her to do something useful, besides keeping us from being sliced and diced. *Find out where the hell we are? Or if we even* are *in Hell?*

I felt her face twist into a frown. But she obviously

wanted to know as much as I did because she complied with my demand.

"Where are we?" she asked Miles.

"We are in NetherHell, milady."

"What part of Hell is that?"

"It's not. It's another separate realm. What inhabitants call the Cursed Realm."

"The Cursed Realm?" Shock and fear strummed through both of us. I screamed inside, a long soundless scream—*No!*

"Are we dead?" she asked, ignoring my inner howling.

Miles nodded, his face bleak.

Ask him to take us to Hell.

"You must bring me to Hell," Mona Louisa repeated.

Coarse sounds came from behind Miles. I—or rather she—looked and saw that we had more company. Pietrus and the other two bull dheus had decided to grace us with their attention now that their other prey had flown the coop. It took a moment to realize that the coarse snorting sounds they were making was laughter.

"Look at what we have here. A Monère Queen," Pietrus said. His eyes had filled with more intelligence. Pity. I liked him much better stupid. "Or would that be two Monère Queens? Two for the price of one." He guffawed a few more times, laughing at his own joke, then strode up to Miles and cuffed him in the head. The light blow knocked Miles down like a bowling pin tipped over onto its side. "Up off your knees. One good thing about this cursed existence is that we no longer bow down to Queens."

Miles lurched to his feet, fists clenched, but he didn't challenge the bigger bull dheu.

Were all the bull dheus here former Monères? I wondered.

"Is this your former Queen, Miles?" Pietrus asked.

"She is."

Pietrus grunted. "Much better looking than the other one. This one's beautiful enough to warrant our lord's interest instead of selling her to the slavers." He turned and gazed at Mona Louisa, all mirth dying on that new smooth face. "There is no escape from this realm. But your fate, if you are fortunate enough, will be easier than that of the men we captured. You may even retain your beauty," he said, reaching out to stroke a rough finger over our cheek.

Inside I shuddered. Mona Louisa bore the caress without flinching. "Then bring me to the one you serve," she said haughtily. It was weird hearing her cool voice issuing out of my mouth. No matter the shape of the lips, wider than my own, I still saw it as my mouth, my body.

Anger flared in the bull dheu's eyes. But instead of striking Mona Louisa, he wrapped huge fingers around her jaw. Both Mona Louisa and I felt the punishing power in that grip. "If you wish to keep your lovely face intact, do not presume to issue me orders."

Wisely, Mona Louisa kept her mouth shut.

"Bring her," he snarled at Miles. Releasing our face, he and the others strode away.

"Milady," Miles said, kneeling back beside us. "I must straighten your leg before it begins to heal."

The lower half of my right leg was bent out at an angle that no normal leg should have been able to achieve. Mona Louisa stared down at it unflinchingly. I, on the other hand, felt my stomach pitch and heave at the gross sight. Trying to stand on it had definitely not been one of my better ideas.

Mona Louisa nodded her consent and much too soon, before I was ready, Miles realigned the broken pieces with one sharp pull. Outwardly, Mona Louisa didn't make a sound. Inside, I screamed for the both of us.

Miles ripped off his sleeves, tore them into four strips, and used his sword and sheath to splint our leg. His bared arms showed the same repulsive growth that was sprinkled on his face. Mona Louisa stared fixedly at the unsightly blemishes, her jaw clenched tight, as he moved to our left leg and examined it. "Did this leg pain you when you stood?"

"Yes."

"Then the long bone is likely cracked, but still intact."

Exactly what I had deduced without all that poking and prodding.

"Hold on to me, milady," Miles said, and lifted her into his arms with gentle care. It was one of the most bizarre things, to be carried by your enemy, held so tenderly by him. I felt emotion move like a soft wave in Mona Louisa, and she lifted a hand, ran it lightly over the ugly, bumpy growth that had begun to crust over Miles's face. No words. But that touch was an unspoken apology. Not for the part she had played in his death—that she still believed had been her right as Queen, to command and have him blindly obey. But remorse for his death . . . yes, she felt that now when she hadn't before.

"I'm sorry that you are here in this realm," she whispered. "But I am glad that I am not alone."

Good old Mona Louisa, I thought. Selfish as always.

Miles's reaction, though, was vastly different. He stopped, held motionless for a second, as if he wasn't used to having her apologize or speak to him so. Or maybe he simply hadn't expected her to touch him, as blemished as he was. With that same careful gentleness, he turned his face and brushed his lips lightly against her fingers, before continuing to walk.

You're wrong, she thought. *I'm different. Such words and actions are not my usual habit or inclination. More like yours.* She seemed surprised, thoughtful. *It seems inhabiting the same flesh, sharing your thoughts and emotions, as well as your body, has affected me more than I was aware of.*

It didn't cost you much, did it, I asked, *that gesture, those words?*

Kindness is not my usual nature. She spoke matter-of-factly. *But it is yours.*

Not always, I answered, thinking of the brutal, violent part of myself had been was emerging.

No, not always. I am quite aware of your ruthless side. But even that you wield for others, which is very odd. Against our nature.

Her comment puzzled me. *Why?*

Because it is not conducive to survival.

Her answer shut me up. I couldn't argue against that, not considering where I was.

In the fifteen minutes it took us to catch up to the others, both of my legs had healed. The swelling was absorbed, the bruising faded away at a far more rapid speed than I was used to. She wiggled her toes and we felt no pain. Sweet.

"I am healed," she said. "Put me down."

Miles stopped but didn't set her down. "We are almost to the others. If I may, I would like to hold you a little bit longer."

Not carry. But hold.

He stood, waiting silently for her reply, and again she surprised me . . . and perhaps herself. She nodded her consent.

Miles hesitated, as if expecting her to abruptly change her mind. When she didn't, he continued walking.

As you said, came her voice inside me, *it does not cost me much. He serves me still. Gives me care and respect when he no longer needs to. A moment more in his arms is not much to give in return.*

What? I asked dryly. *You no longer consider his services, his respect, your simple due?*

Her answer was pragmatic. *It is a different realm, with*

different rules and different rulers. The only thing familiar to me is this man who carries me and the three others who once served me. Her next thought was more misty feeling than actual words. *Small wonder that I should want his arms around me longer for comfort. To cling, as he does, to what is familiar.*

Lucky you, I whispered, feeling true envy. I had nothing. Everyone that I had loved was gone—my life, my people, my lovers. Even Halcyon and Gryphon were lost to me.

Being dead in the Cursed Realm sucked.

Yes, it does came her agreement. But her hand stroked that blond hair and through our shared feelings, I knew that even caked with dirt, the strands still retained a hint of their silky softness. The part of me that was Mona Louisa remembered doing that in the past, stroking her fingers over her men's hair, part ownership, part simple enjoyment of the soft sensation.

Miles released a near silent sigh.

The sounds and scent of blood grew stronger as we crested a ridge and saw the others. The more senior soldiers walked ahead, while Gilford, Demetrius, and Rupert herded the captives from behind. The frequent crack of their whips drove the prisoners at a fast, shuffling pace. All the prisoners were roped together, even the two men forced to carry the limp form of the unconscious man the inmate had beaten to a pulp. They were tethered to their burden, one roped to the unconscious man's bound hands, the other to his feet. If they tried to run, they wouldn't get far, not roped as they were to their heavy burden. The inmate and the two others struck down by swords stumbled along, hunched over, pushed and pulled by the other prisoners tied in front and behind them.

"They are not healed yet like I am," Mona Louisa observed.

"Humans heal slower and are less strong than Monère.

The same in death as it was in life," Miles said, setting her on her feet. The gentle, careful way he handled her touched her against her will.

You have made me softer, she hissed.

Sometimes you find greater strength, greater power in softness, I replied.

Miles knelt, unknotting the cloth ties and removing the sword splint from her leg. I—or Mona Louisa, rather—walked the rest of the distance on our own two healed legs.

Gilford, Demetrius, and Rupert glanced back and saw her. Startled, shocked expressions crossed their faces, almost as if they were seeing a ghost.

Mona Louisa laughed in my mind. *They are, silly Mixed Blood. They are seeing a ghost.*

They almost knelt, a knee-jerk reaction that had carried over from life into death. They were stopped by a low growl from Pietrus, who watched us. They dipped their heads down instead.

"Milady," Gilford said respectfully as we walked up beside him. Sliding off the extra supply sack he had carried on his shoulder, he passed it to Miles. "What of the other Queen that we saw, Mona Lisa?" Gilford asked in a low voice.

A brief, awkward moment of silence, before Miles said, "She shares the same body as our Queen."

"Cursed Light!" Gilford exclaimed softly. "So what the other prisoners said about her is true—that she is two people in one."

Apparently Juan and Charles had tattled on me. *So much for loyalty,* I thought.

You are a fool if you expected anything more from them, replied Mona Louisa.

What about you, with your four men who are no longer your men? You still expect their loyalty.

That is one of the many points where we differ. You are

wrong. I do not expect loyalty from them. There is only one rule here, and that is ensuring your own survival. All other cares and concerns or feelings do not matter.

Not even Miles? I asked. *I can feel your affection for him.*

Not even Miles.

But I was inside her. Part of her truly believed what she was saying, another part of her was not quite so sure anymore. I caught her thought: that she had expected to be roped and bound with the other prisoners. But Miles made no move to do so. Neither did the other three men.

Calling a halt, Pietrus walked back to us with a heavy tread. The bull dheu was an odd mix of both beauty and horror now with his coarsened features covered by smooth, unblemished skin. A preview of what Miles and the others would look like soon. They were already taller, and thicker bone structure had already begun to alter their faces and body builds. But no horns sprouted yet from their heads, and their skin tones were lighter than the mud-brown leathery coloring of the others.

"Bind her," Pietrus said.

"There is no need," Miles said in reply. "She will not try to escape."

Pietrus froze into ominous stillness, obviously surprised that Miles had challenged his order. Both Mona Louisa and I held our breath.

Your man Miles doesn't seem to share the same sentiment about ensuring his own survival first, I noted.

He is a reckless fool. But I felt her gratitude toward him—that he would risk himself for her when she could no longer offer him any benefit in return.

To our surprise, Pietrus didn't strike Miles down with his huge fist or draw his sword. Maybe it was the intelligence gleaming in those eyes now, noting Rupert's, Gilford's, and Demetrius's waiting tenseness, and that the three more senior bull dheus were a significant distance away.

"If she tries to escape, I will cut off your head and feed it to the desert scavengers," Pietrus said before returning back to the front of the line.

A collective breath eased out from all of us.

"I will not try to escape," Mona Louisa promised quietly.

"I know," said Miles. And perhaps he knew her better than I gave him credit for, because he added, "There is nothing out here in these barren lands for you, milady. Your best chance of survival lies with our lord."

TEN

THE HIGH LORD didn't reopen the gate so much as cut open a new doorway through the sealed passage. Walking from Hell to NetherHell was like passing through a thick, suffocating force of immense pressure and utter darkness. Then some of the pressure eased and the absence of light faded away. They were met with a blaze of reddish light when they stepped out onto the other side and found themselves atop a ledge of a steep mountain cliff. Two odd-shaped suns glowed down on them in terrifying brightness. Gryphon cried out, expecting to feel the stinging bite of light upon his skin. But there was none.

"The light here cannot hurt you," Halcyon reassured him.

"I saw what sunlight did to you in the living realm. It might not sting anymore, but I know that it can soften demon flesh."

"The living sun does. Not Samice and Samí, the two suns here."

"How the fuck do you know?" Gryphon demanded.

"For a moment, you sounded just like Mona Lisa," Halcyon said. "And I know because demons used to walk this realm."

Gryphon's panic ebbed a little. "I didn't expect it to be this bright."

"One of the lures of this place. To walk in light once more and not fear it. We learned too late that it is the place itself that we should fear."

"Enough morbid talk. What do we do now that we are here?"

"We climb down this cliff," Halcyon said, suiting words to action. "And we let our bodies adjust to the denser atmosphere here. One of the many unpleasant aspects of this place, this thickened air. Some noted in the old journals that it was like swimming through honey. Likening it to mud would be far more accurate."

Now that he mentioned it, Gryphon became aware of a soft, pulling resistance on his limbs as he climbed down after Halcyon. "It feels more like honey to me. Not that uncomfortable."

"Your newer transitioned state. The discomfort is felt less by the younger dead."

Gryphon shot him a grim smile. "So you feel your age here, do you, old man?"

Halcyon grunted, and concentrated on the downward climb. When they reached the base of the cliff, they found themselves on a mountain that was jungle thick with plants and foliage. They began walking, Halcyon moving in an awkward fashion, completely without his usual fluid grace. Gryphon was affected much less so, walking almost normally. He soon found himself unexpectedly in the lead and stopped, waiting for Halcyon.

"Go on," Halcyon said, waving him on.

"It's pointless for me to lead. I don't know where I'm going."

"Neither do I."

"What?"

Reaching Gryphon, the Demon Prince dropped to the ground, resting for a moment. "It has been almost a millennia since my people walked this realm. Records from that time are scarce. Even were they abundant and detailed, things may have changed greatly."

"So what is our plan? And please say that there is one."

Halcyon gave a small, tired smile. "A vague one. The separate regions of this land were ruled by different warlords. That type of structure remained stable during the time my people roamed these lands. Presuming that things haven't changed much—and yes, I know that is a big assumption—my plan is to find one of these regions and look for Mona Lisa there."

"How many warlords were there?"

"Six, though that—"

"—may have changed," Gryphon finished for him. "Six." Gryphon blew out a breath. "Damnation. We don't have enough time to search through six different territories."

"We probably won't have to. Our best bet is to search the nearest one. Mona Lisa will likely be there."

"And where might that be, oh lord and master?"

"Your guess is as good as mine, my friend." Halcyon rose to his feet and they continued walking.

Two separate and equally difficult tasks faced them. Finding Mona Lisa, and bringing her back before the gate closed to them forever. Unspoken between Halcyon and Gryphon was that while they might accomplish the first task, given enough time, the second was far less likely in the brief amount of time they had. But even with the burden of that knowledge, the thicker air, the unnervingly bright sunshine, it was impossible not to see and appreciate NetherHell's strange and savage beauty. The foliage was different from any Gryphon had ever seen.

Some plants were edged with spines, others tipped with thorny leaves that were lavishly colored purple, burgundy, or black. Other vegetation appeared orange or crimson-red like the scarlet sky. It all bedazzled the eyes—eyes that had dwelled in twilight darkness for over a month now.

The animals that inhabited this realm were as equally strange, savage, and bizarre. He caught glimpses of ratlike creatures that hopped like rabbits on hind legs through the thick foliage and dense brush. One hissed at him, displaying a jagged row of sharp teeth. But it was the bigger creatures that proved the most dangerous.

A large, orange-furred beast vaguely resembling a giant sloth leaped out at him. Purple fur lined the animal's back and formed striped patches over the animal's eyes. Its brows and belly were yellow, blending it perfectly among the bright leaves of the foliage where it had been concealed. Long black claws tipped its giant paws, and its snout was short and blunt instead of thin and long. Another big difference was the huge teeth and sharp aggression of the animal. It moved with wicked quickness, springing at Gryphon. With a cry, he fell back and rolled on the ground. A powerful jaw snapped shut much too close for comfort.

It wasn't anything Gryphon did that saved him. It was Halcyon who came to his rescue. The Demon Prince may have been struggling physically in this new and strange environment, but his mental power was unimpaired. Psychic energy swelled on the thick air, gathered like a hard invisible fist, and punched the giant creature, tossing it back away from Gryphon. It squealed, grunted with pain, and loped away through the thick foliage at an awkward canter.

"Thank you for your timely intervention," Gryphon said, picking himself up off the ground. "Good thing you came along, I guess. Do all older demons retain their mental strength here?"

"Most do, not all."

"Yet you stepped toward it, not away, when you did not know if you had the means to fight the creature."

Halcyon shrugged. "It moved faster than I could; no use trying to outrun it. My only option was to stand and fight."

"Or let it eat me, and slip away while it was busy feasting on my flesh."

"Mona Lisa would kill me if I let that happen," Halcyon said dryly.

"You're already dead. So am I, for that matter."

"There's dead. And then there is true death," Halcyon said, offering Gryphon a hand up.

"Well, here's to staying in the first state and avoiding the second one. So how are you feeling?"

"I am better, less tired. My body is adapting slowly."

"Well, tell it to hurry up."

"As you wish," Halcyon said with a smile that made Gryphon realize how out of character he was behaving. Quick, glib remarks were less his style and more Mona Lisa's. Caution had been the hallmark of his previous self. Caution in what he said, what he did, even what he thought. The only time he had stepped away from that lifelong caution was when he had met her, Mona Lisa, and wanted her above all else, even his safety. Some of his confusion must have shown on his face.

"Your new demon nature is more aggressive, less controlled," Halcyon said. "Being in NetherHell brings that out more."

"It doesn't seem to affect you."

Halcyon shrugged. "It affects me as well, just not as obviously. One benefit of my greater age."

"So you become evil less quickly here," Gryphon said.

"Let's say that I am more slowly amenable to its influence.

But, eventually, it will have just as marked an effect upon me also."

"Great," Gryphon said. "Then let's get going. Time, as they say, is a' wasting." It certainly wasn't their friend.

ELEVEN

O NE MOMENT, NOTHING, just a vast rolling stretch of barren, dry land. Then we dipped down a valley, ascended a rocky rise and suddenly, spread out before us was this huge metropolis encircled by walls. From where we stood, we could glimpse the tiny movements of the crowded populace that dwelled inside. In the center of that walled city lay a large golden lake.

"Is that water?" Mona Louisa asked—her words, my thought. The odd brilliant gold color of the water threw us both.

"Yes, the only water source available for a two-days' journey," Miles said. He passed a skinned water pouch to her, almost as if he knew the sight of water would trigger her thirst. Sure enough, it did, an almost unbearable urge rising. Hands trembling, she pulled out the cork stopper and drank. Sweet liquid wetness splashed down our throat.

The other bull dheus stopped and gulped down water also. The prisoners moaned at the sight of us quenching our thirst. Whips lashed out, and no more sounds were heard.

Mona Louisa poured some of the liquid out into her cupped hand. The water glittered yellow gold. She handed the water skin back to Miles. As he drank, she turned back to study the sprawling city down below.

A huge palace was erected closest to the water, occupying almost an entire side. The other half of the lake was edged more distantly by tall terraced buildings and round domed homes. More houses and buildings fanned out from there in an orderly mass. Lush plants and spiky palm trees were sprinkled like colorful jewels among the buildings. It was a most unexpectedly colorful and crowded oasis.

"Our city-state," Miles said, slinging the water pouch back over his shoulder.

A city-state indeed. Much more sophisticated and larger than what Mona Louisa or I had imagined from the bull dheus' primitive appearance.

The two suns had set, and three moons had risen in their place when we finally reached the closed gate. Up close, the walls that had seemed so tiny in the distance loomed tall above us, over thirty feet high. At a shout from Pietrus, the metal gate swung open with a creaking groan. We marched inside.

Traveling down the wide central street, we caught glimpses of men and women, but no children anywhere. The people, unlike the guards manning the battlements, were of normal size with lightly tanned skins, not the dark leathery hide of the bull dheus. But all had the same barnacle growths covering their skin. The women wore veils but the men's faces were left uncovered. All looked hideous, no matter how prosperous-looking or beautiful their attire. They had the bored look of city people who had seen it all, and scarcely glanced at the prisoners as they shuffled by. Their cold and shrewd gazes slid over Pietrus's smooth face. But when their gazes fell upon Mona Louisa's ivory-white skin and perfect flawless beauty, their eyes, both men and women, filled with lust and envy, hungry desire. They stopped whatever they were doing and crowded around her.

"Stand back!" Miles growled, pulling out his sword. But still they came closer, hands reaching out, as if their compulsion to feel that smooth loveliness was stronger than their fear of his sword . . . until it began to swing and cut. Demetrius joined in, adding the threat of his whip. It whistled through the air, cutting both skin and cloth as he shouted, "Back away!"

Through it all, Mona Louisa stood cool and dispassionate, her composure as smooth and unblemished as her lovely skin.

Why aren't you afraid? I asked.

Because my men will protect me.

Such assuredness. Almost arrogant in her certainty.

Why aren't you surprised at the people's reaction to you? I wondered.

One glance at them, and you can see plainly what draws them—the beauty of my unblemished skin.

At her words, I was suddenly, painfully, aware of how much of that unblemished skin we were exposing. Not just hands and face, but a lot of bare leg, too. The cloth I had ripped off the bottom half of my dress left the new hemline at mid-thigh. Not terribly immodest but compared to the men and women here, who were covered from head to toe, some of them even wearing gloves . . . compared to them, Mona Louisa was almost flauntingly naked.

Beauty and unblemished skin—they are one and the same here, Mona Louisa observed.

Not quite the same, I returned dryly. Much as I had hated her, I could not deny her beauty—it was of the jaw-dropping variety. I sincerely doubted the crowd would have had the same visceral reaction to my plain face and less well-endowed body, perfectly smooth though my skin might be.

And yet with your plain face and flat-chested body, you managed to captivate your men as I never did mine. Until now, she thought, remembering when she had touched Miles's face and seen how he had looked at her. *He loves me now, as he never had before.* Her thought was both pleased and sad.

He didn't love you before? But he was loyal to you, even unto death.

Obedience and loyalty are not the same as love.

And the others?

They do not love me, not as Miles does was her cool observation. *Their loyalty is more to him, although they no doubt feel a certain nostalgia for what I once represented. But it is him now that they follow and obey, not me.*

I was surprised at her clear and accurate surmise of what she so possessively still thought of as "her men." I had wondered, for a moment, if she had deluded herself to the strength of their feelings for her.

I am not one to dodge the truth.

Her calmness, I realized with greater respect, was based on her sureness in Miles, that he would protect her, and that Gilford, Demetrius, and Rupert would follow his lead.

We pushed through the crowd and were suddenly standing before the grand palace. More bull dheus, tall and brutish-looking, stood guard at the entrance. A few came to our assistance, keeping back the large crowd that had followed us.

Stepping inside the palace was like entering a completely different world of beautiful, savage splendor that was both civilized and primitive. Life-sized statues of half-animal, half-man creatures stood in the corners of the grand entryway in all sorts of different poses, their faces terrified, twisted in pain. But it was the statue of the gargoyle in the center that drew the eye most strongly. His strong face, his large powerful body with wings just starting to unfold, was rendered in perfect, lifelike detail. But all else was far from perfect, I saw, as we walked down the wide hallway. There was dust and dirt everywhere. Bits of filth and neglect evident among the opulent luxury of the palace. The gaudy was mixed among the tasteful. Fine paintings hanging next to primitive pagan artwork, evidencing the varying tastes of the different warlords that had conquered and ruled this city-state. I wondered which most accurately reflected the current ruler, the gaudy or the tasteful. But whatever his taste in art, the untidy condition of the palace itself spoke poorly of the present sovereign.

At our approach, the looming doors at the far end of the hallway opened, and we stepped into a room so big, it made you feel small and insignificant. A red carpet rolled out like a flat tongue for a very long distance, leading to a raised dais. We were in the throne room. And upon the throne sat something I saw through Mona Louisa's eyes but didn't fully see or perceive, because it did not sit so much as slouch in the chair, still and unmoving, like one of the statues we had passed. For a moment, I thought it was simply that, a statue, until it stirred, stretched, and sat up, taking lazy notice of our presence.

A gargoyle. But one so unlike the one that had tried to rescue me. As frightening as my first glimpse of a real gargoyle had been, I was immensely glad that I had seen Ghemin's father first. Otherwise I would have thought that the deformed monstrosity before me now was the truth of their kind. Only the color of his skin—a dark charcoal gray—and the black horns—thick and wide and fully developed—were the same. All else was vastly and completely different. The purple robe and fine silk garments only served to highlight the ugliness of the wearer. Lumps and bumps inches thick, not the thin surface crust visible on the bull dheus, covered every inch of that gray skin like a repulsively warty exterior. He was hideously ugly. As if coral had floated out of the sea, adhered itself to the surface of his skin, then died there, giving up all the beauty and life it had possessed in the sea, leaving behind only crumbled skeletal remains.

The creature's eyes alighted upon me—upon Mona Louisa, actually—and I felt the caress of those dark eyes stroke across our skin. As dead as the rest of him looked, his eyes were stunningly alive, dark and intense, gleaming with intelligence and cold calculation. A perfect match for Mona Louisa, those eyes, I would have said before . . . before I'd gotten to know her more intimately than I ever could have imagined. I'd called her the Ice Queen for her cool cunning, for her cold and heartless beauty. But she was me now. We shared the same body, felt one another's thoughts. I did not want her to be a match in any way with that repulsive grotesquerie sitting upon the throne, looking at us like a tasty dessert that had just been brought before him.

"Ah, wonderful," the gargoyle said in a deep rumble, rising to his feet, looming tall as a tree over us as they lined the prisoners up before him. "Fresh dead you bring me. Enough of them to spare you my touch." He lumbered heavily over to stand before them, looking like something out of a nightmare, a creature horrific enough to frighten even the most calloused warrior or hardened criminal.

All he did was stretch out a finger and touch the first man. But that one touch was horrible enough. The surface of that thick barnacle growth on his skin crumbled, melted off him, and moved like visible black sludge down his hand onto the skin of the prisoner he touched.

The gargoyle moved on to the next prisoner before the

first man realized what had been done to him. Looking down at his hands, seeing the dark bumpy growth coating his skin, he gave a horrified screech.

"Unless you wish more of my touch," the gargoyle said with sinister menace, turning back with raised finger, "cease that noise!"

The scream shut off abruptly, and painful, throbbing silence filled the chamber.

Mona Louisa looked at Miles and wondered if he had betrayed her in the worst possible way. If he had chosen this terrible way to repay her for his death.

He shook his head, a slight bare movement. *Just the men,* he mouthed silently.

The roped line of prisoners swayed to the left, away from the gargoyle and his poisoning touch. No screams, no squeaks of sound. But they could not help that instinctive move away from his reaching hand.

Instead of just the bare touch of one finger, the gargoyle grabbed the next cowering man with both hands. Grabbed him and lifted him back into place, jerking the rest of the roped prisoners upright once more. With the greater contact, a darker, heavier layer of sludge moved off the gargoyle onto the prisoner he held, smearing the prisoner with an even thicker layer of crust than the previous man. The second prisoner stared at his changed hands, the defiled skin, and opened his mouth in a silent scream.

"That's right," the gargoyle said in a voice so deep that it resonated in the chamber. "Do not move, do not scream, unless you wish me to share a harder touch with you."

The next man in line bore the gargoyle's touch with a trembling but straight body. The rest stayed stoically still. Or as still as their shivering, shaking bodies allowed them. One touch, and a thin layer of dark sludge covered Juan, and then Charles.

With each layer shed, the gargoyle's skin became

smoother, less ugly. When he finished touching the last prisoner, the gargoyle had only a thin surface bumpiness remaining. Even more startling than the smoothing of his skin was the lightening of his spirit, as if the deformity had burdened mind and soul, as well as body. He was lighter, freer in his steps, graceful now in his movement. Turning, he strode lithely to the beginning of the line. To Pietrus. Stopping before the bull dheu, I saw then what I had not seen before: the uncanny resemblance of the bull dheus to the gargoyle, their maker. Their bigger, bulkier build. The darker color of their skin. The broadening of their features. Even the little horns sprouting on top of their head. He was slowly transforming them, making them take on his more powerful build and features bit by bit, blending it with their own.

The gargoyle gazed at Pietrus's smooth face. "What interesting thing did you find out there in the desert, my hunt captain?" he asked in a deceptively idle voice.

"We captured these prisoners and a Monère Queen, Lord Gordane."

"A Queen, most interesting. But tell me, what else did you encounter in your hunting raid today?"

Pietrus swallowed hard before answering. "A small child like yourself, my lord."

"A young gargoyle." He smiled. The scary sight made Pietrus blink nervously. "That's right. You can use the proper name in front of me. You found a young gargoyle and you touched it, obviously."

Pietrus gave a jerky nod.

"You had it in your hands? In your grasp?"

"Yes, I-I touched the child before I knew what it was, my lord," Pietrus said, falling to his knees. "Forgive me. I shot down an imp carrying the boy, and the imp claimed that the child was his own young. I would not have touched it otherwise."

"Rise," Lord Gordane commanded.

Pietrus rose hastily, standing with his back straight at attention.

"Your error was not in putting your hands on the young gargoyle," his sovereign informed him, "but in not bringing him back to me. Please do not tell me that you simply let the gargoyle child go?"

Pietrus shook his head. "The Monère woman . . . the other one . . . she fought us and ran away with the child."

"Speak clearly, Pietrus. What are you blubbering about? Where is this other woman?"

"There," Pietrus said, pointing at me, or rather Mona Louisa. "The woman who rescued the gargoyle child shares the same body as this one, my lord."

Gordane arched a thick brow. "What wild tale have you concocted to try to save yourself, Pietrus?" he asked softly, causing the big captain to tremble wildly.

"It is true, my lord," Pietrus said desperately.

"Pietrus speaks the truth, Lord Gordane," said the bull dheu whose teeth Pietrus had sent flying. "This woman is like none we have ever seen. She changes entirely—face, hair, voice, and body—and becomes a completely different woman than the one before you now."

"You say that she rescued the gargoyle child?"

"Yes, my lord. She ripped off the lower half of her gown, wrapped the child up in the fabric, and ran off with him."

"Where is the child now?" Gordane demanded.

"Another gargoyle, an adult male, flew off with both the child and the woman," Pietrus said. "We managed to pierce one of his wings with an arrow, but the woman, the other one, released the gargoyle and fell away from him. Without her weight burdening them, the gargoyle managed to escape with the boy."

"He dropped the woman, you mean," Gordane corrected.

"No, my lord. The woman . . . the other one, not the one you see here . . . she let go of him. He tried to grab her but she twisted out of his reach and told him to save his son."

"What a strange tale you bring me. Not the typical actions of a dheu," the gargoyle mused, looking at Pietrus. "But before I turn my attention to this interesting woman—or women, if I believe you—I have one last touch to give. One last touch I saved just for you." Reaching out, he laid a gentle finger against Pietrus's smooth cheek, and the last layer of blemish swirled off the gargoyle and onto the bull dheu. Pietrus shuddered, his eyes dulling a fraction as the defilement coated him.

"That small taste of me is to impress upon you to never fail me like this again," Gordane said, lifting his finger away. "Should you ever come across a young gargoyle again, you are to keep him in your possession. Touch the child as little as you can, and bring him here to me. Do you understand?"

"Yes, my lord" came an echo of voices.

"Good. Because should any of you fail me in such a manner again"—his eyes swept with quiet malice over each one of his men—"my touch shall be the last thing you feel. And it will not be light or gentle like this."

All the soldiers dropped to their knees. "Yes, my lord!" they chorused. At his gesture, they rose again. There was a silent sigh of relief when he turned his attention to me and Mona Louisa.

I trembled inside. Cringed when he walked toward us. Rupert, Demetrius, and Gilford backed respectfully away at his approach, and had I been able to, I would have backed away also, but I was stuck inside Mona Louisa. Stuck in our body. Miles stayed by our side. Gordane shot him a hard, considering look as he came to a looming stop before us.

Mona Louisa stood straight and tall. Coolly serene before the huge creature. *No use trying to run from him* came her voice inside me. *When escape is not an option, you face your enemy with dignity.* But despite her brave words, I felt fear, both hers and mine, flutter through us like butterflies. Frankly, I thought we should have tried to run away instead of putting on a useless brave front.

He laid his hand upon us, and we both felt it, his touch and something more. Something that reached down and found me hidden deep within Mona Louisa. Found me, grabbed ahold of me and *pulled*, yanking me out. I fought against it, but his hold was relentless, his power ruthlessly strong. I screamed inside her, long and echoing. Then found myself screaming with true voice as I exploded out in a quick and brutal transformation.

It hurt, dammit! My entire body felt bruised, beaten. And I was coated with a wet and sticky substance. My first thought was that it was blood, but it was clear fluid. Plasma maybe. It might as well have been blood, so severely weak was I, barely able to stand. Looking up into those black baleful eyes, I shivered.

"What do we have here?" Gordane rumbled. "Indeed, another woman sharing the same body . . . no, an entirely different body. Much less attractive than the other one."

If I wasn't so tremblingly weak, I would have lunged at him and tried to hurt him. Anything to chase away the fear of what he had just done so easily to me. But since taking a swing at him required more strength than I had at present, I used the only other thing left to me—my mouth. "Fuck you and the bat wings you flew in on."

His hand shot out and grabbed me. *Okay, maybe I shouldn't have mouthed off like that,* I thought, as he lifted me off the ground with barely any effort. It was highly uncomfortable, dangling like that, but it didn't really hurt. His hand was a loose collar around my neck, not squeezing yet as we both waited for each other's next move. It was only when Miles dropped to his knees before Gordane, begging, "My lord, release her please, she does not know who you are," that I began to have an inkling that maybe this wasn't about me at all. That maybe it was a test to see how Miles, standing so protectively nearby, would react. A test that Miles had just spectacularly failed.

Anger pulsed like hot lava through Gordane, and that big hand collaring my neck squeezed down, more in response, I think, to Miles's telling reaction than from any real intention of hurting me. But whatever the reason, I began to feel a highly uncomfortable choking sensation. *I don't need to breathe, I don't need to breathe,* I told myself. But even so, I felt like I was choking. My eyes bulged and my body gathered itself to fight. Before I could move, a bright light flashed between us and heat blasted against my neck, coming from my necklace. It was hot enough that it should have seared my skin, but it didn't. It burned Gordane instead.

The gargoyle gave a roaring bellow of pain, and released me. I dropped like a brick, sprawling on the floor next to Miles. Smoke drifted up from Gordane's hand. I smelled burned flesh, and saw a long angry welt seared diagonally across his fingers.

A very big, very angry gargoyle grabbed Miles around the neck—it seemed to be a favorite hold of his—lifting him up as easily as he had me.

"What did you do to me?" Gordane snarled. His face was a frightening mask of fury.

Miles choked out a strangled sound. Nothing understandable. Everyone in the room was deathly still, like rabbits freezing motionless in the presence of a lethal predator.

"He did nothing. It was my necklace, I think, that injured you," I said in a husky croak, picking myself off the ground. A part of me wondered what the hell I was doing, trying to save Miles, a man who had been my enemy! But he'd tried to protect me. I couldn't leave him out to hang like that—in the most literal sense.

"Show me!" Gordane snarled.

With shaking hands, I pulled my silver necklace out from beneath my dress, spilling it into view. Gordane's eyes fell on the cameo dangling at the end, and all that thick swirling anger suddenly dissipated.

"Um . . ." I looked at Miles, dangling helplessly in Gordane's hand. Reminded—he seemed to have forgotten him—Gordane tossed Miles away, and he went sailing into the line of prisoners, knocking them all down like a house of cards.

That great horned head lowered frighteningly close to me as the gargoyle bent down to examine the image carved on the cameo. A dark gray hand reached out to the necklace but stopped just short of contact.

"I think the silver must have burned you," I said, my voice husky from that brief, accidental (I'd like to think) moment of strangling me.

"I am not Monère," Gordane said, all the furious rage curiously drained from him. "It is not the silver but something mixed into the metal that hurt me, reacting when it sensed harm to you. I have heard of this but had never seen it before."

Halcyon hadn't mentioned anything special about the necklace when he had given it to me. But then we never really had the chance to talk privately. Maybe he'd been planning on telling me about it later.

"You are the chosen mate of Hell's ruler," Gordane said. "The one whose name means darkness."

"Actually, I'm Halcyon's mate. Not Blaec's."

"This proclaims you to be the royal consort. Does the Dark One not rule Hell anymore?"

The *Dark One*. I presumed that to be Blaec, whose name meant darkness.

"No, his son, Halcyon, does now." It felt really weird

discussing realm politics with Gordane. Especially after he'd just thrown us around like rag dolls.

"Your actions are peculiar," Gordane said, frowning. "So unlike the dheu who come to this realm."

I thought what was really odd was that such obvious intelligence could coexist with such primitive rage.

"If I may touch you once more," Gordane asked, lifting his uninjured hand.

I didn't shrink back, but I really, really wanted to. "Why?" I asked in a small voice.

"To examine you."

I really didn't want him to, after seeing and feeling what he could do with just a touch. But from Gordane's expression, I doubted I had any choice. I could run screaming away from him and have him chase me down. Or I could hold still with some shred of dignity. "Will it hurt?" I asked, unable to keep the little quaver out of my voice.

"No, it will be a harmless touch."

I nodded, giving my permission—no other choice but to.

His touch was harmless, as promised. No pain, no ugly crusting of my skin, no shoving me back inside and yanking Mona Louisa out of our body like a poorly played game of musical chairs.

He drew his hand away, much to our relief. "This part of you is not dead," he said.

"What?" I asked, not sure I had heard him correctly.

"You still live."

"But . . . but I'm not breathing. And my heart isn't beating."

"I feel your living essence," he marveled, then frowned. "You should not be here. But the other woman, the one inside you, she is true dheu, meant for this realm."

I was alive! My heart gave a great big giant leap of hope. "Can you take me back to the living realm? Or to Hell?"

"No."

One word and I felt all that buoyant hope come crashing down. "But you said I do not belong here in this realm."

"Apparently more than I ever imagined. But the Dark One himself sealed shut the gate between our two realms, an act that they say fractured our sky and split our sun into two broken halves. None who comes here now can leave."

A wild, silent scream rose up in my throat. *Noooo!* I wanted to scream, to cry, to break down in despair. But had to push that aside for later when Gordane suddenly asked, pointing at Miles, "What is this bull dheu to you?"

"My enemy," I said in an empty voice, numbed by that brief wild yo-yoing of hope and crashing despair.

"You lie."

I was heartsore. Achingly weary. "I have no reason to lie," I said in a dull, flat voice. "He detests me and I him. He was Mona Louisa's guard. It was her he was trying to help, not me."

"Does she speak true?" Gordane asked Miles.

"Yes. Forgive me, my lord," Miles said, dropping to his knees. "I feared harm to my Queen if you damaged this one."

"Your Queen." Menace seeped back into Gordane's voice like an ominous black tide. "You have forgotten who you serve now."

Miles flushed and I winced at his slip of tongue. Even in my half-numbed state, I was aware of the verbal damage Miles had just committed on top of his damning physical actions.

"Loyalty is admirable," Gordane said. "Nay, an essential requirement to me, but only if it is to *me*." He sought out Pietrus, standing with the other soldiers, all of them uncomfortable silent witnesses to this drama. "Take Miles and prepare him for tonight's games. He is to fight in the arena."

The punishment must have been worse than it sounded,

because Miles threw himself at Gordane's feet, prostrating himself. "My lord, please. A slip of the tongue, old habit. It is you who I serve."

"Words can lie," Gordane said with chilling coldness. "Actions never do. Take him away!"

Miles didn't fight when Pietrus and the other bull dheus seized him. Just looked at me with a mournful intensity that made me ask as he was dragged out of the chamber, "What will happen in the arena?"

"He will fight against the werebeasts."

It didn't sound like a joyride but neither did it sound like final death.

"Take this woman"—me, apparently—"to the women's quarters and have her prepared. I want her brought before me in an hour's time," Gordane proclaimed and returned to sit at his throne. We were apparently dismissed.

The prisoners shuffled out, and I felt like one of them, even though I wasn't tied up like they were. Frankly, I'd have rather gone with them. Their fate sounded preferable to mine.

We parted company near the front entrance. The prisoners were herded back outside, while two new guards accompanied me down another wide hallway. I turned my head, my eyes lingering on the departing group, watching as all I knew in this realm disappeared out the door— Gilford, Demetrius, Rupert . . . the disloyal Juan and Charles . . . poor loyal Miles.

We made our way to the other end of the palace and passed through a towering archway. Two guards stood at attention before a closed set of doors, their horns even more prominent than the two bull dheus that accompanied me. At a gesture from one of my guards, they swung open the heavy doors, their thick muscles bulging with the effort.

There was the impression of a large airy foyer, richly

decorated, with an order and cleanliness that had been lacking in the rest of the palace. A young and pretty woman, unveiled, rose from where she had been sitting behind a desk. I saw with surprise that her skin was flawless, unblemished. She looked normal, human. Staring at me with as much interest as I stared back at her.

"We brought a new woman."

"I will find the *maistresse*," she said, nodding. With her eyes carefully averted from the bull dheus, she left, slipping through another door in the back. A few moments later, an older woman appeared, her gray-flecked hair bound up in an intricate coil that was both artful and severe. Her skin was also without blemishes, but unlike the other woman, she was Monère. There was no strong resonating vibration of like to like, nothing of what I was used to sensing, but I knew it somehow, the same way I knew that all the guards I had encountered so far were also Monère.

The woman inclined her head politely to the two guards. "What is our lord's desire?" Not exactly the best words for my peace of mind. I'd been trying not to think about that—his desire . . . and how it might relate to me.

"She is to be brought to him in one hour's time."

With a curt nod, she dismissed them. They left, the heavy doors closing behind them, and then it was just her and I. She looked me over from tip to toe, taking in my wet, dirty, bedraggled appearance with a sour expression.

"An hour's time," she muttered. "He expects me to perform a miracle in that spit of time. This way," she snapped, walking through the same doorway she had come through.

The impression of entering another different world hit me again as I followed her and found myself suddenly in an open lounge. It wasn't the large space, so much as the inhabitants that filled it, that made me feel like Alice falling down the rabbit hole. Women, both human and Monère,

were strewn on and around cream-colored sofas and chairs.
The walls and floors were the same pink and ivory-white
coloring, and it was like being inside a giant oyster shell.
Only instead of pearls there were women—so goddamn
many of them. All beautiful, some stunningly so. All with
perfect skin. They sized me up with bored, jaded eyes. Titters and giggles sounded as they took in my dirty appearance, my far from dazzling looks. One brief glance and
they dismissed me. Not just the human women but the Monère ones as well that I sensed scattered among them.

The *maistresse* waited impatiently for me at the other
end of the room. A sharp gesture from her got my feet
moving again. She led me into yet another oysterlike
lounge filled with even more women. They, too, had pure
unblemished skin, but the women here were down a notch
or two in the looks department, more pretty instead of
beautiful. I belonged here, more with this group than the
other—and that was only with lots and lots of help.

They seemed a friendlier bunch. A few of the women
even smiled at me as I passed by. Then I was out that room
and into yet another part of the *hareem,* which was what
Lord Gordane seemed to have himself here . . . with me as
his newest addition!

"What's with the two separate rooms?" I asked the
maistresse.

"The first group of women that you saw are for Lord
Gordane's exclusive use. The second group are used to
pleasure visitors, guests, and a few of his men that he re-
wards with the privilege—those who serve him well."

Wonderful. You either got to be Gordane's exclusive
whore, or that of any Tom, Dick, or Harry that he chose to
give you to. It was hard to think and process everything. I
had questions, so many of them, and needed at least some
of them answered before I decided what to do next.

We finally reached our destination, the bathing chamber. It was larger than my entire apartment back in Manhattan had been, and was comprised of a tiled portion where a stool and several buckets of water sat, and the actual bath itself, which had to be the size of ten Jacuzzis put together. A veritable pool. I half expected it to be filled with frolicking, nubile young women, but it was thankfully empty, the bath itself. Not the room. The bathing chamber came with attendants. Two of them. Older, no-nonsense women like the *maistresse*. Their eyes honed in on me like laser beams sighting their target. A few words spoken in French, I think, from the *maistresse,* and they advanced on me and started stripping me. I had a moment to decide whether to cooperate like a smart, grateful, new *hareem* addition, or to shrug off their hands and start screaming at them to stay away from me. I'd like to say that I consciously decided to behave in a smart and civilized manner, but it was actually expedience that won me over. I was exhausted and upset—the numbness was wearing off—and I wanted out of my wet and dirty, ripped gown. I could have probably undressed myself, but only with a great deal of effort. The damp cloth felt glued to my body. Why fight them when they were doing what I would have done? And doing it much more efficiently? My only fuss was when they tried to take off my necklace. "No," I said, knocking their hands away. "The necklace stays on."

The two attendants looked to the *maistresse,* who nodded her impatient agreement. They left the necklace alone but laid hands on everything else. In the blink of an eye, they had that wet, sticky fabric off of me. I was stripped naked with assembly-line efficiency and sat down on the stool.

I looked at the golden, glittery bath longingly but stayed obediently still as they scrubbed me clean from head to toe, even shampooing my hair. Only after they had rinsed me off thoroughly two times did they finally allow me to enter the pool of water.

Delicious coolness surrounded me the moment I stepped in. I sank down and immersed myself in the clean, liquid embrace, sliding under the soothing water for a long, blissful moment before resurfacing. The sides and bottom of the pool were smooth, polished stone. A shallow underwater ledge hugging the side of the pool made a perfect seat. I sat there and a large goblet of golden water was placed in my hand. Good thing because otherwise I might have simply drank the pool water, so thirsty was I.

I downed the contents in three big gulps, and had another goblet handed to me. Knocking that second cup back like a shot of whiskey, I leaned back with bliss, closing my eyes. Ah, the miracle of water, no matter how weird the color. Drinking it . . . even more, immersing myself in it, felt like a slice of heaven down here in NetherHell. It was almost a criminal waste of water, the many gallons needed to fill this overgrown tub. Such luxury and power. I mused over that as I soaked in the precious water.

This safe, protected kingdom, sitting in the middle of a barren desert land, had water, beautiful women, and military might. Lord Gordane seemed to have himself a real cozy setup here in this oasis city.

I had all of two brief minutes to unwind and relax before I was urged back out into the women's hands. Most of my weariness had been washed away with the dirt. I wasn't completely recovered yet, but close. I was renewed and refreshed, more than I expected to be. With enough energy to shrug off their hands and dry myself with the thick bath towel while the *maistresse* watched with sharp eagle eyes and clucked with disapproval and impatience.

"This way," she said, walking out of the room.

I left the bathing chamber with a towel wrapped like a sarong around me, and another towel covering my wet hair. My torn dress had been left on the floor, no doubt destined for the trash. I'd always hated those long, black formal gowns that Monère Queens wore. And yet now, I almost felt a sentimental fondness for that torn scrap of a dress—my last link to my former life. No matter what Gordane said about my still being alive, I felt dead inside . . . dead and lost to my people in this new harsh realm.

I was hustled through to another room where more attendants waited—the grooming ones. The towels were whisked off me. I'd never been comfortable with casual nudity, but for some reason it didn't bother me now, maybe because it all seemed so surreal. I was in a *hareem*, for God's sake.

The new attendants, three of them this time, were briskly impersonal, drying off the wet spots I'd missed on my back and arms. I lay down on a raised platform they urged me onto, with neat rows of bottles lined up along the top and bottom edges. It was only when an attendant picked up a thin, flat, rectangular stone, sharpened at one end to a wicked knife's edge, that I stopped being the nice, cooperative, new *hareem* addition and sat up.

"What the fuck is that?" I demanded as my hand shot out and wrapped around the woman's wrist.

"It is to remove your unsightly body hair," the *maistresse* said, lips thinned.

"Where?"

"Where what?"

"Where exactly is this unsightly hair?" I asked, nice and patient.

Her patience, though, seemed to evaporate—what little there had been of it. Throwing up her hands in hot agitation, she said, "I have no time for this foolishness! There is still so much for me to do, and only three-quarters of an hour left!"

"That blade," I said uncompromisingly, "is not touching me until I know exactly what parts of me it is going to be touching."

Her eyes narrowed down into slits. "I can force your obedience."

My fingers found a pressure point, dug into it, and the attendant dropped the stone blade with a cry, her hand spasming. I caught the blade before it hit the floor.

"You're certainly welcome to try," I said, giving a few quick slashes in the air to test the weight and balance—easy blurring movements that had the attendants backing away in fear.

"Not quite the usual blade I'm used to," I said, "but I could work with it."

"You waste time!" the *maistresse* cried. And made it sound like the worst crime.

"No, actually you do," I said, my voice hard. "Where?"

She hissed out a breath. "Your legs, under your arms, the curls between your thighs."

"Between my thighs? You've got to be kidding me."

"It is our custom here."

"Legs and armpits are fine. Not between my thighs."

"That is non-negotiable."

I considered the hard resolve on the *maistresse's* face and saw that she wasn't going to budge on this matter.

"Very well," I said. "My cooperation if you answer a question."

"Were we not so short on time, I would not need your cooperation," she said in a low, heated voice.

"But time *is* short."

"What is your question?" she snapped.

"How do I leave this realm?"

"You cannot," she said. "None of us can leave here."

Not the answer I'd been hoping to hear. "How long have you been in NetherHell?"

"Over eighty-five years."

"And Lord Gordane? How long has he been here?"

"The eldest here say that he has ruled for over a century. Others whisper two centuries. Their kind—gargoyles—exist far longer than we do." She made a gesture with her hand. "That is three questions I have answered—two more than you bargained for. Waste no more of my time. You will have plenty of your own time later to seek answers to your foolish questions. Lie back."

A deal was a deal. It wasn't her fault that her answers weren't to my liking. I'd keep asking, but there seemed to be a depressing consensus so far. No way out of this realm.

I handed the flat, polished stone razor back, and the attendant took it from me with wary caution.

"Be careful," I admonished, lying back. She was. Not a nick or a scratch on my legs or under the arms. But when the blade scraped firmly over my mound, I flinched; tensed a little when they parted my folds and carefully shaved off every single piece of hair down there. Then it was over. A light fragrant oil was rubbed all over me. My hair was combed out, dried and styled, and I was dressed in this tiny scrap of cloth that they called a dress. The bottom of the material skimmed the tops of my thighs, barely keeping me decent. It bared most of me—my neck, throat, the top of my chest, my arms and entire back, and lots and lots of leg. Only two thin straps held up the itty-bitty dress. The color, though, was a beautiful shimmery rose, and the fit was surprisingly good. The material clung snugly to what there was of my bosom. No bra or underwear underneath. Nothing to impair Gordane's hands from touching me anywhere he damned well wanted to. Or maybe undergarments just didn't exist here, for *hareem* women anyway.

It wasn't until powders had been dusted on my face and eyes, and stuff rubbed on my lips, that I was led to a full-length mirror and got the whole effect. I looked at the utterly feminine, delicate creature reflected back, and didn't recognize her as me.

An abundance of pure white skin was showcased by the tiny dress. The rest of me had been done along the same general theme. My black hair was pinned up in an elegant coil, revealing the delicate curve of my neck, the gentle slopes of my shoulders. Shadow deepened my eyes, made them larger, darker, more mysterious. Blush made my cheeks glow. My lips were painted red. I was an artwork that had been splashed with three essential colors—creamy white skin, dark hair and eyes, and rosy red cheeks, lips, and dress . . . and the purple-red bruises ringing my throat. The distinct imprint of each separate gargoyle finger could be seen on my neck; no attempt had been made to hide them. The primitive markings of violence were more eye-catching than any jewelry would have been. And bespoke somehow of ownership.

I looked soft, fragile. Delicately feminine.

"A remarkable transformation in such a short time, is it not?" said the *maistresse*, coming to stand behind me.

"A miracle. You made me something that I'm not. I didn't know I could look like this."

"Like a woman?" she asked, voice dry.

"Like a fragile, easily breakable one."

"All women, no matter how strong they perceive themselves to be, are fragile, easily breakable, even Queens. Perhaps especially Queens. Keep that at the forefront of your awareness; it will serve you well in your dealings here in this realm. Come," she said briskly. "It is time for you to go to him."

Our return trip garnered different, varying responses. The second group of women looked at me with more intense speculation than friendly smiles now. The first group was outright hostile. A honey-haired beauty rose to her feet, blocking my path. "He summoned her?" Anger sharpened her words. "It should have been me that he called."

"I would not have prepared her otherwise, Mathilde," said the *maistresse*.

"But she is not as beautiful as I. Nor any of the rest of us!" she wailed, looking like a little girl stomping her feet and crying—*no fair!* "You aren't half as lovely as any of us here," she said hatefully to me.

"I agree." My easy answer made her frown, but only for a moment before she continued her sulky tirade. "It's only because you were a Queen!" Mathilde said, making me suddenly aware that she was Monère, one of the few I sensed among them. None of them were Queens, as far as I could tell.

"He will sample you once for the novelty. Then cast you aside to be used by others. You are not beautiful enough to hold him."

"Why would I want to hold his interest? I would have expected you to shrink away from the horror of his touch instead of fight for it."

Surprise and confusion flickered across Mathilde's exquisite face, then finally understanding. She laughed, and the other women laughed with her. Irritating titters with a spiteful edge. "You think yourself smart, but how stupid you really are. You are not worthy of his touch."

"Again, why would I even want it?"

More laughter, as if what I had said was beyond funny.

"What's the joke here?" I asked, tired of the nonsense.

"The joke is that Lord Gordane's touch is what keeps all of our skins unblemished," said the *maistresse*. "He absorbs our defilement onto himself."

I remembered Pietrus touching Ghemin, the young gargoyle. The transfer of slurry darkness. I remembered also how monstrously ugly Gordane had looked the first time I saw him, his skin thick with layer upon layers of warty bumps.

"But I saw him touch the prisoners they captured. Saw him touch them and transfer all that ugliness onto their skin."

"That ugliness that you speak of is what he took from us yesterday. You saw the inhabitants outside when you entered the city, did you not?"

I nodded.

"It is the environment, the very air of NetherHell itself that layers the blemishes across our skin. Lord Gordane's touch cleanses us from that defiling growth. Without his touch, ugly growths will start to show on your skin in less than a week."

My vision shifted, readjusted itself. "So he's not really the cause of the unsightly blemishes. He's the *cure* for them. Is he the only cure?"

"Yes," said the *maistresse*.

A most depressing answer.

"What about other gargoyles?"

"He is the only one of their kind who roams the lower lands."

"Lower lands?" I asked.

"Gargoyles usually reside on the highest mountains, beyond our reach."

I felt Mona Louisa stir within me, felt her sharp interest. It mattered to her, this piece of news. But I wasn't exactly sure how much it mattered to me.

"Move aside," the *maistresse* snapped at Mathilde. "You delay us. And you risk our lord's displeasure."

Shooting a final venomous look at me, Mathilde swished aside, and I followed the *maistresse* out into the airy foyer. A sharp knock by her, and the *hareem's* closed doors were swung open by the two guards standing outside.

"Take her to Lord Gordane," the *maistresse* instructed crisply. "He awaits her."

The taller of the two ended up as my escort. The other bull dheu remained at his post.

"How long have you been here?" I asked the guard as we walked down the long corridor. He was silent for so long that I thought he wasn't going to answer me.

"Thirteen years," he finally said.

"Why do you stay here?"

He glanced down at me. "I am most fortunate to be within these walls. It could have been much worse."

"How? In what way?"

"I could have been eaten by the wild creatures that prowl outside these walls."

Okay, I guess that did sound much worse.

We turned down an unfamiliar corridor. I stopped. "This is not the same way I came."

"I am taking you to Lord Gordane as instructed."

"This is the wrong direction."

He frowned as if he wasn't used to the women he accompanied balking. "No, this is the correct way, leading to his private living quarters."

His private living quarters. That would have been nice to know in advance, to prepare myself for. I'd thought we were going back to the public throne room, although how public and how safe was a matter of debate. Technically, he could rape me in the throne room, in front of his men, just as easily as in the privacy of his bedroom.

I was suddenly, abruptly aware of how vulnerable I felt without any undergarments on, my pubes shaved, not even hair to cover me. It unsettled me suddenly in a way that I had been trying to ignore up to now.

Should I run? Try to make a break for it?

To where? Mona Louisa asked scornfully. *Here is much better than out there. We have food, water, luxurious accommodations, and freedom from the blemishes that will eventually coat our skin if we leave this place.*

My body won't be a hostage just for the sake of your vanity, I said. *We can search for a way out of this realm. Try to return back home.*

Our home now is here was her pragmatic reply. I caught the rest of her wispy thought. That at least here there were those she took comfort in, those who cared for her—Miles and the other three.

And for that, for them, you would willingly sleep with Gordane? I asked.

I would sleep with him for just one of those many things he offers.

You may be willing, I told her, *but I sure as hell am not.*

Oh, for the Blessed Moon, Mona Louisa hissed with exasperation. *If you are so squeamish about it, I'll sleep with him!*

You'll still be using my body, I retorted.

My muscles tensed. I was recovered enough to take on the guard. I had a feeling I'd stand a much poorer chance against Gordane. I made my choice. To fight. To flee. But my body wasn't cooperating. It froze, my arms and legs locking into place, unmoving.

"Keep walking," ordered the guard, making a hysterical giggle well up inside me as panic mounted. Because even if I wanted to move, I suddenly couldn't. What in the world was happening to me? *Is that you? Are you sabotaging my body?*

I'm saving it, Mona Louisa replied. *And it's my body, too, now.*

Like hell it is. I fought against her will. And found it impossible to break that frozen state she had immobilized me into.

Yes, she thought with grim satisfaction. *My presence, my strength, is as strong as yours here in this realm.*

"Move along," the bull dheu commanded.

"Give me a moment," I snapped.

You are fortunate to have garnered Gordane's interest, said Mona Louisa. *I will not let you ruin things for us now.*

I can do the same thing to our body, I told her. *Keep us locked like this in a battle of wills, indefinitely if I need to. That alone would ruin things quite nicely, don't you think?*

She snarled. *If you truly desire to seek a way out of this miserable realm, then our best chance lies with Gordane. He alone may be able to provide answers others cannot give. He is gargoyle. Has existed longer than they. And he has wings, you imbecile. Flying is much faster than walking. And much safer, if you wish to risk our neck outside of these walls.*

Unfortunately, what she said was true. He might have answers others could not provide. Whether he would give them to me was another entirely different matter. But there was only one way to tell.

All right. I'll go to him.

At my grudging concession, my limbs unlocked and I stumbled into abrupt motion. Frowning, the guard hurried to catch up to me. In far too short an amount of time, we arrived in front of another set of doors similar to those of the *hareem*, only far more grand. The door frames were ornately gilded, and the dark red wood was elaborately carved with winged creatures, gargoyles—adults at work, children at play, some tumbling in the air, others frolicking on the ground.

My escort nodded to the two guards stationed in front of the thick doors, and one of them knocked.

"Enter," called a deep voice from within.

They swung open the doors and I was pushed through. The doors closed behind me and I was left standing alone in the room, if room was the correct word for it, so large and vast it was. The ceiling above me was domed, made entirely of colored glass. On the glass, I saw with wonder, was skillfully etched yet another picture, this one of a beautiful city set atop a vast mountaintop, with winged gargoyles flying to and from it. I had only a moment to glimpse it before a sound, a movement, pulled my eyes back down to what had to be the artist of both pictures, rendered with such love and detail. Only Gordane could have done them.

I tried to imagine that large gargoyle hand, the same meaty fist that had wrapped around my neck with brutally careless strength, delicately etching out these images.

"You drew these pictures. The one etched on the glass, and the one outside, carved on the door."

He stood on the balcony, his powerful gargoyle body framed in an open archway. "Yes," he said, stepping inside. "What you saw on the ceiling was my home, Mont Felleur."

"It looks like a beautiful place," I said as he made his way to me with an unhurried, deliberate stride. I was acutely conscious once more of his enormous size. It was hard not to back away from his approach. He stopped three feet away from me—which would have been more reassuring had his arm span not been that exact length.

"Why did you leave your home?" I asked, softer now with him standing so close.

"Because I was young, foolish, and arrogant, and thought that there was a much more exciting world to explore beyond our isolated mountaintop."

"You want to go back."

Some unnamed emotion moved through his eyes. "I can never go back. This city-state is my home now. Has been for a very long time." His hand lifted and I felt his fingers graze over my sensitive skin, over the marks he had left on my neck. They slid lower. Touched the silver necklace. It lay quiescent. No flash of light or heat.

"Fascinating piece of work," Gordane said quietly. "It reacts against malintent."

If so, the absence of a reaction was heartening. He didn't want to harm me. Not at the moment, at least.

"Does it hurt much, these bruises?" he asked, his fingers continuing to trace over them.

"No." I found it hard to hold his gaze when he touched me like that. Gentle, careful, intimate. So different from his previous rough handling of me.

"What do you want of me?" I asked in a low voice.

"So bold and blunt. Are you always this straightforward?" he asked with some amusement.

"Most of the time, yes. I like honesty and appreciate it in others."

"Straightforward," he mused, letting his large hand drop back down to his side. "But not unskilled in the dance between male and female. And it is a dance, is it not? Our words, our actions. You indicate that you would like honesty, and now wait to see if I will give it to you. If I answer as you wish, with plain speaking, it will tell you that your feelings, your concerns, matter to me, and you will have a certain power over me because of that. And yet, you are here, perfumed and prepared for me, indicating a readiness to engage my interest."

"It's not a power game to me." The cynical look in his eyes prodded me into my next words. "I almost didn't come. For one moment, out in the hallway, it was my intent to bolt, to escape and leave this place."

"Why?" A quiet rumble.

"Because all this preparation at your command, having me dressed, shaved, and perfumed like this, indicates that you want to have sex with me." I took a deep breath. "And I'm not ready for that."

"Plain speaking, indeed. Why did you not try to run, then?"

"I did, but Mona Louisa stopped me. She seems to think our best chance of survival lies with you. I happen to disagree with her, but her will is strong enough now to hamper me physically."

"Two clashing wills stuck in the same shared body. That must be an interesting experience."

"You have no idea." I took another breath, more out of habit than real need. I might still be alive, but it was in an altered state that didn't require me to breathe. "I've answered your question, and would appreciate it if you would answer some of mine. Again I ask you, what do you want of me?"

His eyes were darkly intent upon me—I couldn't read their expression. "I will give you the plain speaking you desire. I wish your affection, your love, your devotion to me."

It became immensely difficult to hold his gaze. "That's a large request for someone I've only just met, and not in the kindest of manner. Why would you want something that your entire *hareem* of women can give you, all of them much more beautiful than I?"

He smiled, a nice smile instead of a scary one, and it was a drastic transformation, changing him from menacing into surprisingly benign-looking. "You are lovely in a way that none of them are."

I snorted. His smile widened.

"You are lovely in your spirit, and in your refreshing honesty. And what I want most from you, none of the women here can give me. I want a child."

His words stirred pain, invoking memory of the baby I had briefly carried and lost. "Wh-what?"

"I want a child, and only you can give me that. All the women here, beautiful though they may be, are dead. There is no life in them, no ability to bear life. Only you can do that."

I stumbled back until I hit the cushioned edge of a divan. I sat down, my knees, all of me trembling.

His lips twisted, his brows drawing together. "Does the thought of lying with me frighten you that much? Am I so different, so ugly to you?"

"It's not that. I was pregnant once and lost the baby. It was . . . grief at that memory that caused my reaction to your words."

An uncertain moment of silence passed before he sat down beside me, his heavy weight sinking the cushions down and sliding me closer to him. I didn't try to shift away.

"You are not ugly," I told him. He was a fearsome thing, immensely intimidating, but not ugly.

He lifted a thumb and testingly stroked it over my hand. "You do not think me odd? Repulsive looking?"

"You are gargoyle. Yes, your features are different from ours. But there is nothing grotesque about you. Your great strength, large size, mature horns . . . I imagine you would be considered quite a handsome gargoyle," I said, smiling at him. His wide lips curved up in response.

"Did you leave behind children in the other realm?" he asked.

"No." A sad smile.

"Do you want children?"

"I don't know. You've sprung it on me so suddenly. It was the last thing I imagined you wanting from me."

"Sex I can easily get," Gordane said, showing that he could be as equally blunt as I. "But a living mother for my child . . . that is not as easy to come by."

"Lord Gordane—"

"Just call me Gordane."

"I'm not of your kind. Wouldn't you do better seeking out a female gargoyle?"

"I am the only gargoyle here in the lower lands. There are no females of my kind available to me. Only you."

"We might not be compatible. It might not be possible for . . ." I was going to say, *For you to get me pregnant.* But that would be putting the onus too much on him. "I might not be able to become pregnant with you."

"We can only try. If you desire a child, you should be aware that I would be your only chance of bearing one. No other male here can give you that."

"Why can you?"

"Because I am a natural creature of this realm. I am not dead as the other inhabitants here are. My kind is capable of reproducing life, as you saw in those pictures."

I slid my hand out from under his and placed it against his broad chest, confirming by touch what my ears had already told me. "But your heart doesn't beat. And you don't breathe, other than to speak."

"Neither do you, yet you still live."

"Are you sure?" I asked, drawing my hand away.

"You are alive as surely as that other woman who shares your body is dead."

If that was so, then we were important to each other in a way no other in this realm could be. We were each other's only chance of having a real family, a child. It changed things between us. Made me look at him in a far different light.

"Yes," he said, satisfied. "You see me now, what I can be to you. What we can be to each other."

He bent his head down to me, and my hand lifted back up to his chest in a stopping gesture. He obeyed the silent command, halting though he didn't need to.

"Will you not let me kiss you?" he asked, his mouth hovering just above mine. "See and know for yourself how we feel against each other? I can please you," he murmured in husky promise.

The laugh I gave was a bit breathless. "With all those women in your *hareem*, and all the years of practice you must have had—"

"Centuries of it."

"—I do not doubt that you can be good. I just . . . everything has happened so fast. I was torn from my people, taken from my other life, and came here expecting to be raped by you, not courted. What you said about a child . . . yes, I do want one."

Triumph made his dark eyes glitter.

"And I know that you are the only one who might be able to give me that child. But I need a little more time to get to know you. To grow more comfortable with you."

"In other words, no sex today."

I blushed. "If you don't mind."

"I do mind. Very much so." His eyes flashed with heat as he held himself frozen above me. "I have not had to hold myself back from anything I desired in a very long time. It does not sit well upon me."

"I'm sorry." Fear edged back into me. Fear more of what would be lost if he tried to force his will, his body on me, when I was not yet ready. Fear of breaking that tentative trust that glimmered like a faint promise between us.

"A compromise," he said, his black eyes gleaming down at me.

"W-what?"

"No sex, that I will grant you. But I would have you give me something of yourself willingly in return."

"What do you want?"

"I would see you unclothed, your body bare, before you leave me this night."

I wasn't sure if I could do that. Then I considered the alternative, considered what else he could have asked of

me, or not asked, simply forced me to do. In light of his
restraint, long unpracticed, showing him my naked body
was not much to ask for really. Highly unlikely that my
paltry offerings would trigger him to uncontrollable lust. A
good thing.

"Do you agree?"

Conversely, it would have been much easier to comply
with his request had I been more centerfold material. Oh,
God.

"Yes," I said, agreeing to his terms.

He eased back away from me and stood, giving me
room. "Go on."

I'd never done this before, deliberately strip for a man.
Gargoyle he might be, but he was still very much male,
more powerful and domineering than I was used to. And
the look in his eyes said that he very much considered me
a female, one he was attracted to. Oddly enough, having
him look at me like that, with anticipation, made it harder.

I stood, feeling awkward and uncertain. "In this dress,
you already pretty much see everything," I said, stalling.

"You agreed," he rumbled in warning. "Do not make
me ask you again."

Crap. His patience and mercy were apparently at an end.

I didn't disrobe slowly. I did it quickly, like ripping off a
Band-Aid. I slid the straps down my shoulders and that
was all it took. Without that support, the dress slithered
down my body, falling in a poof around my feet. I stood
there, eyes downcast, and sensed him move closer to me.

"Lie back on the divan," he said roughly. "I want to see
you displayed there."

My eyes darted up in a quick peek. If he was disappointed in any way, it was not evident. On the contrary,
desire had pulled the strong bones of his face even more
prominent. His expression was intently male, savagely so,

as his eyes moved slowly down my body . . . sending my feelings flip-flopping from fear of disappointing him to fear of being taken again against my will.

"Don't make me fight you, please."

"I will not touch you with my hands," he murmured in reassurance.

Trusting in his promise, I lay back down on the divan, my body trembling. The smooth flat surface felt too much like a bed, as did his next request. "Open your legs for me."

My eyes shot to his.

"Let me see you," he demanded.

Slowly, I let my legs fall apart.

His eyes roved intimately over my smooth, shaven folds. Over the soft, hidden flesh I bared to his eyes.

"Wider," he said, voice thick. And the rough maleness of his voice, the hot desire I saw in his eyes . . . it sparked my own desire. That dark, contrary part of me that liked the taste of danger flared to life, and I was suddenly, abruptly, turned on despite my helpless, submissive position. Or maybe because of it. An exquisite feeling of vulnerability danced with a sense of wielded control. Safe danger. My favorite kind.

I spread my legs farther apart, and he shifted, bracing himself over me in the space I had made. With my wide open display and his close viewing of that display, he could not help but see the dewy response starting to seep out.

"You like this," he rumbled thickly, and I bit back a moan, fought not to open farther to him.

Tease him too much and he will take you, a voice inside me warned. My own voice, not Mona Louisa's.

"Yes," I murmured, "a part of me is very attracted to you. To the situation. But my mind still says no. Not yet, at least."

"Not yet, but soon."

I laughed hoarsely. "Yeah, at this rate, probably real soon. Just . . . not today."

"I have already given you my word."

"I just wanted to be clear. No matter how my body, uh—"

"Responds . . . and how sweetly it does." His head lowered down until he was poised right over the most secret part of me—shaved, no longer hidden—lying glisteningly wet, open and exposed to him. The thought of him looking at me *down there* was enough to tighten all the muscles of my body.

He blew a soft, deliberate breath over me. *There* where I was so freshly bared and so incredibly sensitive. I moaned, I couldn't help it. I moaned at the feel of that delicious puff of air ruffling over my heightened nerve endings. The sight of his massive head with his two thick horns poised between my legs—talk about phallic symbolism—brought forth another gush of arousal. Welled up another moan inside me.

No! Don't move. Don't make a sound, I told myself as my body clenched, both inside and out. I tried, I honestly did. But when he blew again, a second deliberate puff of air that riffled like a thousand fluttery fingers across my skin *there* where all my nerves seemed to have swollen up and gathered, my body no longer listened to me, was no longer in my control.

I came in a brilliant, shocking, shuddering climax, twitching helplessly. He blew again, a third hard jet of air against the most sensitive part of me, moving the current of air over me like a stroking tongue, milking out the orgasm, drawing it out longer, playing me with merciless expertise. Cries spilled from my throat as pleasure—God, such pleasure!—wracked my body.

When he finally raised his head, lifted that incredibly

stirring breath away from me, I felt like a puppet sagging limply on its loosened strings.

Oh my God!

I must have said it out loud because he smiled. With the musky scent of my release perfuming the air, with his skin stretched so taut over the broad planes of his face . . . those dangerous phallic-shaped horns, the rawly sexual look in those black eyes fixed so fiercely, possessively on me, he looked thrillingly, primitively, dangerously male.

"Imagine if I had actually touched you . . . licked you . . . sucked you."

His words and the provocative images they invoked rolled a second small orgasm through me—like the slap of a tiny wave that catches you unaware after the big wave had passed by you, and you thought yourself safe.

I gasped, shuddered, writhed beneath him, a guttural moan spilling out from me. "Mercy," I cried hoarsely. "No more."

He smiled, stretching his lips wide, making me suddenly want to taste them . . . to taste him. I sat up and he started to draw away. My hands grabbed him, stopped him. He was no longer smiling. Slowly I brought my face closer to his until my lips almost touched those wide mobile lips. My tongue flicked out and I licked him, tasted him, made a pleased sound. Another lick, another taste, and then another until I had traveled from one corner of his mouth to the other, leaving my wetness, my own taste, behind.

I pulled back to watch his own tongue emerge, lick his lips, sample the flavor of me.

"Thank you," I said in a husky voice. "That was unexpectedly lovely, both the pleasure and the keeping of your word."

He stared at me for a long moment and stood back up,

the cushions shifting under the withdrawal of his weight. I stood as well, and found my legs thankfully up to the task of keeping me upright.

A dark gray hand picked up the little scrap of cloth that was my dress and offered it to me. I took it and found that dressing was almost as easy as undressing. Lift the cloth over my head, drop it down over my body, and like that I was covered once more, outwardly clothed, excruciatingly naked underneath. A little bit like how I felt toward him now.

There was still the remembered fear, the memory of violence and pain that I had suffered under his careless hand. But now coating that like a soothing balm was this new memory, this new knowledge—of his tenderness, his restraint, of our intimacy. Of his word given and kept. Of his breath, just his breath, wringing such pleasure from my body. Of my tongue licking over his lips, tasting him. And of him tasting me in turn. The baring of skin and flesh—it was an intimate act that drew you closer to the male you made yourself vulnerable to, if he treats you with care. And he had.

"Come." He held out his hand and I took it, and the gesture and my ready response pleased us both. The impressive cockstand that tented his pants was a little hard to ignore. But if he could do so, then so could I. I wasn't quite ready yet to offer him ease.

He opened the doors much sooner than the guards standing outside anticipated, I think. There was a brief look of surprise before their expressions smoothed out and they came sharply to attention.

"I shall walk her back to the women's quarters," Gordane informed them, a statement that flashed another brief look of surprise across their faces. Apparently not something he did for the other women.

"I wish to see you again tomorrow," Gordane said as he

led me down the wide hallway. And even though he said it forcefully, like a statement, I sensed the question in his words. Just a short time together, and already I seemed able to read him more easily.

Would I be ready to return some of that pleasure tomorrow? I wasn't entirely sure but . . . "Yes," I answered. The visit—and its orgasmic aftermath—was utterly different from how I had imagined it would end. I certainly hadn't thought I'd be walking back holding hands with him.

To distract myself, and because I was curious, I asked, "Why are things so messy here in the palace?"

"Messy?"

"Dirty, dusty. Neglected looking."

Gordane gazed around him as if he was only just now seeing the heavy dust coating the furniture, the bits of dirt and debris building up in the corners. He frowned, and the expression was no longer as frightening as it used to be. "The palace steward foolishly stole from me. I hadn't gotten around to replacing him yet."

"How long ago was this?"

"A hand span of days. Perhaps two."

"It looks much longer than that."

"Perhaps it is. I do not keep track much of time."

"What happened to the stealing steward?"

"His punishment was the same as all who betray me. The arena."

"More merciful than I would have expected from you."

"Merciful? In what way?"

"I thought you would have killed him, so to speak. Ended his existence instead of just punishing him."

"I did."

His answer made me stop. "What?"

"You look suddenly pale. Are you not feeling well?"

My fingers tightened around his much bigger hand. "Miles . . . you sent him to his death?"

Gordane's brows drew together. "Yes, I thought you knew. Was aware of what the arena meant."

"No. I thought it was just a punishment, not his final death. My God . . ." My voice trailed off as I remembered again that last frantic look Miles had given me, as if he'd never see me again. He'd known. Dear Goddess, he had known, and thought I had, too. That I had stood quietly by and let him be led to his death—again.

Within me, Mona Louisa whispered, *Am I to be the death of him always?*

You didn't seem to regret his first death, I answered.

I did not. But I do now. You have changed me. I would not willingly be the cause of his death again.

"You can't kill him," I said urgently to Gordane.

He looked down at me, his ebon eyes dark and enigmatic. "I thought he was your enemy."

"He was . . . he is. But Mona Louisa . . . she cares for him. And he was trying to help me. To help her, really, but also me. Please. You must save him if you can."

"It may already be too late. The werebeasts may have already torn him apart."

"You have to try to stop it."

He came to a swift decision. "I will take you back to the women's quarters, then go."

"No time! Take me with you."

A brief hesitation and then he turned and started running back in the direction we had come from. My hand wrapped tight in his, we veered around a couple of turns and came to the grand entryway with all those odd statues. He swung open one of the heavy doors with an easy pull, and we charged past the startled guards outside.

"Hold onto me tightly," Gordane said as his wings unfurled and lifted us into the air. We soared up thirty feet . . . fifty . . . with two strong flaps of those powerful wings. The force with which we cut through the air brought tears

to my eyes. I hung onto Gordane as he had commanded.
Plastered myself to that strong body, and felt his big arms
wrapped tightly around me. And I marveled at the strength
of those wings, able to take our combined weight so easily
airborne like that. Marveled that such a huge span, more
than twice my height, could fold up so perfectly flat onto
his back so that it was neatly hidden and almost forgotten
until he spread it open once more.

The speed and power of our flight buoyed up my hope,
until a crowd's roar came floating up on the winds to me. I
peered down and felt dizzy at how high up we were. I saw
the arena down below us, the vast amount of people filling
its seats. In the center pit was Miles, injured, his left leg torn
and bleeding. He was armed with a sword and shield, but
grossly outnumbered, surrounded by a dozen creatures . . .
just like the statues in the entryway! Only these were not
frozen stone figures. These were flesh and blood, moving,
bleeding, savagely attacking!

Werebeasts, Gordane had called them. Mutant monstrosities would have been more apropos. There were
freakish half-man, half-animal forms. Also mixed animal-
animal forms, like the lizard-snake thing I had encountered in the desert, only worse, much worse. A few looked
as if the heads of wolves had been ripped off intact and
planted on top of human bodies. There were even more
disturbing hybrids, everything from buffaloes and lions to
snake heads. Even more nauseating was the reverse
combination—human heads atop animal bodies.

We flew over the nightmarish creatures in a dark swoop
of wings, drawing attention so that all eyes were lifted to
the sky. In a sharp descent, Gordane flew down into the
stadium crowd and dropped me into the surprised hands of
some of his guards.

"Keep her safe," he ordered, and flew off to the center
of the arena. He swooped down toward Miles, but Miles

was either unnerved by the gargoyle's approach—and honestly, who wouldn't be, seeing a huge horned creature bearing down on you—or he mistrusted Gordane's intent. Whatever the reason, he raised his shield, blocking Gordane's grab for him.

"No!" I cried. "He's trying to help you, Miles." But my words were lost in the excited shouts of the spectators. Another roar of sound as the werebeasts sprang at Miles, attacking him desperately from all sides, as if they sensed the imminent loss of their prey. His sword slashed in a circle, cutting open several werebeasts, but the rhino werebeast—a rhino head atop a horse's body—charged from behind and caught him up on his horn. The sharp tip emerged out the front of him. Blood burst out, and I screamed, the sound lost amidst the frenzied shouts that rose from the crowd. Miles somehow heard me. His head turned in my direction, his eyes searching, finding me. Our eyes were locked together for one brief instant, then the contact broke as the rhino-beast tossed Miles off his horn. He went airborne—ten feet up in the air, falling back down. Gordane turned in mid-flight, sharply changing direction, but he was too far away to catch him. Miles fell and hit the ground in a bloody crumple, and only Gordane swooping down to hover over him like a giant winged bat kept the other werebeasts from pouncing on him.

The gargoyle had no weapon, nothing more threatening than his spread hands. But that seemed to be enough to keep the werebeasts back, as if they sensed something about Gordane that I couldn't see. And they were not the only ones afraid of him. Miles had somehow managed to hang onto his sword and shield. He raised both weakly now against Gordane, as if the greatest threat to him was from the hovering gargoyle above instead of the gnashing, howling werebeasts circling him. He seemed to fear Gordane even more than the grotesqueries waiting to tear him apart. Looking at Gordane, the powerful intimidating bulk of him, I wasn't surprised that he inspired fear. I was surprised, though, that he inspired more fear than the rabid werebeasts. It was obvious that Miles wasn't going to let Gordane touch him, just as it was obvious that Gordane would not be able to hold them all back for much longer.

Save him, Mona Louisa urged within me.

How?

Fly to him.

Her words didn't make sense. My other form was a Bengal tiger. *I can't fly,* I told her.

But I can.

Mona Louisa was a vulture in her alternate form. Since pulling her essence into me, I had often dreamed of flying in my sleep—her dreams, her remembered thoughts. She wanted me to shift into her vulture form. Something I didn't know if I could do or even *wanted* to do. If we ventured into the arena, and one of those werebeasts got a hold of us . . .

She tried to shift. I resisted her.

Do this for me, and I will be in your debt, she urged me.

I was surprised, shocked actually, that she cared enough to risk both of us to save Miles when once she had sacrificed him so easily to the Council.

You wouldn't have tried to do this before. To try to save him.

No. Nor would you have hesitated before. We have bled parts of ourselves into each other. I absorbed some of your love and caring for your men, your people. You now have some of my callousness. You show caution where you once would have charged forward without hesitation.

If she was trying to shame me, it wasn't working. *You forget that the guy you're asking me to risk my life for once tried to rape me.*

Grant me this and I promise you that I will repay you

this debt. Please, she begged with a humbleness that I
would have said was not possible for her. Not for the Ice
Queen.

I stopped resisting. *Okay,* I told her. *Go ahead. Shift.*

She did. No hesitation. I felt her push out of my body
like a snake shedding an old skin, and emerging with a
new one. Maybe it was knowing and understanding what
she was doing and not being panicked by it. Whatever the
reason, the change occurred easily. Or should I say, the
half-change.

I felt my upper body shift, my height shrinking as my
spine shortened. My mouth and nose curved into a hooked
beak as wings pushed out my back, stretching the straps of
the dress out to the side but thankfully not breaking them.
Feathers emerged and covered my upper body. The lower
part of me, though, didn't change: two legs, I saw, looking
down. Shifting my gaze higher, I saw a clear demarcation.
Above the waist, I had the feathers and body of a large
bird, a vulture. Below the waist, I was still human. With
dawning horror, I realized that I had shifted . . . and become just like those mutant werebeasts! I screamed, and a
vulture's raucous cry came out of my parted beak. With a
powerful flap of wings, I launched myself up into the air,
leaving my stunned guards, and soared skyward, my human legs dangling, flying to where Mona Louisa's heart
urged us even amidst my panic.

We're like them, the werebeasts! I screamed inside.

*We're not like them. We're still sane. They're not. Keep
sharp. We're going in.*

Another raucous shriek alerted Miles to our coming.
He looked up and he saw us. Gordane, too. On Miles's face
was a look of recognition and relief. Of welcome. He
pushed himself weakly to his feet, his shield still raised
against Gordane, but he left himself open to me as I
swooped down, his body turned to me, his sword holding

back the werebeasts. Gordane moved back, giving me room to come in. Only as I made the swooping dive did I realize I had a problem.

How in bloody tarnation was I going to grab Miles and carry him away? I didn't have hands anymore, just wings, and human feet, which just weren't that good for grabbing things.

Miles would have to grab onto me and do his best to hold on.

He is too weak, Mona Louisa said. *He can barely hold up his sword. Shift into your tiger's feet. Do a partial change.*

I don't know how to do a partial change, I said wildly.

What state do you think we are in now? The lower half of your body remains in your control, not mine. Shift! Shift now.

I tried, because I couldn't think of any other option. Miles was less than twenty feet away. I pictured it in my mind, a partial change, feet only, and a burning, prickling sensation started in my toes and swept swiftly up my feet. I looked down and watched with a kind of fascinated horror as I shed human feet and began sprouting orange and white fur up to my ankles. Watched as my feet morphed into hairy tiger's paws. Watched as long, wicked black claws sprang out from each toe point.

I flew in with speed, with dexterity—remembered instincts coming back naturally. Instincts that were not from me but from her. I reached down with my tiger claws, flying in on my vulture wings, as if I had done this a thousand times before, and deftly snatched up my prey. I felt my sharp claws sink deep into flesh with almost melting ease. A sudden forceful jerk as I came up against his unmoving weight, met it and overcame it.

With a straining flap of wings, I heaved him up off the ground and into the air.

Two werebeasts leaped up after us, their foam-flecked teeth zeroing in on Miles's dangling legs. Gordane swatted them away from us with two quick blows. The other werebeasts howled, seeing their food escaping them. In mindless hunger, they turned on each other with tearing teeth.

I glanced back once. Saw Gordane following us, his winged presence blocking most of the carnage down below from sight. *He risked himself for me,* I thought, that part of me that was still me and not the vulture—not her.

As we flew over the high walls of the arena and landed on the other side, soldiers came pouring out, now when we had no need of them. But who could blame them for not venturing into the bloody arena pit? Hearing the terrible squeals and shrieks coming from the other side of the wall, I wondered how I had dared fly down so close to those frightening mutants. Then again, who was I to be talking when I looked just like them! Maybe even worse.

My tiger claws retracted as I dropped Miles lightly onto the ground and landed with spread wings that folded in to lie neatly against my vulture back. Such a nifty invention, wings. With a mental willing, or rather a thought more like *Okay, enough of this bizarre bird form*, I shifted back. Feathers melted, reshaped into skin. My spine lengthened. Furry paws morphed back into feet. Wings transformed into arms and hands. Everything went like clockwork. Only Mona Louisa emerged, not I.

"I didn't know," she said, dropping down in front of Miles. "I didn't know the arena would mean your final death. As soon as I realized, I came."

He gazed at her with surprise, fierce tenderness, with devotion and adoration, as he lay there gored and bleeding. "You came for me."

Looking down into those expressive eyes, I felt something soften in Mona Louisa, and used that moment of weakness to push her back down, and myself out. Face and body transformed as I emerged.

The reaction of the watching soldiers was dramatic. They gasped, took a collective step back away from me. Some made a warding sign.

Ignoring them, I said, "You should thank Lord Gordane. He was trying to help you, you idiot. Why did you keep blocking his attempts to reach you?"

The look of adoration faded from his eyes at my appearance. In their place, though, was something I never expected to see—respect. "Forgive me, milady. I was not certain of his intent."

"What other reason could he have had for flying into that pit and risking himself like that?"

Miles pushed himself painfully up enough to kneel at Gordane's feet. Blood spurted from his wounds, but he was already bleeding less, starting to heal. "Forgive me, my lord, for not trusting you as I should have."

"It was understandable," Gordane said.

Maybe to them—not to me. A part of me wondered what Gordane could have possibly done to Miles that would have been worse than being eaten by werebeasts. Another part of me thought it might be better if I didn't know. I shook my head at both of them.

"Are you going to punish him further?" I asked Gordane.

Gordane looked questioningly at me. "Do you wish me to punish him further?"

"No! Definitely not."

"Then there will be no further punishment."

It should have ended there, but this was NetherHell. In a dramatic turn of events worthy of a Hitchcock thriller, the already dark sky darkened even more as huge winged creatures—gargoyles, scores of them—flew over the arena

wall in a frightening swarm. They were dressed in dark
armor, with black swords and knives strapped to their huge
bodies. They caught sight of us, and like a flock of birds—
big, scary ones—they veered down, landing in a loose circle
around us. Not only did they outnumber the dheu guards,
they outsized them in both height and weight. Two gargoyles
flew to block the entry and exit points of the arena, preventing more guards from rushing to our aid.

"Hold!" Gordane commanded his soldiers. They had
drawn their weapons but were cowering back away from
the gargoyles. At the same time, they were careful to keep
an equal distance between them and Gordane, as if being
touched by any of the gargoyles was equally bad.

"We come for the woman," one of the gargoyles said.
Even with him looking straight at me, it took a full second
to understand that the woman he meant was *me*, and to
recognize him, so different did he look from when I last
saw him.

"Ghemin's dad?" I said as recognition kicked belatedly
in. Recognition and the sudden understanding that this
was a rescue, not an attack.

"You cannot have her. She is mine!" Gordane growled.
He stood protectively on my left, while Miles positioned
his bleeding, battered body on my right side.

"You are Gordane, the outcast," said the gargoyle.

"And who are you?" asked Gordane.

"I am Vlad, the gargoyle king."

The king of the gargoyles, who had been dressed only
in old trousers the first time I saw him. Still I should have
suspected. The air of command in Vlad was unchanged—
still bossy. It fit him more appropriately now, though,
dressed in the trappings of war and armed to the teeth with
wicked weapons.

"This woman saved my son's life," Vlad declared. "She
does not belong here."

"She is to be my bond-mate," Gordane said in turn—a statement that obviously took Vlad by surprise. "You cannot have her. With all the female gargoyles that you have to choose from, you cannot take this one from me."

"I do not desire her for myself," Vlad said calmly. "I wish to return her to where she belongs. She is not meant to stay in this realm."

"You can return me?" I asked.

"Yes," he answered.

"A part of her is dead, truly dheu," Gordane said tightly.

"But that is not all that she is."

"The living part of her doesn't mean she will be able to cross," Gordane said.

"The demon part of her will allow her to," Vlad said.

Gordane fell silent. "That may be," he finally said, "but the gate is still closed between our realms."

"A scout reported the presence of demons in the high mountains."

Vlad's words sent a small thrill through me. "Which means the gate is open," I whispered.

He nodded.

"Even so, will I be able to leave this realm?" I asked.

"I cannot say for sure," Vlad replied. "I only know that long before, demons walked our realm at will, entering and leaving during brief periods of time when our seasons shifted. Such a period of time we are now in. But that time frame is a narrow one, soon to end."

"How soon?"

"When this night ends, and a new day reddens the sky, the period will end. If you wish to go, we must leave now."

Inside, I felt Mona Louisa's resistance, and caught the turmoil of her emotions, enough to know that she did not want to leave this place, this realm. She was stronger here.

I'm calling in your debt, Mona Louisa. I'm asking you not to stop me from trying to leave this realm.

We gazed at Miles, the man she had bargained with me to save.

As you wish came her unhappy response. *I will do nothing to hinder you.*

The locking down of my muscles that she had begun faded away. One problem down. Onto the next one.

"Vlad, I would ask of you a favor, if I may."

"I do not comprehend your meaning."

I searched in my head for another word beside *favor.* Mona Louisa supplied it. "I would ask a boon of you."

"What boon would you have of me?"

"That you allow Gordane the opportunity of finding a bond-mate among your women."

My request seemed to stun all the gargoyles.

"Gordane didn't do anything really bad, like kill some of your people, did he?"

"No, he simply left." Vlad make that sound like the most heinous crime. "He chose to leave and willingly become outcast."

"He was young and foolish, his own words to me. He's older, much older now, and he's been alone a long time, with no chance of a family, no chance of having a little Ghemin of his own. Couldn't you grant him a royal pardon or something?"

Vlad fixed his eyes on the other gargoyle. "Do you wish to return to us?" he asked.

A slew of emotions chased across Gordane's face—arrogance, pride, uncertainty, then yearning. "Yes," Gordane grated out. "I would desire that greatly. I do not wish to stay there—I could not leave behind all I have attained here. But to come and spend time among the gargoyles once again . . . yes, that would be my heart's desire."

"Then it shall be granted," Vlad said.

Gordane bowed to his king while I made an awkward half-curtsy, half-bowing gesture. Straightening, my eyes fell upon Miles and deep inside I felt Mona Louisa's grief. "I'm sorry, Miles," I said. "If it were up to her, Mona Louisa, she'd stay here with you."

"But it's not up to her," he said.

"No."

"Then go. I . . . wish you well. And should you return, I will be here."

Never in a million years could I have imagined feeling what I did—regret at leaving this man who had so recently been my enemy. A large part of it was Mona Louisa's emotions, but a tiny part of it was my own feelings.

"I wish you well also," I said softly, and turned to say good-bye to the other man at my side.

"No farewells yet," Gordane said. "I am going with you."

I blinked up at him, and found the idea attractive—having him there as we headed into the unknown. "I'd like that."

With Gordane beside me, I walked to Vlad. "Okay, I'm ready to go."

Vlad smiled and took my hand, causing the gargoyle warriors around us to give little grunts of surprise. I'm not sure at what. Because he'd touched me? Or that I'd allowed him to?

"Like before," Vlad said. Lifting me up into his arms, he cradled me against him in the same way he had carried his son. "Hold on tightly." He launched his powerful body off the ground and his great wings unfurled, spreading wide, snapping taut like dark sails catching the wind. Soaring through the air with him was different this time. His body was encased in armor that looked like metal but felt more like leather to the touch, hard with some flexible give to it, and very, very slippery. It was his grip on me rather than mine on him that kept me from falling. Peeking over his shoulder, I saw the other gargoyles spread out in winged escort behind us. The walled city-state, that great oasis, grew smaller and smaller with each strong surge of Vlad's wings.

I closed my eyes as the sight—the sheer *height*—somersaulted my stomach. I hadn't felt that way before when I had wrapped myself tight as a burr around him. But I'd had a solid grip on him then. Not now, hence the queasy feeling.

"How is Ghemin doing?" I asked to take my mind off of matters beyond my control, and because I really wanted to know. The boy had been hurt badly by Pietrus's slurrying touch.

"He is weak but well, by the grace of your timely intervention."

I lifted my face from where I had rested it against that slippery armor. Watching Vlad's face outlined against the black-scarlet sky was much better than watching the ground fall farther away beneath us. Focusing just on his face, it hardly seemed as if we were moving.

"I would have come for you sooner," he said, his dark eyes troubled as he glanced down at me. "But my first responsibility was to see my son safely to my people first. After doing so, I gathered my warriors and came here as soon as I could."

"I'm fine," I said, patting him on the chest. "I didn't expect you to come back for me. It never occurred to me, actually, that you would."

"Then your sacrifice was even greater than I originally thought. It was a noble but foolish thing you did, falling from such a height. You could have died."

"I thought I was already dead. What else was I to think, finding myself here in NetherHell?"

"But you are not."

"Thank God. Or maybe I should say—thank the Goddess."

"Do your people pray to the Moon Goddess?" he asked.

"I don't know. I do sometimes. I'm not sure about the other Monères. What about you? Who do you pray to?"

"A different moon deity." He smiled at my astonishment, his face crinkling up in a cute-ugly sort of way. "Our people, too, are descended from the moon. Did you think Monères to be the only species originating there?"

I shook my head, marveled silently. "I guess I did."

An animal's blood-curdling roar abruptly ended our conversation. It came from the foot of the tall mountain we were approaching. A second bellow tore through the air.

"Jesus freaking Christ!" My arms tightened around Vlad's neck in a near stranglehold. "What on earth is that?"

"An obor," Vlad said as the treetops below shuddered and shook as something very, very large disturbed them. "It is not a creature you would find anymore in your realm. Vicious beasts you want to avoid, if you can."

Our flight shifted and we started to descend . . . right toward where those treetops shook so ominously.

"Uh, then why are you going *toward* it and not away from it?"

"Because I believe it is your demons that likely stirred the obor from its slumber. The realm gate lies on the cliff above. They would have to pass this way to reach the desert plain."

We neared enough so that I was able to see the creature—as big, mean, and nasty-looking as Vlad said it was—and see what it battled.

My breath caught as my eyes fell upon the two tiny demons defending themselves against the giant obor. "Gryphon!" Another whisper, "Halcyon!"

"You know them?" Vlad asked.

"Oh, yes, I know them. Like my own heart. They came for me," I said, an astonishingly wonderful and terrible thing. Terrible because what they faced—a great behemoth of a creature—reared up and tried to stomp them with its huge forelegs.

Gryphon darted nimbly out of the way with his usual fluid grace, slashing at the giant beast with his sword, slicing into the thick skin. Halcyon also moved, but much more slowly, his movements sluggish and tired, not fast enough to evade that huge descending foot. Gryphon yelled, struck out with his sword again, trying to distract the beast away from the Demon Prince but the obor's attention didn't waver from Halcyon. Just before the foot slammed down on him, Halcyon threw up a hand and hurled out a pulse of power that mixed with my cry.

The power was enough to deflect that giant foot to the left, so that it smashed down on the boulder beside him, crumbling it to dust less than a foot away from Halcyon. Another gesture from that elegant hand, another sharp pulse of power from Halcyon, and a large slash opened up on the trunk of that leg, gaping like an obscene mouth spilling out blood. The creature screamed in pain. Jerking away from Halcyon, it turned and charged at Gryphon— easier prey that did not slice open its flesh with invisible power.

Halcyon lifted his face up. He'd heard my cry, or maybe just sensed our movements. He looked up and saw us. Saw me.

Instead of urging Vlad away, I urged him now down toward the monster. "We have to help them!"

"As you wish," Vlad said. The air whistled by as we swooped down. He touched down upon the ground, and set me down on my feet, much too far away from where the battle raged.

"Stay here," he ordered as the other gargoyles landed in loose formation around us. I opened my mouth to argue, when my eyes were drawn beyond Vlad as if pulled by an irresistible force.

I met Gryphon's eyes, so shockingly blue. Looked upon that beautiful, dear face once again. Felt love—first love—wash over me. Remembered the shocking devastation of his death. And could only say—only think—one word: "Gryphon."

TWELVE

MAYBE IT WAS being dead that made Gryphon feel so suddenly alive. It was certainly that—being demon dead—that twisted his priorities around enough so that he was fighting this prehistoric creature, trying to keep its stomping attention away from his Demon Prince, instead of running to Mona Lisa.

Sweet night, how beautiful she was, even surrounded by those menacing winged creatures who, thank the heavens, did not look as if they meant her harm . . . whereas this big sucker in front of him clearly did.

Thump! Another near squishing stomp of that big foot. Much too near a miss. Gryphon slashed his sword across that thick hide and leaped away, feeling like a tiny gnat stinging a giant human. Another bellowing scream from the bizarre-looking beast that looked part woolly mammoth and part something else he'd never seen before.

"Move it, Halcyon!" Gryphon yelled, adding further clarification in case his ruler prince didn't get it the first time. "Move your ass out of there!"

"I am hustling as you speak," Halcyon said. "You would do very well to take your own advice." But Gryphon couldn't. And Halcyon wasn't hustling as he said he was. If he was, it was an old man's hustle—a sluggish walk instead of a run. They were probably lucky to have even that. It was as if the Demon Prince suddenly felt every single one of his six hundred plus years down in this cursed stinkhole of a realm. A place that seemed to spawn these great mutant monstrosities that apparently liked to tenderize their meat before they ate it by crushing it first.

Whomp! Another near miss, close enough to keep the nasty behemoth's attention focused on him instead of the exhausted Demon Prince making his not-so-quick escape.

Hurry, Halcyon, he mentally urged. A trumpeting screech, like rusty nails scraping across a chalkboard, set his nerves even further on edge as he dodged the ugly beast and at the same time tried to keep an eye on the winged creatures that surrounded Mona Lisa. He watched some fly toward him and the beast, others wing toward Halcyon. It was too many things to try and keep an eye on. Something big smashed into Gryphon. A sideswipe from a tree trunk of a leg, and he went flying. Right into the arms of something that was too small to belong to that one-ton leg, but plenty big in its own right. Much bigger than him, at least. It caught him neatly like a baseball flying into the pocket of an outfielder's glove. Grinning—an expression that flattened the creature's pug nose even more and revealed sharp teeth—the winged thing said, "We are here to aid you at your lady's request."

Batlike wings flew him safely away from the rampaging beast as others of his kind engaged the creature. For a second, there was just that beautiful sense of flight. Sweet heaven, how Gryphon missed the falcon part of himself lost with his death, like a piece of his soul ripped away. He craned his neck and saw Halcyon scooped up in another's arm and carried as he was, like a baby. Easier to tolerate when the ruler of Hell was being transported in similar manner.

Gryphon found himself deposited a safe distance away, with Mona Lisa to the distant left of him, and Halcyon at a third triangular point. In their center was the mammoth beast. Gryphon could appreciate the move—spreading out their risk. But it grated on him to be so close to Mona Lisa and still so far away from her.

"Stay here. We gargoyles are better equipped to handle the obor." With that terse order, his rescuer flew off in a winged rush, flying to where his companions engaged the obor with their dark swords, deadly no doubt to another creature similar in size to them—man-sized or, more accurately, gargoyle-sized—but not to the obor, which towered over the gargoyles, making their swords look like tiny matchsticks.

How in the holy darkness did they expect to handle the obor? Gryphon wondered. Even with a dozen gargoyle warriors harassing the beast, hovering around it like fat-bodied, charcoal-gray moths, they seemed inadequate in number to take down the obor. It was simply too big.

Even more perplexing, the gargoyle who had rescued him didn't draw his sword, though it was there, belted at his side. And he was the one the woolly creature struck at the most with his flying front feet, as if somehow sensing he was the greatest danger. The obor held him at a stalemate, so that no matter which way the gargoyle darted and twisted, it could not get close to the creature. Whatever his gargoyle rescuer had planned to do, it obviously wasn't working.

THIRTEEN

HALCYON MENTALLY CURSED the weakness of his body. The mutiny of his physical strength, which had always seemed so endless and abundant. For the second time in his long afterlife, he knew what it was to be weak. And like the first time around, he found it a most inconvenient state. Even his mental power had started to drain by the time the gargoyles had flown to their rescue.

He recognized exactly who and what had come to their aid. And the reason for it—Mona Lisa—did not overly surprise him. He was grateful for their timely intervention. Even more grateful to have them as friends instead of enemies. Halcyon knew of the gargoyles from his demon past—from demon legend. He doubted, however, that Gryphon had any inkling of what kind of power they were capable of wielding. If they were lucky, that power would be demonstrated shortly. Unfortunately, luck did not seem to be much in evidence at the moment. The giant obor had apparently encountered their kind before; it didn't allow any of the gargoyles near enough to touch it, especially the gargoyle that came deliberately at it with bare hands.

Halcyon had known that the Nether Realm affected the oldest demons most severely—the first to feel the new realm's denseness, the last to recover from it. It was part of the reason he had allowed Gryphon to accompany him here, pairing Gryphon's youthful strength with his older mental power. But in truth, had it not been for Gryphon's presence and his surprising loyalty, Halcyon would have long ago been devoured by the obor, weakened as he was from the arduous trek down the mountain. So much time they had wasted half a day doing just that.

The odds had been against their finding Mona Lisa before the doorway his father had carved out closed with finality between their realms. Their chance had grown even slimmer with Halcyon's growing fatigue and ever slackening pace.

"Go back," he had told Gryphon when they had stopped yet again for a rest.

"Fuck you, my lord," had been Gryphon's polite, impertinent response.

He'd been about to order Gryphon back when the obor had sensed them and attacked. Now, miracle of all miracles, Mona Lisa was here, safe, and they had several hours yet to reach the doorway. They had a chance, a very good chance of making it, if only they could neutralize the one obstacle in their way—the giant obor.

The obstinate beast wasn't cooperating. Far from it. A lucky swat with its thick tail struck a gargoyle, sending him tumbling down to the ground, his weapon knocked from his hand. The creature wheeled about, its two front legs lifted up to crush the downed gargoyle. Shouts of alarm sounded from the others, but they were all too far away to be of help, and none of them were successful in distracting the beast's attention away from their fallen comrade. As those two massive legs came crashing down, something darted in.

The ground shook like a small earthquake at the stomping impact. And there was a shocked, still silence as dust swirled up violently from the ground. The obor lifted one giant leg and then the other, backing away. And all peered down at the ground. Nothing. No trampled body. No crushed gargoyle.

From behind the huge body of the beast, a gargoyle flew into view, the one who had stood beside Mona Lisa dressed in royal purple attire. In his arms was the fallen gargoyle he had plucked out from beneath the obor's descending feet. A few words spoken to the other gargoyle he carried, awake and conscious now, and his arms dropped away as the other gargoyle spread wide his wings. The two of them flew, weaponless, near the head of the giant obor, one on either side of the big head, like fat teasing moths.

The obor gave an enraged shriek, snapping its sharp teeth at them. They flitted away, one up, one down. As the massive jaws crunched on empty air, the gargoyle dressed in purple slapped his bare hand upon the obor's heavy snout. The creature's angry roar changed to a horrible, high-pitched shriek of terror as it froze, unable to move, and began to solidify in a visible wave moving down its body. Immobilizing death was spread with that one touch. Or a state as close to final death as you can come here in this realm without reaching that actual state.

The spreading petrification was like a giant, unstoppable wave that undulated slowly down the creature's body, turning it into solid rock. Another gargoyle, the one who had rescued Gryphon and flown in Mona Lisa, laid his hand on the obor's massive rump. The twitching tail froze and turned to rock and, unbelievably, the petrifying process began from that end also. Life leached out, or life as it existed here in NetherHell. It slipped away from the hardening flesh, froze

out all the suppleness from the skin. The second wave of
stony transformation washed through to the center of the
massive body and met the first wave. For a second the
obor was captured perfectly still, like an exquisitely carved
rock sculpture. Then the creature exploded as the two colliding forces met. Fragments of rock flew in all directions.
Dust filled the air. When it settled, there was nothing left
of the obor but crumbled pieces of stone spewed out over a
hundred-foot radius.

The gargoyles looked shocked. For good reason, Halcyon thought. Because only one gargoyle, the king, was
supposed to possess the ability to turn flesh into stone.
And yet two gargoyles here had wielded that ability. Which
of the two, then, was the gargoyle king?

FOURTEEN

WE WERE SAFE, the obor vanquished. But tension still rang in the air like a thick toxic cloud after the threat was gone. A different sort of tension from before when they had been battling the creature.

I had watched with bated breath as Gordane left my side and flew in to save the fallen gargoyle. Watched as the obor barely missed smashing them both into a bloody pulp. Watched as Gordane had slapped a hand on the obor's snout, and it had started to turn to stone. Watched as Vlad had laid a hand against the rump and done the same from the opposite end. I had glimpsed the final solidified product for one frozen blink of time, and in that moment, knowledge had suddenly dawned. The bizarre statues that I had seen in the palace had been actual existing creatures frozen into stone by Gordane!

I had a moment to think—*No wonder Miles wouldn't allow Gordane to touch him in the arena.* Another moment to puzzle over why being eaten alive by frenzied werebeasts was preferable to being frozen into stone by a gargoyle—it seemed a relatively painless death, as such. There had to be something more to it. Then a ghastly thought entered my mind.

Did the frozen creatures continue to remain aware, even after their physical body had been turned to stone?

I watched as the obor blew apart into a million dusty stone fragments, and thought, *Well, no suffering or lingering awareness for that one.*

Before all the dust had finished settling on the ground, I was running across the rocky debris. Gryphon met me halfway and swept me into his arms. God, how wonderful they felt—solid, strong, real.

"Mona Lisa." His voice sounded the same, the same sweet dark melody I had missed so much. His arms held me tight, his body pressed to mine . . . all that was unchanged, just no heartbeat. But, hey, I didn't have one either. I giggled a little hysterically at that thought, and Gryphon pulled back to gaze at me.

There. Another change: his eyes. Once a lovely azure blue like the sky on a clear spring day, they were lighter and brighter now, almost shockingly vivid. And there was a light tan on his skin. But, oh, he was still Gryphon, still my lost love. Tears filled my eyes.

"Don't cry."

"Gryphon." Wiping my tears away, I saw Halcyon come to us. With one hand wrapped around Gryphon's waist, I drew Halcyon into our embrace. "You came," I said, drawing back to gaze at them. "You both came for me."

"Of course," Halcyon said. "We will always come for you."

"How long before the doorway closes?" Gryphon asked, gazing at the Demon Prince.

"What doorway?" I asked.

"The one my father opened in the sealed gate between

our realms." Turning to Gryphon, he said, "A few hours before it closes. We had best start making our way back."

My frown cleared. "Oh, we have plenty of time then."

"Not if we have to walk," Halcyon said.

"Don't be silly," I said, squeezing his hand. "Our gargoyle friends can fly us there. We don't have to walk."

"We may need to." There was something in Halcyon's eyes, some knowledge that unsettled me, as he said, "We should go now before another battle begins."

"Another battle?" I asked.

"Between the two gargoyles who turned the creature to stone."

"Between Vlad and Gordane? Why would they fight each other?" I asked, and became aware once more of that odd tension. A tension that stretched thick and tight like an invisible rope between Vlad and Gordane as they stared at each other from across the obor's crumbled remains.

"Only one gargoyle among their people should have the power to turn flesh to rock—their king. The two may fight each other, to see which of them will be the gargoyle ruler," Halcyon said.

Sucking in a breath—habit again—I broke away from Halcyon and Gryphon and rushed between the two gargoyles who were approaching each other like gunslingers, hands by their sides. Not drawing yet, but ready to.

"Gordane. Vlad. Tell me you two aren't going to foolishly fight each other." Only now, after Halcyon's revelation, did I see how evenly matched the two of them were—in their powerful physiques, in the proud full curve of their horns, larger and thicker than the other gargoyles.

"I do not wish to fight you," Gordane said, speaking to Vlad over my head. Both had stopped several feet away from me. "It was not my intent to challenge you, only to aid you in immobilizing the beast."

"In doing so, you revealed possession of a power that only a true king should possess," Vlad said.

"Because I am a true king, of my own city-state. And I am loathe to forsake that title and position, already secured, for something I am far less certain I can attain. I am content with my kingdom here in the desert lands. I have no wish to try for your crown. My only desire is to seek a bond-mate from the females of our kind."

"Upon further thought," Vlad said slowly, "any female gargoyle you choose will be unlikely to leave her home in the clean high reaches for the cursed lower grounds, no matter how lavish your desert palace may be. I would not force her out against her wishes, nor could I tolerate your returned presence to our mountaintop, now that I am fully aware of your power. It would be foolish of me to do so."

Vlad's words had both Gordane and I tensing. *Vlad, what are you doing?* I silently screamed. Gordane might not fight Vlad over the crown of gargoyle king, but he would fight him for access to a female of his kind. If the only access to them was by being king, then he would challenge Vlad for that right.

Mona Louisa said, *Vlad would rather meet the challenge and decide it here and now.* Her voice startled me. I'd forgotten her for a minute.

So Vlad is deliberately goading Gordane into challenging him? It seemed rather stupid to me, but seemed to make complete sense to Mona Louisa.

"Sire," Gordane said, dropping his head down in a deep bow. "My oath upon our most sacred high eyrie that I am no threat to you or your rule." His head lifted. "Not unless you deliberately make me one. I ask for only a short period of time to seek out a bond-mate among our women."

They assessed each other, two powerful gargoyle rulers.

"King Vlad." I didn't know his proper title but it had to be something close to that. "Please. You promised that Gordane would have that chance."

"So I did," Vlad murmured, studying Gordane intently. "And so he will, but only for a fortnight," he said finally. "Is that agreed?"

Gordane nodded. "Agreed, sire. I offer you my deep gratitude."

"Do not thank me yet. I allow you only opportunity. The rest—convincing the female you have chosen to leave with you—will be entirely up to you."

"Opportunity will be enough," Gordane said.

"We shall see. You have been long away from our people. Your skills may have grown rusty."

"What skills?" I asked.

"His sexual ones. That is how we court among our kind," Vlad explained.

"Oh, well, I'm not sure about the charm, Gordane may have to practice up on that," I said, making Gordane scowl. "But I can vouch for his sexual skills. He's had plenty of practice." A low growl, *two* low growls behind me, suddenly made me realize how my words could be taken.

"I meant plenty of practice on *other women*," I hastened to add, looking exasperatedly at Gryphon and Halcyon— where the growls were coming from. "He has an entire *hareem* of at least eighty women, for Pete's sake."

Thankfully, the menacing growls subsided.

When the hell had they become so jealous? I wondered. Gryphon, I could understand, he'd shown signs of jealousy before. But not Halcyon, not from him.

"When we entered this other realm," Halcyon said. And I felt him then in my mind, in that demon part that was his own blood. "I'm sorry. Being in this realm has changed something in me. Made my control more slippery."

I eyed him uncertainly. "Then perhaps it would be best if we left right away." I turned back to the two gargoyles. "Everything square with you guys?"

"Square?" Vlad asked.

"I mean, is everything agreed between you two?"

Vlad nodded.

"Okay, great, now back to our regular show," I said, and got strange looks from the two gargoyles. "Too much television," I said, confusing them further. "What, no television down here? Well, that settles it. I definitely can't stay now." Heady relief mixed with something else, something that had to do with Gryphon, with seeing him, being so close to him once more, seemed to make a giddy stream of nonsense pour out of my mouth.

I closed my mouth and focused on the most important thing now. "Can you guys give us a lift to the gate . . . the doorway . . . whatever it is that will allow us to leave this realm? I could probably shift into my vulture form"—my mutant vulture/human/tiger form, to be more precise—"but I'd rather not make two trips carrying first Halcyon and then Gryphon. Plus, more important, I don't know where we're supposed to go."

"Of course," Vlad said. "We shall gladly take you there."

"Sire, if I may, I would ask to fly Mona Lisa this final distance," Gordane said, bowing as he made his request.

Vlad nodded, cordially enough, if a bit stiff. "Of course, you may carry her. And I and my men will assist the demons."

He paired up with Halcyon, another gargoyle with Gryphon, and then we were off the ground, into the air once more, with Gordane's arms secure around me, my own clinging tight to his wide shoulders.

"Why?" Gordane asked softly.

"Why what?"

"Why did you intercede on my behalf with Vlad when you had nothing to gain by helping me?"

"Because I was here, and able to."

"You are kind."

"Why does that surprise you?"

"Because *kind* is not a word many would use to describe me." He touched my neck, stroked delicately over where the bruises had been, faded away now.

"You're kind when you wish to be," I murmured as memory of that brief and intimate time of sensual pleasure flashed between us.

"Only when it serves my needs."

I laid my hand over his stroking fingers. "You should try to be kind more often, Gordane. It sits very well upon you. As a ruler, you have a duty to show kindness and mercy to those under your care."

"You see me that way. As under your care," he said perceptively.

I flushed. "Before, when I thought that this was to be my life . . . I would have accepted what you offered. Maybe even created a child with you." Poignant knowledge swelled between us for a moment. "But this way works out much better for everyone."

"Perhaps. Or perhaps not. We shall never know."

"No," I said softly, maybe even a bit tenderly. "We'll never know now."

Then the time for more words passed as we neared a small open ledge on the side of the mountain. Gordane shifted down toward it.

"Is that where the gate is?" I asked.

"Yes, our time together is almost at an end, and I find myself surprisingly sad to see you go."

"You flatter me," I said as we touched down featherlight on the narrow ledge. "I hope you find what you seek," I said softly as he set me down on my feet.

A cocky male grin creased his face. "I shall certainly have fun trying." Then more seriously. "And you, will you be happy?"

My gaze fell on my dark and beautiful Gryphon, on Halcyon, my elegant Demon Prince, as they landed on the ledge beside us a short distance away with their gargoyle escorts. "Oh yes. I will be very happy."

"The gate is just within," Halcyon said, walking inside.

The cave was much larger than it appeared on the outside, twice our height, with more than enough room to accommodate two demons, three gargoyles—the others still cruised on the winds above—and myself.

The gate, or rather the doorway, was just within, as Halcyon had said. Near the back wall, an eerie black field of energy undulated, like ore would look if it were melted into flowing form. A gargoyle, the one who had flown Gryphon, gasped at the sight. Vlad spoke softly to him, and the gargoyle backed out of the cave and hastily left.

"There is no need for you or Gordane to remain, either," I said to Vlad. "Thank you for bringing us here. For coming to Halcyon and Gryphon's aid. For everything you have done."

"Do not hasten us so quickly on our way," Vlad murmured. "We will stay until we know what your fate is to be."

Oh, yeah. That wasn't quite certain yet.

"Come," Halcyon said, apparently not seeing any point in waiting.

He held out a hand to me and I grasped it, felt Gryphon grip my other hand. Secure between the two of them, I walked to that eerie liquid doorway. Halcyon didn't stop. He didn't say any special incantation or exert any special power that I felt. He simply continued walking and passed right through it, disappearing from sight until all that remained of him was his hand wrapped around mine, pulling me forward until my fingers reached that black undulating essence and stopped there like it was something solid I could not pass through. Hot blistering pain had me screaming and releasing Halcyon's hand, wrenching myself violently back, cradling a hand that sizzled and burned with horrific pain.

Gryphon cradled me as I rocked in agony and awful discovery. "I can't pass through," I muttered, tears streaming down my face. Part of me had believed, had utterly believed that I would be able to walk through that doorway just like Halcyon. It was a staggering shock to find myself unable to. To find myself stuck here forever in NetherHell.

"I will stay here with you," Gryphon murmured in my ear.

"No!" I fought free of his arms and stood cradling the burnt, charred mess that was my hand. "No, just go, Gryphon. Leave!"

Halcyon stepped back through the gate, and I marveled at how easy it was for him to pass in and out of that black barrier. "Once the gate closes, it will not be reopened again," he said, looking at Gryphon and I.

"Just say the word, Mona Lisa," Vlad said, quietly drawing our attention to the two watching gargoyles, "and it can be as it was before with Gordane."

"What?" I had no idea what Vlad was talking about, and found it hard to concentrate on anything other than the blistering pain emanating from my hand.

"Your arrangement with him before. To become his bond-mate."

Gordane's face had gone utterly still.

"You're asking me to release you from your promise. To give Gordane a chance of finding a bond-mate among your people," I said slowly to the gargoyle king, finally comprehending what he proposed. "So Gordane would have no other option but to choose me as his bond-mate if he wants any hope of having a family, a child."

"You would be his queen," Vlad said.

"I would be his curse. No." I shook my head fiercely. "You promised him a chance. I ask that you keep your word. My not being able to cross the gate—it changes nothing."

"It changes everything," Vlad answered. "This is a hard realm. You must begin to think of your own survival here—what you will do, where you will go."

"I will be beside you," Gryphon said. The determination in his voice, his eyes, was frightening.

I might be stuck here, but Gryphon didn't have to be. God! The ways this realm would change him—had already changed me—were too awful to imagine . . . or perhaps to easy to.

"We should first determine if you are truly stuck here," Halcyon said.

I stared at Halcyon. Raised my burnt hand up to him. Half of the blackened, blistered skin had split and peeled away from my fingers, exposing raw, gooey flesh, naked tendons and joints, uncovered bone. "I think this pretty much tells me that I am."

Halcyon knelt down beside me and gently cradled my injured hand. I felt him move within my mind, his presence like the gentle brush of a bird's wing.

The wrenching pain faded away.

The sheer relief of it contrarily caused more tears to spring up in my eyes. "You took away the pain. I didn't know you could do that."

"Only with you, because of our link. The pain is still there. I just blocked your mind's reception of it."

"Whatever you did, Halcyon, it feels wonderful. God. Thank you."

"Do not thank me yet. I may be about to cause you even worse pain."

I brushed the tears away. "Worse pain? I don't think that's possible. What do you mean?"

"There is one other thing we can attempt, Mona Lisa. But it depends on how badly you wish to return to the living realm."

"Pretty damn badly. What other thing can we attempt?"

"I can try to separate Mona Louisa's dead essence from your living one. I believe that is what prevents you from crossing."

And he might be able to do that, I realized, because part of her dead essence was him, his own blood. I felt Mona Louisa's attention sharpen within me.

"What will happen to her—to Mona Louisa?" I asked. "Will she be able to exist here separately?"

"I do not know. Nor do I know what will happen to you. If you will even survive the sundering of your spirits. Even if you do, you may still not be able to cross the doorway."

"Put like that, how could I resist?" Yeah, there was some sarcasm, but it was truthful sarcasm on my part. Any chance, any chance at all, I was willing to take. Still, the concept shocked me: separating out the demon dead part that was Mona Louisa from the rest of me.

"But wouldn't taking out her demon part be defeating the whole purpose?" I asked. "Isn't being a demon what allows you to cross this doorway?"

"The gate is more of a barrier to keep in the condemned—in this case, Mona Louisa's dheu spirit. I believe that is all that prevents you from crossing the doorway, but it is only speculation on my part. I do not know for certain."

Within me, I felt Mona Louisa give her consent. *Yes,* she thought, *I will risk the sundering. The possibility of existing here separately, as my own individual being once more, is worth the risk.* She thought in this realm, with her greater strength, she had a chance of existing apart from me.

Gryphon saw my answer in my eyes. "No," he said, his blue eyes glittering with that eerie brightness. "Don't risk yourself this way. We could stay here together in this realm."

"No, we can't. You can't stay here, no matter what happens to me. This place changes you. You don't know the horror you would become."

"Mona Lisa." He grasped my uninjured hand, held it tightly. "I beg of you. Do not risk this sundering of yourself."

"I have to, Gryphon." I pulled my hand gently out of his. "You know it's not in me to do anything else. It's all or nothing for me." With my eyes, I implored him to understand and forgive me.

Turning, I walked to Halcyon. "Okay, let's do this." Brave words. But when the moment came—and it came all too quickly, with the bending of his head and the lowering of his lips to mine—fear stabbed through me.

Halcyon did not kiss me or touch me in any way. He simply brought his lips down an inch away from mine and inhaled. With that first breath, I felt a tugging within me. Not a gentle tug, but a hard steady pull, as if a giant fish-hook had latched into me and was starting to peel away my innermost lining, ripping it out. I swallowed the screams until the pain became too much to bear anymore, then I threw back my head and screamed—terrible shrieks, guttural cries, instinctively pulling away from Halcyon. He touched me then, gripped my shoulders to hold me still. To keep me close to him as he continued to rip Mona Louisa out of me.

A white vapor condensed in the air. Slowly became visible as he drew her out. It felt like I was being torn apart, sundered in truth. It was terrible agony, unbearable pain. Worse than any she or I had ever known.

We won't survive!

We cannot survive this!

Our twin voices screamed the words through our

minds. Then the words spilled out of our mouths in two different voices, startling us. A brief flare of hope—*he's succeeding!*—then spasms began to shake our body as he continued to split us apart. Spasms that became alarming convulsions.

He's killing us!

I opened my mouth to scream: *No! Stop!* But another convulsion seized me in its grip and shook my body so cruelly I couldn't speak.

With a final yanking pull, Mona Louisa was brutally torn free of my flesh, leaving behind a jagged tear that I felt deep inside. All ceased—the screams, the violent paroxysms of my body. All froze for one suspended moment. Then I breathed, took in a shuddering breath, and found myself outwardly whole. No blood splattered my body. No innards were pulled out, hanging obscenely outside my body.

I breathed, not habit but need, real need, and sank slowly down to my knees. In front of me was Mona Louisa's vapory form. She shimmered for a moment like an ethereal spirit, the detail and outline of her sharp and vivid. We stared at each other, amazed, awed. Then her shimmering form dulled and she began to fade, to disappear.

"No!" I cried, moving forward. But another reached her first. Gordane stretched out a gray gargoyle finger and touched that fading essence. And with that one light touch, her fading spirit began to take corporeal form. Flesh spilled onto Mona Louisa, filled in the outline of her shimmering spirit. His touch gave her substance, a solid and real body.

"How did you do that?" Mona Louisa asked, standing before Gordane splendidly real, splendidly naked.

With a surprising bit of gallantry, Gordane removed his shirt and covered her with it. "My touch solidifies things. It seemed what your spirit needed."

"Miraculous," I said, awed.

"Not what one often says of our ability," Gordane murmured dryly.

"Thank you, Gordane. You saved her." I was grateful for his intervention. My feelings toward Mona Louisa had changed somehow from hate into something else. She had been a part of me. And that had changed things. Had changed her—both of us.

Gordane shrugged his broad shoulders. "You did not seem to want her to dissipate."

"So you helped her."

"Yes, though she may wish later that I had simply let her go. NetherHell is not an easy place to exist."

"I seem to have a knack for surviving, though," Mona Louisa said. "You have my sincere gratitude, Lord Gordane. Especially if you return me to my Miles."

The corners of his mouth curved up in a slight smile. "My wings are at your service. And you are correct. Miles seems more yours now than mine."

"Despite that, I think both our services will prove quite useful to you," she murmured, sliding her hand through his offered arm.

Mona Louisa was indeed a survivor. And I had no doubt she would see well to the business of surviving here—had begun to, already, it seemed. All that was left was to see if it worked. If, now that she was no longer a part of me, I would be able to cross through the doorway and leave NetherHell.

Gryphon laid his fingers gently on my arm. My hand was visibly starting to heal, bits of blackened flesh falling away, new healthy pink tissue replacing it. A reassuring sight. I had wondered for a moment if the damage would be permanent. "Can you walk?" he asked.

"Yeah, I can walk." I would have crawled had I needed to, but walking was much better.

"Shall we try again?" Halcyon asked. He stood on my

other side, not making any effort to touch me. I'd known he was there. Had been aware of him in a hypersensitive sort of way. But I hadn't been able to look at him yet. I forced myself to meet his gaze now, with the memory of the pain he had caused me still raw and fresh.

The pain wasn't his fault, I told myself. But the sharp, vivid pain memory of my body still made me shrink back from him, unsettled by his nearness.

A wounded look passed through his eyes before he blanked out all expression from his face. He took a step back, and gestured to the black undulating doorway. "Go on."

This time it was Gryphon who led me to the gate. Gryphon who held my hand. He stopped in front of the doorway. "It's up to you," he said, leaving the choice to me. To try or not to try.

With my fingers entwined with his, my hand trembling wildly—his rock steady—I lifted our hands and touched the doorway. Our fingers sank through as if nothing was there, disappearing through the surface. No burning flesh, no flash of pain. Nothing but a mild brush of energy across my skin.

"It worked." I turned back to Halcyon, elated. "It worked!"

Relief filled his eyes, and was the last thing I saw as I stepped through the doorway with Gryphon. It was like walking into the room next door—effortless, pain-free. I left NetherHell, my last glimpse that of Halcyon, passed through smothering darkness, and emerged on the other side with Blaec, the High Lord of Hell—an older version of Halcyon—waiting for us there.

"Thank the darkness. You found her," Blaec said, looked unbearably strained and weary. "Where is Halcyon?"

"Just behind us," Gryphon said. But his voice sounded

funny. His hand, wrapped around mine, clenched tight, painfully tight. "Blood . . . I smell blood." Slowly Gryphon turned to me and said in that funny voice, "Let go."

Every hair on my body was suddenly standing up on end. "What?"

"Let go of my hand . . . and run!"

I abruptly realized why his voice sounded so strangely garbled. He had fangs! The shock of seeing them on Gryphon and realizing again what he was—*demon!*—had me dropping his hand.

"No, don't run!" Blaec said. But it was too late. Blind instinct had taken over. I ran. And Gryphon came after me.

I made it only into the next room before he was on me. His sharp nails sank into my shoulder, my hip. His fangs ripped savagely into my neck. I had a moment to think—*It's not real. It's just a nightmare, a horrible nightmare.* Then blood-filled darkness sucked me screaming down into its scary depths.

FIFTEEN

MY BODY FELT as if someone had viciously pummeled me. *Why do I hurt so much?* I wondered. With that one question, all the recent events came rushing back, hitting me like a sharp, brittle hailstorm.

I remembered the awful, wrenching agony of Mona Louisa being torn out of me, of stepping across the doorway and crossing into Hell . . . of being attacked by Gryphon.

My charred hand was whole and unblistered. And my neck, I found, reaching up to touch it, was smooth, untorn.

"My father healed you."

I turned my head in a swift, startled movement, and saw Halcyon standing there, a towel wrapped around his waist, his black hair hanging wet and damp around his face; he'd obviously just come from a shower. Crossing the room, he disappeared into the closet and emerged a minute later wearing his usual black pants and a white silk shirt that he casually buttoned up as he walked to where I still lay in his bed.

"Can you get this for me?" he asked, presenting me with an undone cuff. Two diamond cufflinks were cupped in his other hand. He looked tired, I realized, sitting up. And he was treating me almost like . . . a wife, with casual intimacy. Maybe another time it would have pleased me, made me happy. Now it just unsettled me, his nearness. Trying to be as casual as he, I retrieved a cufflink out of his hand. But my fingers accidentally grazed his palm and I flinched. With clumsy haste, I fastened the first cuff.

"I'm sorry I hurt you," he said when I began working on the second cuff, which was taking longer than it should have because my hands were trembling.

"It still hurts," I said, not looking at him, "like an open wound inside me." Finished, I drew my hands slowly away from his sleeve, instead of yanking them back quickly the way I wanted to.

"My father healed the surface wounds Gryphon inflicted. Not the inner one caused by me."

I braved a quick glance at his face before my eyes darted away. He looked tired, I thought, the same echo of weariness I had seen on his father's face.

"I'm so sorry." A whispered apology to my bent head.

"You warned me it would hurt. And I know you did it to save me. But God, Halcyon, it hurt so much."

He reached out to take my hand. I shied away from him. And he froze into a dangerous stillness.

"I'm sorry, I'm still a bit jumpy," I said, not looking at him. Not *daring* to look at him. "I'll be better with time."

"That's something I'm afraid we don't have." His hand dropped back to his side and I watched as those long elegant fingers clenched into a loose fist. Noticed, as I had never noticed before, the cutting sharpness of his nails.

I looked up—forced myself to—and as I met those chocolate brown eyes, I realized suddenly that I no longer had that deep and intimate connection with him afforded by the presence of his demon blood within me. It was gone, ripped away with Mona Louisa. I couldn't read his emotions now. Could read nothing on that closed face.

"What do you mean?"

"I had to tear Gryphon off you. The blood on your feet drove him wild."

"Miles's blood." Drawn by my tiger claws when I had lifted him out of the arena.

"The blood flared up his bloodlust when we crossed back into Hell. He's a new demon, Mona Lisa."

"I'm well aware of that!" I said in angry outburst. "Especially after he went all demon on me and attacked me."

"So now you don't trust either of us. Now you're afraid of us both." Halcyon's eyes were hard, cold, his voice flat in a way I'd never seen or heard before.

I opened my mouth to deny his words . . . and couldn't. Actions did not lie, and my body's instinctive reactions around him had told a vivid truth. No, I did not trust them anymore.

"I just need some time," I said in a small voice.

"Time away from both your demons, to forget the pain we caused you. But as I said, I cannot give you that. Yours is not the only pain we must contend with," Halcyon said. "You must address Gryphon's pain first before you run away from us. Otherwise there will be only one demon lover for you to return to, if you ever do."

Halcyon's strange words and strange attitude frightened me. Made my heart race. And I became aware of that wonderful noisy rhythm—my heart was beating again! But elation quickly ebbed and worry took its place as Halcyon's words sank in.

"Are you saying that Gryphon . . . wants to kill himself?"

A twist of lips. "He's dead, remember. But if you mean if he wishes to end his demon existence, then yes."

"Why?"

"Because, as you said, he went all demon on you and attacked you."

I squirmed, hearing my words thrown back at me. "But he couldn't help himself, I know that. I remember how overwhelming bloodlust can be."

"Then you must tell him this. And you must give Gryphon more than mere words. You must make him believe it with your actions."

My fingers went again to my neck, remembering the feel of his sharp fangs tearing into my flesh. Remembering again the pain of his demon nails sinking into me, the frightening strength in those hands. With a deep shuddering breath, I forcibly closed the door on those memories. "Take me to him, and I will convince him."

"How?" He flung out the word like an accusation. "You cannot even convince *me* that you do not think of me as a monster. And I did not attack you or rip into you with nails and fang. How will you convince Gryphon?"

"You're not a monster," I said, flinching at the outburst. "Just someone who is much stronger than I."

"Someone who deliberately inflicted pain on you, like Gryphon." Halcyon's eyes closed, dark lashes coming to a rest in crescent shadows over his golden skin. Then his eyes flashed opened, snaring me. "But what lies between you and I does not matter at the moment. Tell me," he said almost gently. "How will you convince Gryphon that you do not see him as the monster he sees himself as? As the monster you see him to be also?"

"I don't! He's not a monster. Just a new demon with strange new urges and . . . difficulty controlling those urges."

"Is that what you will say to him?" Halcyon gave a hollow laugh. "Maybe I should save us all the trouble, time, and heartache, and simply turn him loose, allow him to seek his final rest. Maybe I should seek it, too."

"Don't say that!" I said angry, bewildered. "Why are you talking like this? Behaving this way?"

"Because I am tired . . . so tired . . . and my own heart aches." He ran a hand through his damp hair. "Forgive me. I am not entirely myself. The other realm drained me more than I thought. I need to rest, and I shall do so, but not until we see to Gryphon first."

I tried to hold onto my anger but it slipped away at seeing Halcyon so unsteady, so agitated . . . so unlike his usual calm and in-control self. "What do you want me to do?" A simple question.

A simple answer in turn. "I want you to be his Queen."

"He is no longer Monère, Halcyon. And I am no longer his Queen."

"You have been his Queen, his lady of light, longer than he has been demon dead."

"Just barely," I said, feeling pain wash through me at that truth. How brief our time together had been.

"He lived for over seventy-five years where his Queen was everything to him, her word absolute. I do not want you to ask him to forgive himself. I want you to command him to. To demand it of him."

"I never demanded anything of Gryphon when I was his Queen. I asked for . . . hoped for things, but never demanded. I was not that type of Queen with him."

"Mona Sera, your mother, his former Queen, was, however. And Gryphon spent many decades serving under her."

"You're asking me to be like her? Cold, cruel, ruthless?"

"Not cold. But cruel and ruthless? Yes, if you need to be. He will respond to that. It is too ingrained in him, and he is only just transitioned. Kindness, sweetness, any hesitancy on your part will not do the job. You must command his obedience."

"That he, what? Not end his existence? How can I convince him to do that? Just telling him isn't going to make that happen, no matter how ruthless, how cruel, how Queenly I command him."

"No, you are correct. Words alone will not convince him that he can trust himself with you again. You must show him with action. Convince yourselves both."

"What action?"

"What is the most definitive act that tells a man that a woman trusts him, that she loves him?"

My lips flattened. "You want me to make love to him?"

"No, making love is too tender an action, an emotion, Mona Lisa. I want you to take him and make him yours again."

"You want me to fuck him."

"Yes."

I blew out a frustrated breath. "I don't know if I can," I said softly. "I keep remembering the way Gryphon looked when he attacked me. That frightening new strength of his."

"He is chained. I will keep him so."

"That doesn't make it better, Halcyon. And . . . I don't want to rape him."

"It will not be rape."

"I don't know if I can."

"Then beat him."

"What?"

"Punish him. You have to do something to lessen his guilt or it will cause him to seek an end to his afterlife. Anything that you can think of that will accomplish this, you must do."

"I can't think of anything other than giving him the words—"

"—which will not do when they are empty! He is hurting, not brainless!"

"Then we have a problem. I don't know what else to do." Other than what Halcyon had suggested. To punish him or take him, as he put it.

"We do not have much time," he warned, making me feel like a clock that he was winding too tight.

"Just give me a fucking moment!" I said in explosive frustration.

"Take your moment in the bath," Halcyon said shortly, as he headed out the door. "You need to wash the smell of blood off before you see him."

"Where are you going?"

"To prepare him," he said and closed the door behind him.

The bath didn't give me any new or brilliant ideas, but it did get me cleaned up, a wonderful feeling all on its own. I walked into Halcyon's large closet with the intent of pilfering some of his clothes. I didn't expect to see my own clothes hanging beside his. Not my old stuff but new clothes made in my size in vibrant colors that would flatter my white skin and dark hair. I slipped into a gossamer dress that fell in a light swirl down to my ankles. It was peacock blue and fit me perfectly. I found Halcyon waiting for me back in the bedroom, the hard look on his face softening when he saw me in the dress.

"You made all those clothes for me," I said, uncertain how I felt about that.

"There are undergarments and other women's apparel in the left bureau drawers," Halcyon said, all his anger gone, disappeared like mine. "But it would be better if you did not wear them. Just the shoes you have on." A dainty pair of slippers that I had chosen from among a dozen others. My shoes set alongside his. Men had shared my bed before. But never my room or closet space.

"You even got me shoes," I numbled.

"Do not look so surprised," Halcyon said. "You are my mate. Of course I would provide for you."

More than provide. He had made room for me in his bedroom. Taken space that had once been entirely his, and shared it now willingly with another. It . . . unsettled me.

"You do not look pleased."

"No, of course, I . . ." I stopped the lie I had started to utter. "It just seems so . . . *married*." A word, a concept, that suddenly made me feel a bit strangled.

"Married is a human concept," Halcyon said with calm reasoning. "You are my mate. Demons provide for their mates."

"Then why are you so willing to have me fuck Gryphon?" I burst out.

"Because in your heart you are also his mate. Come," he said more softly. "Let us go to him."

I almost ran out the door in my eagerness to escape the shared intimacy of the bedroom. Given the choice between facing a chained and snarling demon, and tackling my other issues . . . Well, I'd take the angry demon any day, hands down.

SIXTEEN

O F COURSE I felt completely different when I came face-to-face with Gryphon. He was chained as promised in the lowest level of Halcyon's home. In the dungeon. I didn't know whether to be more frightened that Halcyon had such a place, here where he lived, or over the state Gryphon had worked himself into. He had more than gone demon on me. If he'd still been human, I would have said that he'd gone crazy. Using demon terminology, he had gone into a full demonic rage.

I'd never seen a demon that was totally out of control before. His lips were peeled back in a frenzied snarl, and his blood-stained teeth and fangs on full display as he screamed in a voice gone bone-achingly deep, "Unchain me! Release me!"

His eyes were lava red, and his forehead and temples bulged as if the fury within was shifting his very bones. Muscles swelled his body, thicker than normal, as he viciously strained at the overhead chains that held him suspended almost completely off the ground. His shirt was ripped, hanging in tatters on him. And the neat black pants and polished shoes he still had on, remnants of a more civilized man, seemed jarringly out of place in the frenzied animal state he'd fallen into.

"Let me go!" he howled with spewing hot rage. I was shocked speechless to see him in such a state. Kind and forgiving words, as Halcyon had said, were just not going to do the job here.

"He's shifting into his demon beast," I said, horrified.

"He cannot complete it," Halcyon said. "The chains prevent that."

The chains holding Gryphon were purple, different from the black demon chains I was used to seeing. Of course, black chains wouldn't have been able to contain a demon, much less one in such full-blown fury. The chains rattled violently as Gryphon fought the restraints, both the ones around his wrists holding him up, and the ones binding his ankles, anchoring him down.

"My God, Gryphon," I whispered, completely intimidated by what I was facing.

"Stop it!" Halcyon growled at me. "Stop all the useless, mawkish sentiments, and just *do* something! Be the Queen he needs you to be."

"She is not my Queen!" Gryphon screamed, pain mixed with fury. "Not anymore."

"You're wrong. She will always be your Queen. Your Demon Queen now, as my mate," Halcyon said. "You must obey her as you obey me."

"I've never obeyed you, Halcyon," Gryphon growled, gnashing sharp teeth.

"Part of the trouble. I have been too lenient with you."

Halcyon's words snapped me out of my shock and into the role I needed to play. A sneer twisted my lips that was part Mona Louisa, part Mona Sera, my mother. Most of it, though, was just me. "Look at you," I said with hot, biting contempt. "Look at the state you've allowed yourself to fall into."

Gryphon was surprised enough to still his wild struggle for a moment.

I walked closer, inspecting him. "This is unacceptable, Gryphon," I snapped, the words coming out sharp as a whiplash.

"This is what I am," he snarled back.

"No, you are more than this," I said with a calm certainty that enraged him again.

"I am nothing! Nothing but a danger to you now!"

"You are mine," I said with quiet tenderness, and stepped in close to him. So close that I could have brushed my lips across his fangs, stained with my own blood. So close that those dagger-sharp teeth could have cut into me. But they didn't. My first point.

I stepped back away from him. "I will not let you go, Gryphon. Never," I said in a hard, cruel voice. "No matter how you scream or plead for it." Sauntering behind him, I violently ripped off the remnants of his shirt. Gryphon's body jerked in surprise but he didn't snarl or say anything.

Halcyon watched us both in silence.

I dropped the torn fabric to the ground and circled around in front of him again. "You have been a bad boy," I noted coolly, and watched as the demon redness in his eyes receded, as his vivid blue irises swam back into focus, looking oddly beautiful on that half-morphed demon face.

"You should be punished for hurting me," I said, and my cold decree seemed to calm him even more. The bestial thickness of his face slowly slid away. His face thinned, his bones becoming slim and proportioned once more. But his fangs—they still remained.

I smelled blood wine nearby and spied a chalice set on

a small table against the wall. Picking it up, I brought it to
Gryphon. "Drink," I commanded, lifting the heavy rim to
his lips.

His eyes fixed fiercely on mine, Gryphon drank.

"Good," I crooned as he drank it all down. His long
fangs were ivory white now, my blood washed away. "Why
are your fangs still prominent?" I asked.

"You are standing here, your heart beating, your blood
so near. I can hear it rushing within you," he said, the rumbling deepness gone from his throat, leaving it sounding
more like his normal voice. His words should have frightened me, but they didn't because he was back in control.
His rage had receded, if not his fangs.

Returning the empty chalice to the table, I inspected the
other objects laid out there, and raised a brow at Halcyon.
"Your toys?"

"My sister's."

I wasn't sure if I was pleased or disappointed.

My hand reached down and selected a heavy crop.
Hefting it, I put it back down and picked up the slender
switch beside it. Gave it a few testing swipes. Heard a nice
satisfactory whistle as it cut through the air. "This one, I
think."

I sauntered back to Gryphon, switch in hand. The thin
whipping rod did not feel as unfamiliar as I thought it
would.

The two-inch heels on my slippers thrust my pelvis forward enough to put a nice sway into my walk. Gryphon's
eyes were fastened quite nicely on me. On the soft, flowing
undulation of my body, the promise of it. On the whisper-
thin material of my dress as it molded and clung to my hips,
my thighs. I felt sultry, powerful, and just mean enough to
enjoy the wariness in his eyes as I swayed over to him.

I brought the switch up and whipped it lightly across his

chest to test us both. It left a red mark against his lightly tanned skin. "Do you want this?" I asked.

Eyes narrowed, he slowly nodded.

I moved in close. Watched him grow still and tense. More tense even than when I had struck him. "Are you sure?" I whispered, so close to those threatening fangs.

His body gave an involuntary shudder at the tease of my blood so near him. "Yes," he said roughly. "Just . . . do not stand so close to me."

I threaded my hand through his hair, felt the thick, glossy locks slide beneath my fingers. Grasping those silky strands tight, I yanked his head back. "But I have to," I said, my soft breasts brushing his chest as I pressed myself tight against him. "It comes as part of your punishment."

Those unearthly eyes glittered at me. "Then I refuse it."

"Too late." I smiled coldly. "You already said yes." I eased myself away from him, my hand freeing his head to move, to strike. A long teasing moment before I stepped back out of striking range. For him. Not for me.

"You will take all that I dish out as your punishment, and more. Because I want you to. Because I command you to. Because you are *mine* and I am not giving you a choice." I circled around him, in the periphery of his vision. "But first, we have to get rid of your clothes. You'd hardly feel my little switch wearing these thick pants." I trailed my fingers down around to the front of his waist, and yanked open the top button.

"Why are you doing this?" Gryphon asked, his body tensing so still beneath my touch.

"Because you've been a bad boy, and you must be punished—my way."

The zipper rasped down and his pants fell open enough for me to see that he was semi-hard. Not aroused, but stirred a little. "Yes," I murmured, shoving his pants down to his feet with one swift pull. "Better. Much more skin now."

I walked to his right side, standing slightly behind him. Lightly applied the whistling switch to his thighs, his calves. His buttocks—those lovely round muscular globes—I first caressed with my hands then slapped. *Whack! Whack!* Hard enough to leave the red imprint of my hand on each cheek. I brushed the soft material of my gown against those red stinging marks and circled around to his left. Applied more blows with the switch. Then came around to the front of him.

"Is that your punishment?" Gryphon jeered, taunting me. "Just those light love taps?"

Something in his voice, his sneered expression, triggered something in me, unleashing an anger I hadn't even known was buried inside me. In a blur, the switch came lashing down across his chest in a hard, swift blow. With that first unthinking blow, it was as if a dam was released, spilling hurt and anger out in a roaring mindless gush. Another hard blow, and another! I beat him as I had not intended to—with anger, with real intent to inflict pain, the same pain welling up inside me.

"You bastard!" The words spilled out in a hot tide, mixing with my tears. Another hard blow. Another. "You left me! You died and you left me when you promised me that you would stay with me!"

I hit him over and over again, giving him the beating that he had asked for, the hard whistling sound of thin wood hitting flesh lost beneath my sobs. I hit him, struck him, until I could no longer see clearly, my vision blocked by tears.

Over the broken sounds of my weeping, I heard Halcyon say, "Enough. Enough, Mona Lisa."

His voice brought me back to myself. I wiped the tears from my eyes, and saw with terrible clarity the angry red welts I had left all over his body. Appalled, I dropped the switch and backed away.

"Oh, God," I whispered brokenly. I would have turned and fled up the stairs had Halcyon not done something so unexpectedly shocking that it froze me into stunned stillness.

He released Gryphon.

A swipe of Halcyon's demon nails sliced away the pants at Gryphon's feet; a quick removal of the pin, and the manacles were unlatched from Gryphon's ankles. Another quick release above and Gryphon's wrists were freed.

I stood there and watched Gryphon come toward me, the demon I had just angrily beaten, and made no effort to run away. A part of me feared retribution. A part of me wanted it, felt that I deserved punishment in turn.

The tears would not stop, pouring out of me like clear blood.

When Gryphon took me into his arms, offering comfort, cradling me against him, I wept even harder. "Gryphon." My arms crept around him. "Oh God, Gryphon, I'm so sorry."

"Don't cry."

"I beat you."

"I deserved it."

"I was so mad. You made me so mad, I lost control." A small hiccup. "You should . . . should beat me in turn."

"There are other things I'd rather do to your body. Far better things than beat it," he murmured, and his hands slid underneath the dress, touched bare skin. Just that one touch and my emotions swung from sorrow, guilt, and grief to something hotter, darker, much more base. My hands tunneled into his hair, gripped the silky strands, and pulled him toward me. "Love me," I demanded.

"I do. I will." But he resisted the silent command of my hands, and kept his mouth, those sharp fangs, away from me. It reminded me sharply, vividly, of how much stronger he was than I with his new demon strength and my demon essence gone.

A thrill coursed through me, a sharp zing of lust, of added desire, driving through me with a keen spike of excitement. Nothing like a little bit of danger thrown in with the sex. A residue from Mona Louisa or maybe my own twisted desire, I didn't know and didn't care.

"You like it that I'm stronger than you," Gryphon said, dark knowledge glittering in his blue eyes as he pushed me down and moved over me. Gripping my wrists with a swift suddenness that made me draw in a breath and grow even wetter, he lifted my arms, pinning them above me. "Keep them here," he ordered.

"And if I don't?" I asked, testing him. Testing us both. Taunting him, I lowered my arms back down to my sides. "What will you do? Punish me?"

He moved so fast I didn't see him. Moved with demon speed.

My wrists were yanked above my head with easy brute force. Held there with one hand while his other hand tore the delicate material of the dress from me with one savage, ripping pull. Hot glittering eyes swept down and fixed like an arrow upon that shaven part of me. His hand, holding my wrists, tightened painfully at the sight. "What's this?" he growled.

My desire cooled, seeped away, as pinpricks of red began to fill his eyes. "They . . . they shaved me down in NetherHell."

"Did that gargoyle lord see you like this?"

Fear—not the safe, exciting fear, but the dangerous can-rip-you-apart type edged into my voice. "Gryphon, your eyes are turning red."

"Answer me!"

"Yes, he saw me. But he didn't take me, he didn't touch me." The words tumbled out of me.

His hand left mine, and in that frightening fast way he had of moving now, he sank his hands into the hard ground on either side of my head, burying his sharp nails there, up to his fingertips. His knees spread my legs wide apart.

"Gryphon?" My voice was high-pitched, uncertain.

"I need you," he said hoarsely.

His voice was lowering, I noted with panic.

"Take me," he demanded—a raw plea somehow—and plunged into me.

I gasped as he filled me. Sharp, burning fast, brutally strong. I felt overwhelmed by him . . . his greater strength, his jealous anger, his almost desperate passion.

I was wet. But not enough to take him so forcefully like this. Pain intruded, nudging aside the pleasure, and fear pushed it away even further—a woman's fear of being hurt by a man so much stronger than her when her body was unprepared.

How could he have prepared you more? Not Mona Louisa's thoughts but my own. *He cannot touch you with his sharp nails. Cannot kiss your lips, your nipples, with fangs filling his mouth.*

He drew out of me, and I opened my mouth to scream at him to stop, to tell him to wait, that I wasn't ready yet, when I felt the sensual brush of phantom hands glide over my breasts, brush my nipples, ruffle over my sensitive, bared nether lips. Stroke deftly over the even more sensitive pearl he searched out from my folds. An invisible touch that drew forth a hot wash of tingling wet pleasure.

As my eyes lifted to Halcyon, as my body reacted to his phantom strokes, his invisible caresses . . . as I remembered that he was still there, *watching* us . . . Gryphon speared himself back into me—hard, deep, filling. Sliding into my lubricated sheath with a tight, frictioned burn that passed just barely from the thin edge of pain into ecstasy. I screamed as a sharp, unexpected climax gripped my body, bowed it up. Moaned as Gryphon furiously rode me through my twitching jerks and spasms. As his own body shuddered violently as he heaved and groaned and emptied himself into me.

He rolled off me and my vision was filled with Halcyon as he stood above me, his dark chocolate eyes fierce, hot, wildly possessive as he opened his pants and freed himself. As he came down over me, his hands falling exactly where Gryphon's had been, braced on both sides of my head. As he sank into me with one smooth thrust.

"Come for me again," my Demon Prince, my demon mate, demanded. He drew back and thrust into me in a steady, pounding rhythm, strong enough to move us several inches up with each forceful drive of his hips.

A hand wrapped around my wrist, anchoring my body still, and my eyes were drawn to Gryphon. Each time Halcyon thrust and withdrew, thrust and withdrew, I caught a glimpse of Gryphon's face in a peek-a-boo fashion over Halcyon's shoulder. It was like seeing a slideshow of first one lover and then the other filling my vision. One lover holding my body as another one filled and stretched it. The duality heightened my pleasure, my excitement, bringing me to another swift peak as Gryphon watched—and helped—Halcyon fuck me.

"Again," Halcyon growled, his rhythm, that hard pistoning motion in and out of me, remaining steady and relentless through my writhing spasms.

"Make me," I said, my voice low and sultry.

His dark eyes blazed with heat at my challenge, and a hard-edged smile curled his lips. A smile that was confident enough, ruthless enough, to drive a new frisson of lustful anticipation through my quivering body.

Instead of quickening his rhythm, Halcyon slowed it down so that I felt every inch of his hot penetrating slide into me, his unhurried pull back out. He slid his cock back in, into a tight quivering sheath filled with another man's ejaculate, and the smell of our combined scent, the three of us, the sight of them both watching me, one of them holding me down while the other pumped into me, was both shocking and unbelievably arousing. And I wasn't the only one turned on by the situation.

I moaned at what I saw in Gryphon's eyes, glimpsed in that peek-a-boo fashion over Halcyon's rising and dipping shoulders. Groaned as Halcyon's cock filled me, stretched me full.

"Look at me," Halcyon commanded. When I did, he thrust himself deep. Holding himself still, rooted fully within, he used his power to stroke invisible hands over me. Not in front but behind. Like an invisible lover, he entered me there, not with phantom fingers but a slick phantom cock. I felt him slide through my anus as surely as if he were solid flesh, and I screamed my pleasure, came again as he had commanded.

SEVENTEEN

CLEANING UP AFTERWARD, after gathering all of our ripped clothes—so many pieces scattered on the floor—I fell into a sort of dazed calm. Okay. So two men had just fucked me, one after the other, and I had enjoyed it—immensely. The important thing, the truly important thing, was that Gryphon's rage was gone and his mental equilibrium re-established, along with my own. I trusted him again. And he trusted himself to be with me. As long as Halcyon was there to supervise.

Ironically, it was much easier to look dispassionately at what I had just done than walk back into Halcyon's bedroom. Washing up and walking into that closet again caused that same feeling of suffocation to come over me. Snatching the first dress I saw, I threw it over me and almost ran out of the bedroom. Halcyon mistook it as eagerness for me to leave, and in a way, it was. Just not for the reason he assumed.

Two demon guards joined us outside the house. They were big guys, one with dark gold skin like Halcyon, the other baked a slightly lesser brown. The heat, I think, was what darkened their skin. They were armed. Throwing knives were sheathed in a double row on the wide harness each wore across his chest.

"This is Tuck," Halcyon said, introducing the gold-skinned demon. "And Keven." He gestured to the demon with an ax—a primitive war ax—belted at his waist. Tuck just had the usual sword. Okay, it was more like a machete. A big, heavy, curved thing.

"They will be accompanying us to the portal."

"As will I," Gryphon said, joining us outside. Under that dim twilight darkness cast by Hell's gray elliptical moon, he looked calm and determined. Like the Gryphon I had known and loved and watched die. *So alive* came the sharp, painful thought.

Halcyon glanced at him, assessing his state. Apparently satisfied with it. "You can take Mona Lisa's horse. She'll ride with me." As opposed to riding by myself. Can't say I wasn't relieved.

The horses they had ready and waiting for us were more the kind I was familiar with. With nice saddles complete with a sturdy horn you could grab, and bridles to guide the beasts with. Much better than riding bareback, hanging onto a flapping mane. Nor did the eyes of these demon horses flare red, even when I heaved myself awkwardly up into a wide saddle that made you feel like you were doing a freaking split. But, hey, I was grateful just to be sitting up, and not sprawled facedown on the ground, eating dirt.

"Scoot forward a little," Halcyon said. I scooted and he swung up easily behind me. The two demon guards, even Gryphon, mounted their horses with a casual skill I would have killed for. A graceful rider, I was not.

When our horse lurched into movement, I gripped the horn like my life depended on it. "I hope you know how to drive this thing," I muttered to Halcyon between clenched teeth.

"Relax, Hell-cat. Caine is much less wild than the demon horses my father had you ride the last time."

"Just promise me that this horse won't do that frog-leaping thing in the air."

"I promise that Caine will not be doing any air galloping. He senses your unease and is being very gentle with you."

Hah! That's what Halcyon thought. The horse was ignoring me, clip-clopping along at a fast and eager pace.

I never did manage to relax. Nor did I release my death grip on the horn. The ride there, every jerky, swaying, wild lurch of it, seemed unbearably long. Frankly, I would have rather walked there on my own two feet. When we finally arrived, I dismounted as gracelessly as I had mounted the horse, half-falling, half-flopping off the beast. Caine flicked his ears forward, patiently continuing to ignore me.

"Thanks," I muttered, and lurched away in a stiff gait that was unfortunately bowlegged. The horse snorted, and I could have sworn I heard evil amusement in that sound. It was certainly there on Halcyon's and Gryphon's faces and the other men's eyes.

I glared at them. "Do not say a word," I warned, rubbing my sorely abused posterior. From the corner of my eye, I caught the faint shimmer of the portal. If you looked straight at it, you couldn't see it. Only when you peered sideways at it were you able to catch a glimmer of the portal. There—only a few steps away. It beckoned to me, bittersweetly.

I turned, swept my eyes over Gryphon as he came to stand beside me. Lost to me once, and how terrible that had been. Now found again. I had thought him a fallen angel, kicked out of heaven, the first time I saw him. Now with those sharp pointy nails, present always, even without any fangs on display, he was indeed that—fallen from life into death. My demon angel. My demon lover.

"I'll be back soon," I promised, my voice growing husky with the ache of farewell.

"I'd rather you didn't. Don't come back to Hell again."

I'd known that our good-bye wasn't going to be easy, but this was ridiculous. "What do you mean, don't come back to Hell again?"

Gryphon took my hand in his, ever so carefully, keeping those sharp nails away from my skin. "Exactly that. Halcyon can visit you. There is no need for you to ever return here."

"What about you?"

"You are still my Queen. In my heart, you will always be that to me. I wish your safety first, above all else. I cannot allow you to endanger your life—a life we risked ourselves to save—by returning here." He wrapped his other arm around me and held me close with that careful new strength of his, looking so serious, so somber, so heartbreakingly lovely in a sad, resolute kind of way.

"Nothing," I said, "not even you, will keep me from returning back here, Gryphon."

"Forgive me," he whispered. Lowering his lips over mine, he kissed me. Kissed me with such love, such tenderness, such feeling. As if it was our final kiss. So lost was I in that exquisite kiss, so caught up was I that, when I realized he was walking, moving toward the portal and carrying me with him, it was too late. Only then did I realize his intent: to enter the portal with me.

"No, Gryphon, no! Don't do this!"

"Sorry, my love. Like you, it is all or nothing for me."

It was madness. It was suicide! Only demons old and strong enough attempted the portal, not new baby demons. Then all thought dissolved as the biting energy of the portal slid over me and I felt as if I were being torn apart, not

in big chunks, but in little bloody ones. Like a million rabid ants were chomping down on me. I screamed with pain,
with horror. And that horror was reflected back at me from
Gryphon's mirror-blue eyes.

"What's wrong?" he asked, gripping my hand with concern.

"Nothing," I gritted. "It always hurts like this. But
you . . . God, what have you done, Gryphon?" Fear for him
tore at me even more viciously than the pain ripping at my
body.

"I'm fine." But as soon as he spoke, it stopped being so.
He felt it suddenly then, the same pain that I did. I saw it
screaming out of his eyes, steaming out of his skin. Vapor
rose from him. *Was* him as he became less solid—became
nothing but heat, such heat. Hot enough to burn my hand. I
clung to him. Refused to let go of his hand. "No! Gryphon!"

His eyes grew unfocused.

"Gryphon!" I said sharply enough to pull his attention
back to me. "Hang on. Do you hear me? Hang on!"

Fear, panic, and pain made my heart thump loud as a
drum. And that pounding beat gave me the answer on how
to give a demon more strength. Blood. My blood.

"Bite me, Gryphon."

He looked at me blindly, uncomprehendingly, as he
tried to hold himself to flesh.

"Drink my blood!" I shouted. But he was too dazed, too
weak to understand me. I turned his unresisting hand—a
hand I was starting to be able to see through, dear God!—
and slashed his sharp nails across my wrist. The pain of
that was negligible compared to the pain the portal was
beating on me, like a mosquito biting you while someone
was hacking you into pieces. But the smell of my iron-rich
blood was electrifying to Gryphon as I raised my bleeding
wrist to him. His bright eyes took on a red glow as his
fangs sliced out. This time it was a sight I welcomed. A

blur of movement and his mouth was on me, sucking the dripping blood, then biting down, sinking those fangs deeper into me, drinking more, drawing my blood into him with hard, sucking pulls.

He was insubstantial enough that I could see through him, *into* him. So that I could literally see the redness of my blood pouring down his stomach, spreading out into his bloodstream like red ink, swirling, diffusing . . . firming his flesh. Cooling it so that he felt less molten. The vapors stopped, no long rose from his body, and I felt relief, such giddy light-headed relief, that I no longer tensed but relaxed against the pain bombarding my body.

With a final jolting sting of agony, we arrived at our destination. I pulled us out of the portal, stumbling, falling to the ground, pulling Gryphon with me, attached as he still was to my wrist, continuing to drink from it, his throat working strongly. It made me wonder if maybe my light-headedness wasn't just from relief. If it was perhaps more from blood loss.

"Gryphon . . . Gryphon, enough. Stop!" I yanked my wrist violently from him, and he growled, lifting his head, flashing fangs and red eyes at me.

"Gryphon, we're here. We're here in New Orleans. You crossed the portal, Gryphon. You did it. You're back in the living realm."

His body crouched and, in that moment, he was the exact image of what people pictured demons to be—this preternaturally strong, vicious, mindless beast, fanged and fierce, eyes burning Hellfire red. I don't know if he would have returned to his thinking self. I don't know if I could have fought him off, or if he would have killed me.

Halcyon walked out of the portal's shimmering white mist. "Do not!" he growled, his will so forceful, so strong, that I felt it slam Gryphon back away from me like a powerful fist. Gryphon flew back against the alley wall so violently that bricks cracked and rained down in dusty pieces onto the ground. I'm not sure if it was the blow itself that knocked some sense into him, or if Halcyon's presence imposed some sort of calm over him. When Gryphon regained his feet, his eyes were no longer hazed red, though the fangs still remained.

Gryphon stared, looked at me and saw me. Saw my ravaged wrist, the blood dripping from it. "I hurt you," he said, his voice thick and hoarse.

"No, I did this." The first slice at least. "I cut myself and made you drink my blood when you began to dissipate. Remember?"

He shuddered. "Yes, I remember."

"I didn't know how else to give you strength."

"It worked. Too well. I would have killed you had Halcyon not intervened."

"But I did," Halcyon said. "Thanks to her blood and quick thinking, you survived the portal. Something no demon so young in his afterlife has ever done."

Halcyon walked to me and brought my bleeding wrist up to his mouth. He lapped his tongue over my wounds and I felt a tiny eddy of pleasure swirl through me as he licked the blood clean and stopped the bleeding—only a tiny fraction of the orgasmic bliss he was capable of imparting. Releasing my wrist, he turned back to Gryphon. "What you did was insanely reckless. We almost lost you."

Halcyon's words chased the last lingering pleasure from me and hot, scalding anger rose in its place. I might not be demon fast, but my Monère quickness had me in front of Gryphon in the blink of an eye. I grabbed him by his shirt-front and shook him. "You dumbass! You almost died again. For good this time! Why did you do something so stupid?"

"Because Hell is a dangerous place, not meant for the living. Because I selfishly did not want to wait one hundred years before I knew whether or not I could cross the damn portals. Because I would rather be truly dead and gone to you than exist that long without you. But—" A beautiful smile lit Gryphon's face. "—I did it. I can. I can cross the portal. With your blood and Halcyon's controlling presence, I can cross the portal." He gazed wonderingly about him, took in the familiar alley, the distant scents and sounds of humanity drifting to his heightened senses. Wetness sheened his eyes.

"Yes, with our help you can cross the portal." Halcyon's voice was grave and calm. "But there is good reason why weak demons are extinguished in the portal and not allowed to cross into the living realm. You would have gone on a slaughtering rampage had I not been here, and Mona Lisa would have been the first life you consumed in your mindless bloodlust."

The joy drained out of Gryphon. "You are correct. I do not have the control yet that I need." His face changed, hardened with resolve and hope. "But I can work on that, now that I know it is possible for me to return."

"Oh, Gryphon." I released his wrinkled shirtfront and wrapped my arms tightly around that dear familiar body. "You are such a horse's ass. Promise me that you will wait until you are stronger and have better control before you try this again, okay? It would kill me . . . kill my heart and extinguish all my joy if you died again. If you were taken forever from me."

I felt the light skim of his lips and the harder brush of his fangs against my hair. "I will be more careful with my existence, now that I have this hope," he promised as he stepped back from me, face strained. "I'm sorry. Your blood, the beat of your heart . . . it calls too strongly to me."

"We must return now," Halcyon said, stepping between us.

Dread welled up in me at his words. Another roundtrip torture session in the portal coming right up. Lovely.

I pasted a fake smile on my lips. "All right, I'm ready."

Realization filled Gryphon's eyes. Understanding that I would have to accompany him back, and return yet again. "You are right. I am a dumbass. All that pain you felt—"

"You do not have to return with us," Halcyon said.

"Don't be silly. Who else is going to give him blood? You?"

"Blood will not be necessary. Do you remember how I shielded you once from the pain?"

"Yeah. Real clearly."

"I shared my energy with you. I can do the same with Gryphon. You do not have to return with us."

I shook my head in stubborn determination. "I won't risk Gryphon's existence on theory. I'm coming with you."

"It is not theory," Halcyon said. "It is fact."

"What do you mean, fact?" Gryphon asked.

"I know that it can be done because it has been done in the past—a powerful demon sharing his energy with a less powerful demon to allow both of them to safely cross between the realms. But it is a knowledge that has faded away. Knowledge that I ask you to keep secret."

"You knew that I could return to the living realm, that I could return to Mona Lisa with your aid, and you kept that from me?" Gryphon growled.

"Yes."

"Why?" Gryphon demanded.

"Because poorly controlled demons usually go on killing rampages. Once in the living realm, their bloodlust overwhelms them. Ending a weak demon's existence if he tries to cross the portal is Hell's final safety measure, a fail-safe that should not be tampered with lightly." He let that sink in for a moment before clasping Gryphon's shoulder.

"Come," he said. "You have done extraordinarily well, but it would be prudent not to test your control any longer."

Gryphon regretfully agreed.

I watched them walk toward the white mist of the portal. "Halcyon."

He looked back at me.

"Are you sure Gryphon will be safe?"

"On my life," he said with a wicked, roguish smile.

"Halcyon!"

"On my afterlife," he amended. "I promise you, Hell-cat. I'll get him back safely home."

One last lingering glance shared between us as they stepped into the portal. Then they were gone, and I was left alone, back in the living realm.

EIGHTEEN

BEING ALIVE WAS so different from being dead. Loud and noisy. The soughing in and out of breath. The constant thumping of the heart. The rhythmic swish of blood rushing through the arteries, seeping in the veins. The ingesting of food. The chewing of it, swallowing it down. The digesting of it, then pissing and pooping it back out, burping and farting to help it along the way.

Messy life. How sweet it was—even standing tired and fatigued and light-headed from blood loss in the empty alleyway the portal of Hell had spit me into.

It was night, or more accurately, early morn with the breaking of dawn's first light trembling on the horizon. No sounds rose around me. No heartbeats. None of the immediate noises of life but from my own solitary body. We were in the business district of New Orleans. Closed storefronts, tall office buildings, and ghostly warehouses were all that existed now—empty, waiting walls that would fill again with human noise and bodies when daylight painted the world sunshiny bright once more.

I wondered how Gryphon would have fared had we arrived a few hours later, when the streets were swarming with people, and the thick, heady rush of other blood, not just mine, was near. Wondered and shuddered at the near disaster that could have so easily been. I walked the empty streets, thinking those thoughts and others as I headed toward the French Quarter. Breathing deeply, I savored the thick humid air of Louisiana, warm even now in the winter month of February.

I'm back, I thought. *I'm alive.* And I couldn't wait to get home.

A cab turned the corner and headed down the street toward me. Only then did I give thought to how I looked, wearing attire that was more suited to attending an opera than walking the streets alone in the twilight hours of a breaking dawn. There was also the matter of how I would pay for the cab ride back home with no money, no purse, or even any visible pockets to hold the money in should I have had some. I wondered why the cabbie even bothered to stop when I waved him down. Maybe the novelty of such a sight, although this was New Orleans, the home of Mardi Gras. Not much surprised the inhabitants here, I supposed.

The driver rolled down the window. I leaned in and captured his eyes . . . or tried to. Pain hit me, sharp and jabbing, as I tried to call up power.

"You okay, lady?" the driver asked. He was a middle-aged man in his fifties, with coffee-colored skin and abundant white sprinkled in his dark hair.

"No, I . . ." Hastily, I tried to come up with a plausible explanation. "My date dumped me. Can you drive me home? I don't have any money on me, but I promise to pay you when we get there." I told him the address.

He looked at me like I was crazy. Not because of the

way I was dressed but because I suggested he even do such a thing: drive a woman with no money to a place almost an hour away based on only a promise of payment.

Tears of tiredness, of helplessness, misted my eyes during his long and obvious hesitation. I wondered what I would do if he refused? I didn't even have any money to make a phone call.

"Get in," the driver said gruffly.

"Thank you!" I gratefully climbed into the backseat and closed my eyes in relief and fatigue.

I must have slept.

The driver's voice saying, "We're here, lady," brought me back into waking awareness, and my eyes opened to the beautiful sweeping sight of Belle Vista, the grand plantation house, a mansion really, that was my home now. Maybe it was the near loss of true life that made me see things anew—the grace, the age, the lasting endurance of the house and the surrounding land.

The soaring white columns and granite steps welcomed me now instead of intimidating me. And the people spilling out of the enormous front door twanged another ache in my heart, a good one, blurring my vision with tears. They called my name, shouted it, and I was suddenly in as much rush to reach them as they were to reach me.

I blindly found the door handle, pushed it open. Before I could take even a step, I was swept up in arms almost as big in proportion as the house. Arms that I would know anywhere—Amber, my giant Amber. Other hands touched me and I blindly reached out, touching them in return, laughing, crying, a sobbing snotty mess. I calmed enough to say, "Pay the driver. Tip him well, please. He brought me here, even though I didn't have any money on me."

Aquila's smiling face swam into my vision. "I'll take

care of it," he said, giving my shoulder a warm, welcoming squeeze.

I was swept up into Amber's arms and carried inside, back to my home, back to my family.

"Are you all right?" Amber asked gruffly as he carried me into the front parlor. I nodded, my throat squeezed tight with joy, with thankfulness. *I almost lost you,* I thought. *I almost lost all of you.*

Instead of putting me down, Amber sank onto the sofa and settled me on his lap, holding me as if he would never let me go again. A hand wrapped itself around one of mine, and my brother's face popped into view. "Thaddeus," I sniffed, wiping the tears from my eyes.

"Don't cry, Lisa."

He was the only one to call me that. Just Lisa, instead of Mona Lisa.

"Got a tissue? Maybe the whole box," I amended, sucking back up some snot that had been about to drip out of my nose. Yup, life was real messy. But being back, being alive, was so damn wonderful!

Jamie's red hair and freckles danced into sight as he thrust a tissue into my hand. I thanked him, brought the tissue to my nose, and honked loudly. We all laughed. His sister, Tersa, pushed a tissue box into my lap. "Thanks," I muttered, hugging her, hugging them both—the Mixed Blood brother and sister of my heart.

Their mother pushed her way forward, tall and sturdy Rosemary, whose heart was as big and as broad as her physical self. "Now, now, lass," she said, patting my hand. "Are you all right? You're not hurt anywhere, are you?"

"No, no. I'm good."

Another hand touched me. Many hands did, but this one I knew, could tell apart from all the others because of the uniquely different electrical energy that danced across my skin in a faint buzz of sensation. I turned and saw Dontaine, met those brilliant jewel green eyes of his, and was staggered anew by my master at arms, so devastatingly handsome. Different from the blunt and craggy roughness of my Amber the way a perfectly cut emerald differed from raw amber.

Dontaine gripped my hand, the soggy tissue captured between us.

"My wet tissue," I protested, embarrassed at the thought of my messy snot smearing those beautiful fingers. His face closed down and I knew that he thought I was rejecting him yet again.

I dropped the wet tissue and grabbed his hand before he could withdraw. The impulsive gesture lit up his face again, in a smile, dazzling bright, that showed pearl-white teeth as perfect as the rest of him.

Chami, my chameleon guard, one of my most dangerous men, though you couldn't tell it from his innocent youthful appearance, finally asked what everyone wanted to know. "Mona Lisa, what happened to you?"

I told them.

"NetherHell," Tomas, my other guard, said with a touch of horror and awe. "Were you dead then?"

"I thought I was. My heart wasn't beating, and I wasn't breathing. But Gordane said that I was still alive." I told them about the gargoyle and the vast city-state he ruled.

"Did you see Gryphon?" Dontaine asked. He slept now in Gryphon's room, had taken his place as my lover. No surprise that he would ask about Gryphon.

"Yes. He and Halcyon rescued me, brought me back."

"How is Gryphon doing?" asked Amber. Of everyone here, Amber had known Gryphon the longest, been the closest to him.

"He's doing well," I said softly. And he was, for a new demon. I didn't tell them about Gryphon attacking me when we returned to Hell. Or of his blood craze when we came out of the portal. Come to think of it, I'd left out quite a bit.

"How sad to think of Miles, Rupert, Gilford, and Demetrius in NetherHell," Aquila murmured. His comment made me wonder how close he'd been to the other four men. "And how fortunate, but surprising, that they helped you."

Indeed it was, especially since I hadn't told them the part about Mona Louisa being able to emerge and take over my body. "They were Monère warriors, newly dead. It was probably instinctive, coming to a Queen's aid," I said weakly. I know, pretty lame, but it was the best I could come up with at the moment.

"Gargoyles," Thaddeus said excitedly, thankfully changing the subject. "A rogue and a king." He had been spellbound when I had described the gargoyles and what they could do with their touch. "You meet the most interesting people, Lisa."

"Yeah, but I hope I never see them again. I like it just fine here. Being in NetherHell was pretty bloody awful." A yawn tried to overtake me. I valiantly fought it back. "How long was I gone?"

"Two days," Thaddeus said, more subdued.

"That long? God, I'm exhausted."

"We can see. Enough," said Rosemary, clapping her hands. "Everybody to bed now. Our lady needs her rest, as do the rest of you. They hardly slept while you were gone," she said to me.

"I think I could sleep for twenty-four hours." I lost the battle and a huge yawn split open my jaws. Amber stood, lifting me up.

I closed my eyes, just to rest them for a moment, as Amber carried me up the stairs. Before we reached the second floor, I was sound asleep.

NINETEEN

THE SUN WAS shining when I woke. Not that I could see it—the room was entirely dark, curtains drawn. But I could feel it. Feel the quiet presence of the moon, still there, something most people weren't aware of, that the moon was still there during part of the day, but with only a soft spark of its usual vibrant nighttime presence.

I opened my senses and heard the quiet, even breathing of the household at sleep, the reassuring thuds of their slow heartbeats. The space in bed beside me was empty, but I smelled Amber's scent in the sheets, lingering on the indented pillow next to mine. He'd been here. Slept beside me for a little while. I got up, feeling both rested and tired, and wondered how long I had slept. Judging from the daylight hour, probably only a few hours. But I was wide awake now, bright-eyed and bushy-tailed in a lazy, lethargic sort of a way.

I turned and my eyes fell on a folded note propped on the bedside table with my name addressed on the outside in a bold masculine scrawl. I opened it and read it.

My darling love, it began, surprising me. Had I not smelled his scent on the parchment, I would never have guessed those flowery words to be from my quiet, stoic giant. A man who usually kept his feelings hidden, as did most warriors who had served under my mother—a hard mistress even by Monère standards.

My darling love,

I stayed as long as I could, lying beside you, content just to be in your sleeping presence, thanking the Goddess over and over again in my heart for returning you safely back to us—even as I wondered if she was the one who took you from us. But likely not. It was a black light that took you, not her silver rays. I know you did not tell us all, but that is not important. What I yearn to know most, to be assured of, is that you will not be taken from us like that again.

Forgive me for leaving you before you awoke. You slept so deeply, so peacefully, I was loathe to disturb your rest, so I will leave you with these written words of parting instead of a good-bye kiss. You are my life. My most dearest love. The heart of our people. You are the bravest, fiercest person I know, and the kindest and most generous also, tempering ruthlessness and strength with wise benevolence. You are the Queen that all Monère men dream of serving—one with honor, compassion, dignity, and power. And love, so much love there is in you, unstinting, unselfish, sometimes too much so. I'm a lucky bastard. We all are.

Stay safe for us. Stay well. And come to Mississippi when you can, to me. To your people here. One day a week is too brief a time to spend with you.

Know that my heart is with you always. With love and devotion forever . . .

> *Your humble servant,*
> *Amber*

I folded the note carefully and put it away in the drawer. Tender words he had penned with surprising eloquence. They filled me with warmth and made me sorry I had missed his departure.

Dressing in silence, I made my way out of the sleeping silence of the house to where the sun was bright and glaring outside, dominating the sky. I was more aware of my surroundings, acutely so, maybe from my near brush with death. Every blade of grass I saw, every flower I smelled, appreciative of the scent and sight.

The sultry rays of the sun beat down on me with gentle warmth as I made my way across the lawn to where a lone heartbeat pounded beneath a shading copse of trees—Dontaine, keeping watch while the others slept. I walked to him, and thought him as blindingly bright and beautiful as the overhead sun.

"What are you doing here?" I asked, sitting down beside him.

"Waiting for you."

"You knew I'd wake up so early?"

"I knew that you had to wake up soon. You've been sleeping for almost thirty-two hours."

"That long? You're kidding. No wonder Amber had to leave. I thought it was only a couple of hours. I can't believe I slept more than an entire day away."

"You needed the rest."

"Ugh, no wonder I feel so sluggish. I overslept. How long have you been up?"

"I awoke two hours ago, and relieved the sentry on duty."

"What time is it now?" I asked, glancing up at the sun.

"Almost four in the afternoon."

"What day?"

"Thursday."

"My brother should be out of school now. Probably at the library."

"You want to go see him?"

I nodded. "Yeah, I do."

We took the green Suburban. Dontaine sat in the passenger seat while I drove. "Do you know how to drive?" I asked. Among my guards, only Aquila knew how to drive.

"Yes, many here in this territory do."

"You all have driver licenses?" That was a pleasant surprise.

Dontaine nodded. "It is useful in managing such a large territory."

"So, this *is* a large territory."

"Yes, one of the larger and more prosperous ones. Did you not know?"

"I thought it was, but was never sure," I said, flushing over my ignorance.

"I did not mean to embarrass you. I was simply surprised you did not know."

"Lots of things I still don't know," I said morosely, then shook off the mood. "But I have time now to learn. How's my brother doing?"

"He's doing well, practicing his fighting skills daily with Nolan. Chami hasn't mentioned any further encounters at school. He's been keeping a discreet eye on your brother and should be with Thaddeus now at the library."

"But it's daylight."

Dontaine quirked a brow. "And I am sitting here beside you. We do not melt under sunlight."

"No, but it's painful for you, being exposed to the sun."

He shrugged. "Nothing unbearable. The car windows are tinted, and we keep out of the direct rays as much as possible."

"We?"

"I watch Thaddeus occasionally, to give Chami a break."

I hadn't known, but I wasn't surprised that Chami was keeping a watchful eye on my brother. What surprised me was that Dontaine was as well.

"It has become my habit to wake earlier than the others," Dontaine said. Because of me. Because I sometimes woke up hours before sunset, the time when the others usually rose to begin their day.

"There is no need for you to personally change your sleeping habits, Dontaine. I thought you had sentries posted in shifts, watching the house." Keeping an eye on me, should I rise early and wander outside like I did today, I thought guiltily.

"I did so selfishly, in hopes of spending time with you alone." A pause that stretched out. "Why does that make you so uncomfortable?" he asked.

"I guess because it always surprises me that you would want that. To be with me."

"Why should that surprise you?" asked the man who looked like a sun god.

"Oh, come on, Dontaine. Just look at me, and then look at yourself."

"I am looking, and I still do not see."

"Dontaine, you're one of the most gorgeous men I've ever seen. Me, I'm just average, at best."

"Gryphon was more beautiful than I," he said softly.

"Yes, but he was an outcast, a rogue when I first met him. Amber, too, in his own way, was an outsider. Chami, Tomas, Aquila—all the men I claimed, they all existed on the outer fringes of Monère society. But not you, Dontaine. You were the golden boy, your Queen's favorite."

"And because I am not one of your outcasts, one of the men you rescued, you are not comfortable with me?"

"Not so much uncomfortable as surprised. It's an unlikely pairing, you and me. Like hitching a beautiful race horse with a clumsy nag."

"If you are going to cut me off at the knees, at least be truthful about why you are doing so!" he said abruptly. The sudden spill of hot emotions from Dontaine surprised me enough to pull the car over onto the side of the road.

"What are you talking about, Dontaine?"

"You reject me because you do not trust me! You believe that once a traitor, always a traitor!"

I shook my head, at a total loss. "I don't have any idea of what you're talking about."

"I almost betrayed you once!" he burst out. "I fully intended to. You know that—you had to know that. You had to have suspected."

"Suspected what?"

"That Mona Louisa left me behind in the hopes that you would take me to your bed, so that I could betray you to her." Anger, guilty torment etched harsh lines across his face, and still he remained exquisitely handsome, enough to take my breath away.

"What changed your mind?"

"What?"

"You said you intended to betray me, Dontaine. What changed your mind?"

"You did," he whispered. "You were supposed to fall under my spell. But I was the one bewitched instead. That night when you cared for me after my challenge battle with Amber, I thought you did so with the intention of bedding me to acquire my gift of Half Change." He had the rare ability to arrest his change in a state that was halfway between man and wolf. Not the mutant half-half form down in NetherHell, but a true blending of both states, so that he became the werewolf of human folklore.

I was aghast that he had thought sex my only intent in helping him. "God, Dontaine. You thought I wanted to have sex with you when you were so gravely injured, choking in your own spit and blood?"

"I was willing."

"I know."

"But you didn't want me. You cared for me, washed me, cleaned me with your own hands, saw to my comfort."

"There was no one else. I was the closest thing we had to a healer at that time."

"And when I was healed enough, you elevated my status to your master at arms, even though I had lost the challenge. Even though you had not taken me to your bed, or benefited from me in any way."

"I benefited from your experience, your knowledge, your established relationship with the people here. I trusted you, and you honored that trust."

"But for one moment, just before I rescued you, you thought that I had betrayed you."

I didn't try to deny it. He'd seen that vivid belief in my eyes. "But you didn't."

"No," he said with soft bitterness. "I betrayed my former Queen instead, and damned myself in your eyes as a traitor."

"No, Dontaine, you didn't." I grabbed his hand, and was surprised to feel only a gentle buzz from the contact instead of the usual strong zap of electrical power. I hadn't known Dontaine was able to control himself that well when his emotions were riding so high.

"Then why?" he asked, clearly distraught. "Why do you continue to reject me?"

"Because of what I told you before. I never understood

why you chose me over Mona Louisa. She's beautiful, which I am not, and a Full Blood Monère Queen, which I'm also not. And she favored you."

"Whereas you obviously do not."

"Dontaine . . ."

"Do you truly trust me?" he asked.

"Of course I do. You are my master of arms. You've rescued me, more than once, proven yourself true many times."

"Then that nonsense you spouted before, about my being the golden boy and you being plain . . . that really is why you push me away?"

I nodded and said softly, "I'm sorry, Dontaine."

"You make no sense, you know. I am no longer the most favored by my Queen. But perhaps that is to my advantage. At least I am still by your side."

A cruelly accurate jab. Gryphon was gone, Amber sent away to rule another territory.

"No, don't draw back," Dontaine murmured, his hand tightening around mine. "Forgive me for letting my hurt and frustration spill out like that. Blessed Night. You are so different from other Queens." He looked at me like a puzzle he could figure out if only he could see the pieces clearly enough. Drawing my hand with a thoughtful gesture to his face, he asked, "Would you care for me more if I were ugly? Scarred?"

I jerked my hand away, horrified. "Don't you dare do anything so stupid! I forbid you! No scars, no trying to turn yourself ugly for me." Then some of the panic eased as common sense asserted itself. "I forgot. Monères don't scar. We heal too quickly."

"We can scar. With the right conditions, we can be left with permanent scars."

"Dontaine," I said clearly, carefully. "I *never* want you to do that for me. Your scars would flay me, and my guilt over it would drive me away from you more surely than your handsome face does now. I know my reasoning is not sound, that I probably don't make sense to you, but hurting yourself, leaving visible wounds on your face . . . it wouldn't help. It would only make matters worse, much worse. Promise me that you will never do anything like that."

He bowed his head. "As you command."

"Say it!"

His eyes lifted, met mine. "I will not deliberately try to scar myself."

"Too conditional. Say that you will *not* scar yourself."

"I cannot promise you that. It may one day be another's intent to inflict that on me, beyond my control."

"Then promise that you will do your best never to permanently scar yourself or allow another to do so to you."

"I give you my oath that I will do my best never to permanently scar myself or allow another to inflict that upon me."

Only when he had made that promise did my heart ease.

"Do my looks please you then?" he asked.

When you cared for someone, you should make them happy, confident with themselves, not discontent, not wanting to turn themselves ugly, I thought sadly. I looked at this breathtakingly handsome warrior before me, and did not know what to do with him. "Yes, Dontaine, your handsome face, your beautiful body pleases me very much. I would be very unhappy if you allowed yourself to become damaged on purpose."

My words made him happy. Made him smile. "I will find another way to make us seem more an equal match in your eyes," he said with determination. *An impossible task,* I wanted to say. But I didn't. Silence here was much wiser.

We parked in front of the public library, across the

street from my brother's car. His heartbeat, slower than the other fast beats around him, told me that he was inside. Chami, on the other hand, was not. The sudden flare of his Monère presence next to four human heartbeats had Dontaine and me rushing around the back of the building to find Chami faced off with four high school boys. Yes, boys, even though they were as tall or taller than Chami, and with far beefier builds. Seniors. Big bruisers wearing varsity letter jackets. Football jocks, if I wasn't mistaken. The same ones, I was willing to bet, that had beaten up my brother a week ago.

The realization spiked my anger and also my confusion. "I thought you were going to let Thaddeus defend himself," I said to Chami. My words turned all their faces to me, and I caught sight of a black eye on one boy, and a cut swollen lip on another guy.

"I did," Chami said, "and your brother kicked two of their asses yesterday quite nicely, as you can see. Unfortunately, they did not seem to have learned their lesson. They're back with two more of their buddies. Four against one, boys? Very flattering, but grossly uneven odds against a kid one year younger and forty pounds lighter than any of you."

"So what? The three of you going to take us on?" sneered the tallest brute, the guy with the black eye. He seemed to be the ringleader. To my amusement, he eyed Dontaine warily, mistaking him as the biggest threat, not the slender assassin standing right in front of him.

"No," I said. "That would be unfair. We have to even the odds up better."

The big black-eyed boy hooted. "No way I'm going to have one of my boys leave. You're one man short—two, considering you're just a girl—that's your problem, not ours."

It was the slow heartbeat behind me that let me know

that my brother had joined us, even before he spoke. "I'm here, Jack. I make four," Thaddeus said, coming to stand beside me.

"You mistook my meaning about evening up the odds," I said with a mildness I did not feel inside. "I meant reducing *our* numbers, not adding to them. If the four of us engaged the four of you, it would be a slaughter." Which actually sounded pretty good to me. But no, I pushed aside the temptation. "The three of us will just watch. Chami, these four ignorant bullies are all yours."

Jack and his friends laughed. "Him against us? You consider that even odds?"

"Not really. You'd need two more of your big buddies to really call it fair but I think this is all I'm going to grant you."

With an eager, ugly look on his face, Jack turned and swung at Chami. His fist met only air as Chami took a step back. Moving slowly for him, at human speed, Chami pushed Jack over a tripping foot to land him hard on the ground. Three more twists and shoves, and the rest of Jack's gang were sprawled alongside their leader. Less than five seconds.

Grabbing Jack, lifting him easily with one hand, Chami slammed him back against the side of the building and held him there. "Looks can be deceiving," Chami murmured. "Lesson number one: Training, experience, and a cool head will always prevail over untrained idiots. Lesson number two: I will give you only one warning." A knife appeared in Chami's hand as if by magic, and he threw it behind him without even looking. It struck the ground an inch in front of the boy who had been rushing to Jack's rescue. The boy yelped.

"If you come after Thaddeus again, the next time I will not restrain myself. The next time I will kill you."

Whatever Jack saw in Chami's eyes, it made his voice

rise an octave higher. "We're cool, man! We're cool. Won't bother him again, my word."

Chami lowered Jack back down. As soon as Jack's feet touched the ground, he jerked away from Chami to huddle back against his three buddies, their wide eyes all fastened on the stiletto Chami had pulled out of nowhere and began flipping with chilling, impressive ease.

They eased cautiously around us. Once clear, they ran for the street.

"I think your knives did more to frighten them than your words, Chami," I said.

"Still, I think Jack believed you—the part about killing them," Thaddeus said, grinning. "The way you said it was totally believable, man. I think they'll leave me alone now."

They better, because Chami's threat wasn't the bluff my brother seemed to think it was.

Chami's eyes met mine, and the question in those angry depths—if he could kill them if they overstepped themselves again—I could not answer in front of my brother.

"Well done, Chami," I said for now.

He gave me one of those graceful head dips, understanding that we would talk later. I turned to my brother. "You got any more studying to do?"

"Nothing I can't do later. How are you, Lisa? Everything all right?"

"Everything's fine. I finally woke up and wanted to see how you were doing, which seems to be fine. Let's go grab some coffee, and you can tell me how you kicked their bully asses yesterday."

"After practicing with Jamie under Nolan's instruction, it was easy taking them down," Thaddeus said as we walked out of the alley.

We laughed and chatted for an hour as the sun slowly set, sitting at a local diner where the men drank coffee and I indulged my sweet tooth with a slice of lemon meringue pie. None of the others ate anything, probably in fear of Rosemary's wrath if they ruined their appetite for the main eventide meal, which we would be eating soon.

The laughter and celebration ended in more practical reality as we drove back home. Chami rode with me per my request so we could "catch up on things." Dontaine caught a ride with Thaddeus.

"My apologies, milady" were Chami's first words to me inside the car. "I should not have threatened to kill the human boy without asking you first if it was permitted."

That killing was Chami's first instinctive response was not a surprise. He'd been an assassin, what other Queens had used him for. It was certainly the perfect career choice for him. Chami's full name was Chameleo, in honor of the chameleon gift that allowed him to literally disappear from sight and even more dangerously, from Monère senses, until he reappeared again—the reason for our sudden sensing of him when we had first arrived. To the four boys outside, it would have seemed as if Chami had appeared out of nowhere or snuck up on them undetected. Both were true. What *was* surprising was that it had also been *my* instinctive response upon seeing them and realizing who they were. Frightening how easy the thought of killing was becoming to me.

"No apology needed, Chami. You've displayed remarkable constraint." He had allowed Thaddeus to take on the boys yesterday, much more constraint than I might have shown. I doubted I would have allowed Thaddeus to take on two opponents. Maybe one—and that was a very big maybe.

"So am I allowed?" he asked.

"To do what?"

"To kill them if they bother Thaddeus again."

"A difficult dilemma," I said. "A threat is only effective if you're willing to deliver on the punishment. But . . . if they bother Thaddeus again, let me know and I'll take care of them. Not fighting them," I said when Chami started to protest. "I'll compel them." Force my will upon theirs, something I hated to do, and perhaps even their parents. If I had to, I'd compel them to move away from here. Better than killing them. "But I think we made our point. And Thaddeus said he's no longer helping Jack's girlfriend in math, the reason for the friction in the first place." She'd been using him, Thaddeus had said, enjoying the drama and jealousy she caused and snubbing him at school. A painful first lesson in girls, but at least he hadn't sounded heartbroken. Far from it. He seemed more confident now, at ease with himself. Older somehow.

"Is Thaddeus taller?" I asked, frowning.

"He grew an inch, with more to quickly follow," Chami said, satisfaction evident in his voice. "He's finally entered into his growth spurt. Also starting to put on some weight and muscle from his daily practice with Nolan and Jamie."

"What about Tersa? Is she practicing with them?" She'd shown an interest, and had the most reason to want to learn. She'd been raped, brutally taken against her will by a Monère warrior. I didn't know her before the attack. All I knew was the quiet girl she was now, wary around men, barely speaking to anyone. Only around Jamie, Thaddeus, and Wiley, the wild Mixed Blood stray she had adopted, was she at ease.

"Tersa practices with them most days, not all."

"Good." I wanted her to learn. If Thaddeus's triumph the other day was any indication, Nolan was an effective teacher—as I had cause to learn myself after we finished our main meal of the day.

I'd like to say my people pampered me, but that wasn't exactly the Monère way. They hovered, took care of me, each in their own way. Rosemary made sure I ate everything on the plate. After dinner—or more like brunch, in our case—Nolan stayed behind while everyone dispersed to their separate duties. I, apparently, was Nolan's.

"We're beginning sword practice today," he announced to me.

"We are?"

"Yup."

I smiled at his response. Nolan, his wife, and two sons, had spent a couple of decades living among the humans and, at times, he was more casual in his way of speaking than the other warriors. Not too long ago, he'd also nearly been the grandfather of my child. Would have been had I not miscarried. He had a tie to me that others did not have. It was a connection that made him comfortable enough to boss me gently around, and have me obey him.

So first day rested, miraculously back from the Cursed Realm of the damned dead, I found myself wielding a wooden sword, learning basic sword drills. The scowl on my face wasn't from the ridiculously easy drills. It was from the perceived injury to my dignity.

"Why can't I use a real sword to practice?" I asked after finishing up the first set.

"Because you are a beginner. Until you demonstrate to me that you are more than that, what you hold in your hand will be your practice weapon."

"It's not as if I haven't used a real sword before," I grumbled. "It's demeaning using the same thing a snotty twelve-year-old kid here would use." Come to think of it, I guess I was lucky he wasn't having me train with the beginner's group, which ranged from ten- to seventeen-year-old boys.

"Just because you were fortunate enough to kill your opponents with a sword during battle does not advance you beyond novice status," Nolan said.

"It wasn't luck," I muttered. "What more do I need to

learn than how to swing a sword hard enough to take off
my enemy's head?" Yeah, yeah, I knew better. But I
couldn't seem to help myself. I was embarrassed and cha-
grined by the wimpy pretend weapon I held.

"Okay, show me," Nolan said. He picked up a wooden
practice sword and faced me. No embarrassment on his
face. But then, not only was he a big guy, almost as physically big as Amber, he was a master swordsman. He had
nothing to prove while I, on the other hand, did. Still, this
was far better than doing those embarrassingly easy drills.

I swung full out at Nolan, knowing he could more than
adequately defend himself.

He just stood there and parried the blow with insulting
ease. In a quick countering maneuver he knocked the
wooden sword from my hand and laid his weapon against
my neck.

"All right, you proved your point," I said, swallowing at
the fresh reminder of how lucky I'd been so far. Lucky that
I still had my head attached to my body. "But do I have to
start from the very beginning?" Even to myself it sounded
whiney—I couldn't help myself. It was embarrassing waving around what amounted to a glorified twig, especially
with my men watching from the house, keeping an eye on
me. "If I have to practice with this stupid stick, at least can
we do more challenging drills?"

Nolan was a good teacher. Flexible. "More challenging
drills coming right up, milady." He executed a fluid bow
that was not bad considering he'd been out of practice for
twenty years. "But I want you aware that my healer wife,
as well as your men, will have my head if I get a single
scratch on you."

"No scratch, I promise. Just don't treat me like a baby."

He didn't. For the next fifteen minutes, he paired up as
my partner, and wooden sword went up against wooden
sword, which was much better than thrusting and parrying

against empty air. I was grinning like an idiot until Nolan said, "Good. Now let's pick up the speed."

"What do you mean, pick up the speed?"

"You're only moving as fast as a human. Let me see more speed and force behind your strikes. Don't hold back."

"I wasn't."

His turn to say, "What do you mean?"

"I wasn't holding back."

Frowning, he raised his wooden sword and said, "Again." We repeated the thrust-parry, thrust-parry maneuvers, and I consciously pushed myself in speed, in strength.

"Harder," he said. "Faster."

"I am," I grunted. When Nolan stepped up the pace, I couldn't match him. Nor could I hang onto my weapon when he increased the force behind his strikes. My wooden blade went flying out of my hand to land on the grass.

A chill went through me as I stood there weaponless, breathing heavily. Nolan's breathing wasn't even labored.

"I'm slow," I said, as if repeating that fact out loud could sink the revelation into my brain. "I move as slow as a human, and am as weak as one." I remembered the pain that had slashed me when I had tried to call up power to compel the taxi driver, and had been unable to. I'd thought it was because of my exhaustion from crossing two different realms, journeying back from death to life. But I wondered now if something in me had been damaged. If my Monère strength, quickness, and power had been torn out of me along with Mona Louisa. That inner wound was still there inside me. I still felt it.

"Forgive me, milady. I should have allowed you more time to rest and recover before beginning your training."

As the stunning realization that I had lost my Monère strength settled in on me slowly, I couldn't bring myself to mouth platitudes. Couldn't find anything worthwhile to say to Nolan. I just nodded and left him, walking back to the house.

When I saw Amber waiting for me by the front door, I dashed up the stairs and was caught up in those big arms that always felt like safety, warmth, love—Amber, my rock.

Those giant arms tightened as they lifted me. "Careful, Amber. Gently," I gasped, even though he always was—gentle and careful with me, ever conscious of his strength. After my words, he started to loosen his embrace and draw back. It was I who tightened my arms around his neck and plastered myself against him, burrowing into his bigness. His arms came tentatively back around, holding me loosely as I murmured, "Oh, Amber." Just that, his name and all that he meant to me.

I didn't question his return, how and why he was there when I suddenly needed him. Nor did he question my almost desperate welcome. He was a man more of action than words, and his next actions were perfect. With me clinging to him like a burr, he went inside and climbed the stairs. Only when we were in his bedroom did he speak. "I missed you. I needed you."

"I missed you, needed you, too." He didn't know, I thought, gazing at his clear, untroubled eyes. He didn't know the awful truth that I had just discovered about my strength. I didn't want to think about it or dwell on it, all the worries. I just wanted to feel, enjoy what I had now, for the moment. Kisses followed, far better than words. A meeting of mouths and hearts. Sweet and gentle on his part. Hungry and ravenous, a touch desperate on mine. Still he was careful, gentle, letting me set the pace. Allowing me to unbuckle his belt, push down his pants as he pulled off his shirt. Letting me shrug out of my own clothes with careless haste and abandon. No thoughts, no modesty, no care, just this—his hands running lightly over my breasts, me pushing him back down on the bed, climb-ing on top of him, holding the stiff, throbbing jut of him, slipping a quickly snatched condom over him, then sinking down on that thick, swollen head. Oh! Just so.

"Amber," I murmured, closing my eyes, sinking into bliss as my body swallowed him slowly into me. When I had sank down as much as I could, I gave a little wriggle, a sharp swivel, and deeper still he went. A big man all over was my Amber. Mine. Yes, mine. At least for now. He groaned, I moaned, and together we began to move, him gently, me much less so. I wanted him. Wanted him to wash away all my doubts, fears, concerns. I just wanted him like this—on his back, his stiff rod buried inside me, his calloused warrior hands running tenderly over me, stroking my breasts, pinching my nipples, combing his fingers lightly over the soft mound between my legs, there where we came together, melded with sticky wetness to each other as we rocked together, as I rode him, my strong huge stallion, still gentle in his counter-thrusts while I grew increasingly wild on top of him, plummeting up and down with increasing speed, sliding wetly up and down him. His fingers grew more urgent, harder pinches, more abundant squeezes paced and metered to my cries, my needs, my heated murmured response of "Oh, yes . . . like that . . ." Then just his name, "Amber," and my need to forget, to only feel. A gentle slide up, a harder thrust down, pushing his thick length back in. "Yes." Like that.

Light glimmered through my closed lids as we began to glow. He picked up the rhythm, shoved himself the tiniest bit harder inside me as I rocked and swiveled and gyrated above him. Harder, faster, taking him all, taking him fully, taking him deep, a part of me forever.

"Amber!" I cried as he touched me, the rough gentle-ness of his fingers sliding over my swollen nub, prominent now, button-hard. A sizzling stroke that sent a sharp bolt of pleasure through me, making me gasp, making me open my eyes. A gentle squeezing pinch over my swollen clit, a gentle forceful drive into me at the same time, sending me flying into climax.

A moment of suspended breath, of suspended pleasure.

Then bursting ecstasy, wracking shudders, spilling cries . . . and the horrible realization, as I gazed down and felt him follow me into spilling release, that he glowed—and I didn't!

TWENTY

WORDS CAME LATER with terrible awkwardness.
"Did I . . . please you?" Amber asked uncertainly.
He asked because when Monères had sex, they glowed, but only if they felt pleasure. I hadn't glowed.

"Yes, you pleased me. You saw . . . felt me come."

"But you didn't—"

"No, I didn't glow." My smile was bittersweet as I realized that things weren't as bad as I thought—they were worse. Much worse.

"Maybe I was too gentle."

I laughed, a far from happy sound. "No, you were perfect." I kissed him lightly, poignantly, trying to say *I'm sorry, it's not your fault* in that tender gesture. Maybe even a silent good-bye.

"I'm going to take a shower." I slipped out of bed.

The water ran over me, washing away the musky smell of sex, of remembered pleasure, making me feel washed away as well—washed of everything that I was.

I've lost everything. Everything . . . even Amber.

Human weakness, human frailty—that might have been workable. No matter my other shortcomings, I could have still been their Queen . . . as long as I could Bask. As long as I could draw down the renewing rays of the moon and share it with my people. I couldn't now. I couldn't glow. That inner luminous shine of the moon kept as a reservoir within our bodies was no longer in me. I no longer held the moon's light.

A part of me wondered if I was no longer Monère, just human now. Another part of me said it didn't matter. I was useless to my people. Whatever I was, I was useless to them.

Drying off, I went back into the bedroom and found Amber naked, waiting for me. "Tell me what I did wrong?" he said, eyes worried.

"You did nothing wrong, Amber. The problem is with me, not you. Why don't you take a quick shower," I suggested quietly, pulling on my clothes. "And I'll explain everything downstairs. Not only to you, but to the others also. They'll need to know."

It was the hardest thing to leave, to walk away from him. Shutting the door softly, I walked downstairs.

TWENTY-ONE

ONTAINE AND AQUILA were the last to arrive. All the rest of my family—Chami, Tomas, Rosemary, Tersa, Jamie, and Thaddeus—were already in the front parlor. Nolan and his wife, Hannah, our healer, were also there. They, too, had a right to know. Exactly what, I was still working out. Lots of secrets I had to keep, but some . . . most . . . just didn't matter anymore. If what I suspected was true, I would no longer be with them much longer. So I told them many of the things I hadn't told them before. I told them about Mona Louisa becoming demon dead—not *how* she had become that way, but that she simply was. Everyone just assumed it was through the usual way—that she died and made the transition to demon life.

When I told them that Mona Louisa's demon essence had somehow become a part of me, and my brother asked, "How?" I told him, told everyone, that it was a demon secret I had sworn not to reveal.

"Sworn to who?" Chami asked.

"To Halcyon and to the High Lord."

That I was acquainted with the reclusive High Lord of Hell didn't seem to faze my men at all, though Nolan and his wife seemed shocked by the knowledge. But then my men knew that I had gone down to Hell twice before. They likely thought that Mona Louisa's demon essence had blended with mine during one of my trips there. I could imagine Monère mothers, generations from now, telling their children my sad story as a lesson for living Monère never to mix with the demon dead—both literally and figuratively. Not only had I gone down to Hell, the first Monère—well, the first Mixed Blood Monère—ever to do so, but I had mated with the Demon Prince and become part demon in truth. Just desserts, many would no doubt say.

"Mona Louisa's demon essence inside me was why I was whisked down into NetherHell. That's apparently where she belonged. And the dheu part of her, the damned demon part of her inside of me, was what wouldn't let me cross the doorway back into Hell."

"So how did you come back?" Thaddeus asked.

"Halcyon. He and Gryphon found me. When I couldn't pass through the doorway separating the realms, he ripped the demon part of her out of me. I was able to cross into Hell, and from there, into the Living Realm again. But it seems I'm damaged now, not whole. All that makes me Monère is gone—my strength, my speed, my power, all my Monère abilities. I can't even glow anymore. I can no longer Bask. Without that, I cannot be your Queen anymore."

Pin-drop silence. Then a rising jumble of voices. Hannah's voice cut through all the others. "Mona Lisa, if I may, I would like to examine you."

A hush fell over the others. At my nod, she took the seat that Amber vacated for her. "Here, in front of everyone?" she asked.

"Yes. Why not?"

She lifted her hands and started with my head, giving a gasp when she touched my forehead. I felt the tendrils of her power sink into me like warm, spreading heat. My sense of everyone had been muted, I realized now, but this power, this inner seeking, I felt strongly.

Giving a soft cry, she jerked her hands away from me, not quickly but slowly, as if something sticky tugged her to me and was loathe to give her up.

"What's wrong?" Nolan asked sharply.

Hannah gazed at me mutely.

"Go ahead," I said. "You can tell everyone what you sensed."

"Sensed is a good word," Hannah said, her voice slightly tremulous. "That brief touch only allowed me a glimpse of your inner wounding. Your energy . . . aura, I suppose would be the best word for it . . . is severely damaged."

"Is that why you pulled away from me like that?"

"No, I drew back so abruptly because that wound in your aura drew on my energy with unexpected force when I touched you."

"Is that usual?" I asked, frowning.

"Far from it."

"Then, why did it happen?"

"Your body is trying to heal itself. Do you feel any better?"

I searched inwardly. "No, it feels the same. Like this raw, open wound. How about you? Did touching me hurt you?"

Hannah shook her head.

"Then why are you trembling?"

"Because you siphoned off quite a bit of my healing energy. I wasn't expecting that. Didn't even know it could be done."

She reached her hands out to me once more.

"Whoa, just a second," I said, leaning away from her.

"If I just siphoned off enough energy to make you this shaky, why are you trying to touch me again?"

"I wasn't prepared for it the first time," Hannah said. "I should be able to control it better, now that I know what to expect. I'd like to examine you again, more thoroughly this time, and see if my energy helped you in any way."

Because I wanted to know as well, I agreed. "All right, but if you can't control it, you release me right away, understood?"

She nodded and her fingertips rose to hover just over my face. I felt that warm, healing energy floating just out of reach. She ran her fingers down the sides of my neck, touched briefly. A small jolt of energy passed between us—was drawn out of her. She lifted her fingers away and continued down my body.

"Lift up your T-shirt, please, milady."

When I did, I felt the warm, teasing presence of those hands slide above my abdomen, not touching, just gliding an inch above my skin, assessing my aura. A brief touch over my belly, and another small jolt of energy passing between us. She moved down my legs.

"If you can remove your sneakers and socks, milady."

I kicked off shoes and socks, and lifted my bare feet up. Hannah passed her hands over my toes and continued down over the soles. Lightly, she grasped the bottoms of my feet. One last surge of siphoned energy, and she released me.

She sat there bravely beside me, inches away, while I felt my body's hunger for her energy. Had I been her, I would have scooted back, far out of reach. "What's the verdict, Doc?"

"It is as you say," Hannah said. "You have a raw, open wound, leaking out energy, not just your own but what you took from me as well. All of my healing energy, transferred to you, seems to have washed right out of that hole in your aura."

"So I'm like a broken cup that can't hold water," I said.

"I've never seen an injury like this. I don't even begin to know how to heal it, but I could try."

Try . . . and die, I thought. "No, if what I took out of you did nothing, any further attempts would not only be useless but possibly very dangerous for you." A brief hesitation. "Will I get better on my own?"

"I don't know," Hannah answered. "I would have to examine you over a course of days, maybe weeks. See if you continue to leak away your energy or start to conserve it better."

I sighed. "Nothing to do but wait and see then. I have a leaking hole that you cannot plug. I think if you tried, my body would likely drain you dry, for no purpose, no gain."

"You're not even going to try to let her heal you?" Dontaine asked angrily.

"She just did, not entirely voluntarily, and she wasn't able to heal me. I don't think conventional healing will be able to help me."

"If not conventional healing then what else?" he asked.

"I was thinking of Hell, the High Lord. He's a gifted healer. He may be able to help me. If not," I shrugged, "then NetherHell, if I can find a way to return there. Try to find Mona Louisa and merge us back together again." My announcement seemed to stun everyone.

"How would you be able to find Mona Louisa again?" Aquila asked. A logical question from my practical business manager. "Didn't her essence dissipate when she was separated from you?"

"Ah, no. Once Halcyon pulled her out of me, she became her own separate being." With the solidifying touch of a gargoyle. But no one here needed to know that. Or how unlikely it was that I would be able to reverse the process, if I could even find her, or go back there in the first place.

"But if you fuse her back into your aura, you won't be able to return here again," Thaddeus said. "You won't be able to leave NetherHell."

"That's correct. If I can fix my problem"—and that was a really big *if*—"I'll be stuck in NetherHell."

"How likely is it—returning to NetherHell, finding Mona Louisa, and merging the two of you back together? How good are your chances at accomplishing all of those things?" Thaddeus asked intently.

I took a deep breath. "Not very good."

"Then why don't you just stay with us," my brother suggested. "See first if you can heal this wound on your own."

"Even if I did that, I still have to let the High Queen's Council know of my condition so they can start making arrangements to have another Queen take over. If I still can't Bask by the time the next full moon rises, I'll have to step down."

"I can Bask," Thaddeus said into the sudden silence.

Only Nolan, Hannah, and Dontaine were surprised—the only ones here who had not witnessed that miraculous occurrence. A secret we had kept successfully hidden until now.

"Thaddeus—"

"It's all right, Lisa. You don't have to protect me or keep it a secret anymore. Not now when it's what our people need and something I can contribute. I can Bask but I can't lead our people the way you do. Stay here, continue to be our Queen, and let me Bask for you."

"Thaddeus . . . I don't want to have your life change so drastically."

"It would change as drastically if another Queen took

over," he said. "I doubt a new Queen would let you stay here."

"You could have a normal life," I said. "A normal human life. You could go away to Harvard, like your parents wanted you to."

"And let everyone here be taken over by a new Queen, or dispersed or combined with another territory? Not just ours, Mona Lisa, but Amber's also? Lisa, don't do anything hasty for now. Just give yourself time. Give *us* time. Stay here with us."

"The way I am? Weak, powerless, with no light in me, unable to Bask?"

"You are still our Queen, the one we all look to," Dontaine said, kneeling in front of me. "Let the men and me be your strength and power. Let Thaddeus Bask for you." He took it on blind faith, Thaddeus's outrageous claim.

"Then what do you need me for?"

"To be the heart and soul of our people. To be our Queen, our lady, our familiar head," Dontaine said. "Without your presence, the people might not accept Thaddeus."

Stay here and ease Thaddeus's transition to power, Dontaine was subtly suggesting. Help our people—and the High Council—to accept him. That, indeed, was a powerful inducement.

"Thaddeus," I said, looking at my brother, "your life would change forever."

He actually laughed. "As if it hasn't already, sis. I'm sure about this. It's what I want."

I looked from Thaddeus's earnest face to the others. "What do the rest of you want?"

"The same thing," Amber said. "Be our Queen, our anchor, and let Thaddeus Bask in your place."

"You can still seek help from the High Lord," said Dontaine.

"Hell is fine," Tomas added in a surprising about-face. My men had hated me going down there before.

"Just don't go back to NetherHell," said Chami.

When comparing Hell to NetherHell, I guess Hell came up smelling like roses.

"NetherHell sounds like a terrible place, milady," Rosemary muttered.

"Awful," Jamie said, grimacing.

"Stay," Tersa murmured softly.

All of them in accord.

"All right," I said. "I'll stay."

TWENTY-TWO

I T WAS HARD to be human. I didn't know how normal
people did it, being ill. Waiting endlessly for the days to
pass, to heal, to get better. But unlike a normal human, I
did not heal, not as they did, drearily slow though the process was.

I had been spoiled all my life, I realized now. A funny
insight to have, considering the difficult time I had growing up in foster homes. But I had been. Since I was young,
I had always had my strength, my speed, my sharper
senses . . . always a little bit more than others. A lot more
after I hit puberty. And I'd always been special in some
way. I used to think of myself as different, but different is
special. Only now did I see that, when I no longer was.

A week passed and I did not improve as I had hoped I
would. A small part of me had thought that I would be able
to heal on my own. I was used to being strong. Used to saving the day. Used to being different, even among people of
my own kind. I think that was the hardest part, having that
specialness ripped away from me. What I was now was

weak, normal, mundane. I was common now. No different from three billion other people, no different from any normal Half Blood in terms of strength, of power, of specialness.

I had been arrogant. I'd never known how much courage it took to be the weakest one. To live among others all stronger than you.

When it finally dawned on me that this might be it for me, this ordinariness forever, it changed everything. Nothing else changed, only in my mind. Only in my perception of myself—from strong to weak, from special to ordinary, from Queen to common Mixed Blood. Nothing else really changed, and it was harder than if it had. Like waiting for the other shoe to drop.

My blinders were off after one week of no improvement, of no healing. My people's blinders were still on. Those who were closest to me, they still treated me as if I were special.

Amber was here three days out of the week now, the other four days spent back in his territory. He alternated with Tomas and Aquila, who had become his pinch hitters during this crisis. When he was with me, the other two were in Mississippi. When Amber was gone, Dontaine was there, watching over me. My two Monère lovers. My personal protectors. They both treated me like spun glass, easily breakable. But in all other ways, they treated me the same—as if I was desirable, attractive. As if I were still their Queen.

Oddly enough, it was hardest to bear from Dontaine. Amber and I had a longer relationship, a love more deeply grown. My relationship, my love with Dontaine, on the other hand, was new, freshly fragile, much more easily broken. That it hadn't yet surprised me. That he persisted in his courtship made me feel guilty, if what I was begin-

ning to suspect was true—that I would never again be
what I once was.

I spent more time with Tersa and Jamie, keeping them
company. Or rather the other way around—they kept me
company while they did their chores. They refused, utterly
refused, to let me help them. Had been horrified, in fact,
when I had offered to lend a hand. When I realized I was
not only slowing them a great deal but that my hovering
presence was making them feel terribly awkward, I gave
up my attempt to seek comfort for myself. And it had been
comfort I had been selfishly seeking. I wanted to be with
others as weak as me. To see and understand how they did
it—moved around a world where others were so much
stronger.

My brother was thankfully more comfortable in my
presence, and we carved out a routine, grabbing a drink
and snack at the diner near the library just before sunset,
then driving back home in time for the main meal. I treasured that time spent with Thaddeus, but he wasn't truly
weak like I was. He was a Mixed Blood, but he was special
as I had been and no longer was.

Only among other humans did some of that tension ease
in me. Only among them did I finally relax. Only among
them was I among people as weak as I.

I started venturing out more to New Orleans. Nothing
like the hustle and bustle of the French Quarter if you
wanted to be among people. But not on the days when Amber was with me. On those days, I was, for the most part,
happy and content to stay at home and be with him. I'd
taken him once into the city, into the rowdy French Quarter when I had gotten restless, and it had been a disaster.
Amber had flinched at every sound. Hated the casual
chaos, the vast number of people, and what he saw as an
overwhelming number of threats to my fragile self. He'd

actually growled at people who had lightly brushed me in passing. By the time we left, a short ten minutes later, he had been sweating, his entire body tense as if he had just endured an arduous ordeal.

Funny that what made me feel safe, being lost in a crowd of people, made him feel most threatened—not for himself but for me. One person, he said, could not guard me adequately enough. He had gruffly offered to bring along more guards the next time I wished to venture into the city. I had smiled and said I was happy to stay at home . . . on the days he was with me. When Dontaine was with me, though, that was when I quenched my need to bury myself among people.

Maybe it was growing up here and having so much Monère-owned business based in the city that gave Dontaine the ease he had, moving among the crowded populace of New Orleans—because he'd done it all his life. Whatever the reason, he walked down Bourbon Street, Royal Street, and the rest of the crowded thoroughfares of the French Quarter as if he owned them, guiding us through the crowds with an ease and surety that Amber had not possessed.

The first day we lingered at Jackson Square, listening to a jazz band playing there, then wandered through several antique stores where all the salespeople, for some reason, had been most attentive. In the third store we stopped in, Dontaine asked if I wanted to bring the jewelry box, an exquisite piece that I had stopped to admire, back home with us. I told him that I didn't have enough money on me to make the purchase. Even if I did, I would never have bought anything so expensive. It was fun to look at, but I had no interest in buying anything so pricey. When Dontaine said that I didn't need money, that I owned the store, I suddenly realized why they had all been so attentive. They had recognized Dontaine.

I glanced at the price tag. A mere five hundred dollars—and I wasn't being sarcastic. The jewelry box was one of the least expensive items in the store. A second clerk was busy ringing up the sale of a twelve-thousand-dollar antique writing desk that another couple had just purchased. I know because I had glanced at the price tag when we had first walked in. Frankly, I couldn't imagine paying that much for a desk. To find out that I *owned* the shop, with all its outrageously expensive items, was even more shocking.

"People actually pay these outrageous prices?" I don't know why I asked. Proof was being rung up right in front of my eyes.

Dontaine smiled, while the saleswoman's eyes darted nervously to the couple making the purchase, obviously hoping they hadn't heard my gauche remark, and soured the deal.

"There are always people willing to pay for quality," Dontaine murmured quietly and steered me out the door, to the saleswoman's relief.

"What about the first store? Did I own that, too?"

Dontaine nodded.

When I asked, "Any other stores here?" he pointed out a gift shop and a small bank.

"I own a bank?"

"You did not know?"

"No. Aquila wants to introduce me to all my holdings, but we haven't gotten around to it yet. One thing or another always comes up." More like one disaster after another, but I didn't say that.

"Would you like me to show you all your businesses here in the French Quarter?"

Maybe not my businesses for much longer, I thought.

I shook my head. "No need. Let's just enjoy the night." And we did, wandering leisurely around, soaking in the sound, the music, the atmosphere.

The second night, he drove me to the garden district and parked at a street corner. It was more residential, without the hustle and bustle of tourists.

"What are we doing here?" I asked.

"Do you remember when you said that you did not see us as equals in terms of beauty?"

I nodded.

"I thought of a way to remedy that."

I glanced at the beauty salon where we were parked. "What did you have in mind?" I asked with enough wariness in my voice to make him smile.

"Nothing so terribly bad. Just a haircut and a manicure. Painless procedures."

"Maybe for you," I muttered, "not for me."

I hated change. I really did. Having things change beyond my control was one thing. Bringing about deliberate change when there was no need to—that was another entirely different matter. And not only did I hate change, but I was a miser at heart. I didn't like spending money on myself when I didn't need to. On other people, fine. On myself, no. The jeans and T-shirt I had on were over ten years old—old, worn, and comfortable. Familiar, like old friends. And my hairstyle—long, usually in a ponytail, but more recently left loose to please the men—was not only easy but cheap for me. I didn't have to cut my hair often, just trim it a couple of times a year.

"A haircut and manicure are not going to make me as pretty as you, Dontaine."

"You do not know until you try."

For a moment I thought he was joking, but he wasn't. He was utterly serious.

"Why waste everyone's time, effort, and money on something that isn't going to work?" I asked bluntly. "It'll be a dreadful waste of money."

His answer was just as practical and blunt. "You own

the store, you won't have to pay." His tone softened, turned cajoling. "I know you do not feel inclined to do so, but can you not try this for me? Will you not at least allow me this attempt?"

He was shooting for a miracle, and that just wasn't going to happen, not with just a haircut and manicure. But looking at him, so hopeful, so handsome, so fair, with that tender, hopeful look in his eyes, it was impossible to say no.

"Okay," I said, gritting my teeth, "we can try this."

He didn't wait for me to change my mind. Faster than I could blink, he was out of the car and holding my door open. I found myself hustled inside the salon with almost indecent haste. There were quick hellos—everyone seemed to know Dontaine—then I was seated in a chair, a black cape snapped around my neck quicker than you could whistle. It was a highly effective strategy. Harder to say, "Sorry, I changed my mind," wearing that black cape around you. But then that was just probably my suspicious mind. They were probably as speedily efficient with all of their customers.

Once I was seated and draped, the stylist appeared. He was a trim little man in his later thirties, stylishly clothed and groomed. "Fabulous to see you, darling," he said, air kissing Dontaine's cheeks.

I raised an eyebrow. *Darling?*

Dontaine's laughing eyes told me to behave. "This is Melvin," he said, introducing us. "The premiere stylist of New Orleans, a true artist in the field. And this is Lisa Hamilton, my good friend, the lady I told you about."

"Ah, yes," Melvin said, giving me a quick, thorough scrutiny. "A real challenge, but lots of potential, as you said. Daphne," he said to the young woman who had seated me. "Let Antoine know I'll be busy with her for two hours."

When she left to do his bidding, the premiere stylist of

New Orleans ran his hands through my hair, checking its texture and thickness, lifting it and letting it fall from his fingers.

"You can't cut it short," I said, wanting to make that clear before he started.

"Yes, yes, sugar. I know," Melvin said, still concentrating on my hair and what he wanted to do with it. "Dontaine told me I had to keep it at least shoulder-blade long."

I relaxed and didn't say anything more after that. I mean, what could he do, length-restricted as he was? Not much more than trim it, right?

Wrong. Really wrong. I got an idea of just how wrong I was when he left and returned with a hair-coloring chart composed of different strands of hair ranging from jet-black to white-blond.

"You're going to color my hair?"

Melvin sniffed. "I do not just color people's hair." He held up different shades of brown against my hair, my skin. "I blend colors together like a palette, not just one color but several. Now, hush-hush. Let me concentrate."

I hush-hushed and let him concentrate . . . until he held up some lighter color samples against me.

"Not blond," I said.

"No, sugar." He rolled out the last word, dropping the *r*, so that it came out sounding like *sugah*. "Dontaine said you weren't likely to agree to that." Making me wonder if all that fast efficiency when we first stepped inside hadn't been good strategy after all. "Though you really would look lovely as a blonde," he said hopefully.

"Forget it," I said, scowling.

"Then we will simply lighten the color and add in some highlights."

He lied. It wasn't simple at all. He brushed this alarming rust-colored paste into random bits of my hair, and wrapped it in foil. Then he started to slather this yucky blue paste over all my remaining hair. When I asked if he was dying my hair blue, Melvin laughed, hush-hushed me again, and proceeded to make me look like this bizarrely painted alien antenna. I wondered briefly if all that aluminum foil crunched up around my head would draw lightning during a storm. What a stupid thing that would be, to get struck by lightning. Maybe I was being paranoid but weirder things had happened to me lately. But no storms came. And no angry lightning bolts zapped down from the sky to strike my head.

For once I was thankful for my diminished sense of smell—all my senses were duller now. Even so, the chemical smell was foul. I don't know how Dontaine stood it, but he did, sitting nearby in a chair they had brought out for him. He flipped through a fashion magazine, smiling at me when our glances met—mine uncomfortable, impatient; his soft and tender, indulgent. A look that, along with his attentiveness, screamed *boyfriend*. I got a lot of envious looks from the salon girls, all of them young and pretty. And even from a few older clients busy having their hair done by other stylists.

When Melvin had finally finished applying all the dye, a girl named Tammy came out and did my manicure while the dark wet goop stained its way into my hair.

When she asked me what color nail polish I wanted, I said, "Clear." She glanced at Dontaine. When she got his nod of approval, she briskly and efficiently got down to business, finishing up just as the timer for my hair dinged. They washed the dye out, and sat me back down. I had a brief glimpse of my turbaned head before Melvin spun me around so I was no longer facing the mirror. He took the towel off, and with little scissors in hand, began snipping away. He trimmed the ends, a very simple straight cut across the bottom. I assumed he was finished. He wasn't. He was only getting started. He gathered up a hunk of hair, holding it straight up and out. *Snip, snip* went the scissors, and a clump of hair at least three inches long fell to the floor.

"I thought you were keeping it long."

"I am, sugar. Just adding in some long layers. Lightening up all that thick weight."

He was very detailed and meticulous in his cut. Quite different from what I was used to. At one point, he actually rolled and twisted up different sections of my hair, cutting across the ends of them as he let them untwirl. He spent over an hour on me, the longest haircut I'd ever gotten. No doubt the most expensive, had I had to pay for it.

When he was done cutting, yet another girl came out and set up a camcorder and tripod. She pressed a button and a red light came on.

"You're recording this?" I asked.

"Yes," Melvin said. "So you'll be able to see what I'm doing and duplicate this style later."

"Why don't you just show me how to do it now?"

"It's a surprise, darling," he said, eyes twinkling.

A surprise. Sure. But I could be tactful sometimes. I kept my mouth closed while he gooped up his hands with styling gel, and proceeded to rub it into my hair. Yuck.

The blow-dryer whined as my hair was pulled in all different directions by a twisting, twirling brush. If Melvin or Dontaine thought I was going to do this every day, they were delusional.

Finally, the whining blow-dryer clicked off. My neck was dusted off, and the protective cape removed. Finished, I thought. But I should have known better by now. Before I could move, another little man came striding up. He was pretty like Melvin, and flamboyantly gay. Shadow accented his eyes, mascara darkened his lashes, and ruby color brightened his lips and cheeks. He was darkly complected, both skin and hair, with a slim oval face and these really high, sculptured cheekbones like Prince, the singer, before he became know as the Artist Known as . . . whatever.

He sauntered up to us and air kissed first Melvin, then Dontaine, who stood up to greet him. I stood as well as Dontaine introduced me to Antoine.

Instead of shaking my hand, he kissed it. "A pleasure, mademoiselle." His eyes shifted to Dontaine. "And a real challenge, as you said. Yes, yes." He gave me that same scrutinizing look that Melvin had given me, but this one didn't stop at my neck, it continued all the way down to my feet. "Wonderful, wonderful," he said, eyes traveling back up to my face. "You have begun the process, my dear Melvin. Now I will finish it."

"You will?" My voice was careful. Not angry, exactly, just careful.

"*Oui, oui.* Just put yourself in my hands and all will be fabulous." He beamed at me. I didn't beam back. I just looked at Dontaine. Demanded an explanation.

"Antoine is an exclusive dresser."

"A dresser?" I asked. I'd never heard of the term.

"*Oui,*" Antoine said, nodding proudly. "I dress the rich and famous in our fair city, those fortunate enough to have my services."

Not a shy one, our Antoine.

"He's also a very talented makeup artist," Dontaine continued.

Antoine fluttered his long mascaraed lashes up at Dontaine. "You flatter me, *cher.*"

One look at Dontaine's beautiful, pleading green eyes and all the resistance went out of me. I nodded, giving my permission. Why the hell not? I was here. Antoine was here. I'd had my hair and nails done, why not makeup and clothes? I wasn't entirely pleased at how Dontaine had sprung it on me, bit by sneaky bit, but truthfully, had he tried to ask me ahead of time, I would have likely flat-out said no.

"What would you like me to do?" I asked.

"Just sit. Sit and put yourself in my hands," said Antoine.

I sat. Another seat, a high one, was brought out, along with a table tray for Antoine. He laid out a huge makeup box on the table, filled with all brand-new items.

"First, cleansing." Antoine talked me through the entire process while the video camera blinked red at me. Then face cream was applied. He chose a foundation, the lightest one, smearing it all over my face and neck with a triangular sponge. Ick. I sat through everything he did with a stony, unsmiling expression that must have been perfect for all he did, because he didn't ask me to change it, not until it came time to apply the lipstick.

"Open your mouth a little. That's it," he murmured, penciling in the outline, then filling in the rest of my lip color with a tiny brush.

Eye shadow was simply closing my eyes. Eyeliner was a "Look up" and "Look down." The most uncomfortable part was curling my eyelashes, and then gluing on a set of false eyelashes. It took about thirty blinks to get used to the odd feeling of my eyes after they were applied. I shot Dontaine a glare that said, *I cannot believe I'm letting them put this shit on me!*

Dontaine smiled soothingly, serenely back at me. Easy for him to do. He wasn't getting his face painted or eyelashes glued on him. Crap! I wondered how many times I'd have to scrub my face to get all this stuff off me.

With hair and face done, I was whisked into a back office where an entire rack of clothing hung. Even more clothes had been draped over two chairs.

"I am not trying all those clothes on," I said, flatly balking.

"No, no, of course not," Antoine soothed, his tone distracted as he flipped through the thick rack of clothes. "I brought extra sizes just in case Dontaine's guess was off, but it isn't. Here, try this on." He thrust gold slacks and a light green oriental silk shirt into my hands, and closed the door behind him.

I changed, grumbling a bit, but only a tiny bit. It could have been much worse, like one of the long formal gowns I saw hanging on the rack.

When I opened the door and walked out of the room, the men froze. A look flashed in Dontaine's eyes, something I couldn't read. Something that made me wish suddenly for a mirror so that I could see what he saw.

Antoine clapped his hands and trilled, "Perfect!" Then added, "Well, almost. Shoes. All you need now is shoes. Sneakers so do not go with that outfit." Going to the clothing rack, he unzipped the plastic end section, revealing eight sets of shoes sitting neatly in layered cubbies. He grabbed the ones in the third cubby, delicate ivory ballet slippers, and handed them to me. "Try these."

There was nowhere to sit. Dontaine solved the dilemma by kneeling. "Allow me."

I opened my mouth to say, "Don't be silly, I can put on my own shoes," but closed my mouth, the words unsaid, at that look again in his eyes. It was as if he bespelled me, but he didn't, not really. He just *looked* at me that way, and I allowed him to unlace the sneaker, slip it off, and lift my right foot onto his thigh. He slid his hand slowly up the pant leg until he touched my bare skin. He made the gesture of removing my sock and cradling my bare foot in his hand more intimate than it should have been. In a graceful, chivalrous gesture that made me feel a bit like Cinderella, he slid the slipper onto my foot. A perfect fit.

He lifted my other foot to his thigh, and my hands went to his shoulders for balance. The slight buzz of touching him made my hands tingle. He bared my other foot, cupped it in his hand, then the cool satin lining of the other shoe slid over my skin.

"Perfect," Dontaine murmured, looking up at me.

"What's perfect?"

"You." He stood up and drew me down the hallway. "Come see what I see."

Antoine was waiting for us back in the salon; he'd slipped away without my noticing. I froze as I looked beyond him and caught a glimpse of myself in a mirror.

A stranger looked back at me, and she was beautiful. Strikingly so, like a model. The makeup had been boldly applied, with no attempt at being subtle. Dark eye shadow and heavily smudged liner brought out my eyes, heightened their exotic slant. The long fake eyelashes—that did not look fake at all—made my eyes appear deep, stunning pools of mystery. Blush carved out my high cheekbones, and red lipstick made my mouth fuller, poutier. My hair was full and wild, wisping in artful layers about my face instead of hanging straight and heavy. The color, though, was the biggest change. My dark hair had been lightened to a deep shining bronze, and streaked with blond and gold highlights, a color theme echoed by my clothes.

Under Tersa's lightly applied makeup, I had been pretty. In NetherHell, I had been lovely in a delicate, flawless-skin kind of way. Now, in these clothes, with this bold, unsubtle makeup, I was drop-dead gorgeous. Sensual and sophisticated. Like one of those women that appeared in glossy ads.

"Wow! I don't know what to say."

Others didn't have that problem.

"Stunning," said Melvin.

"Beautiful," oohed the salon girls.

"Divine," cooed Antoine. "Devastatingly divine."

"You guys are miracle workers," I said.

Melvin and Antoine didn't argue with me. Just nodded their heads in preening agreement.

I still couldn't believe what I saw, what they'd made me. I touched a hand to my face to make sure that divine reflection was really me.

Antoine pushed a tissue into my hand. "No touching, *cher.* Wipe your fingers, that's a good girl. You don't want to get any makeup smeared on your clothes." Sitting me back in the chair, he turned the video camera back on and proceeded to give detailed instructions on how to remove the makeup, pointing out different bottles of cleansers to use for each part of my face—eyes, lips, and lastly skin.

"I don't think I'll be able to remember everything," I said, overwhelmed.

"That's why we're videotaping this, *cher.*" Antoine popped the DVD out of the camcorder, slid it into a clear plastic case, and handed it to me like a precious gift. "For you, along with everything here in this case." He gestured to the large makeup box.

"You're giving me all this stuff? That has to be over five hundred dollars' worth of products in there."

"Try a thousand," Antoine said lightly.

I gulped. "I couldn't possibly take it. It would be a waste to give it to me. Even with the videotape, I doubt I'll be able to do what you guys did."

"I'll help you learn," Dontaine said. "Just take it and say thank you." That look again in his eyes.

I said thank you, hugged Antoine and Melvin, and allowed Dontaine to usher me out into the car in a near daze. Antoine and an assistant followed us out, both of them loaded with an armful of clothes, which they laid out on the backseat.

"What's that?" I asked, twisting around to look.

"Some outfits to go with your glamorous new look," said Antoine, winking. "Also some shoes in this bag, and hair care products from Melvin in the other. *Ta ta*, darling. We'll see you in a month."

"A month?" I said.

"Yes, of course. Your roots will need touching up by then." He threw me a bright smile and closed the door.

"My roots?" I asked as we pulled onto the road, waving to a beaming Antoine.

"He meant the roots of your hair, the darker portion of your hair as it grows out."

"You mean I have to do this every month?" I must have sounded as horrified as I felt because Dontaine flashed me a smile.

"Not the whole procedure you went through today. Just some dye along the roots of your hair once a month."

Maintenance—that was a whole other concept I wasn't ready to deal with yet. I was still trying to wrap my mind around the amazing transformation. I flipped down the mirror and gazed at my reflection. "I can't believe that's me," I mused. "It's not, really. It's the clothes, the painted hair and painted face."

"Most beautiful people do not look the way they do without a lot of help," Dontaine observed beside me.

"You look stunningly handsome without any help from makeup."

"But my hair has a good cut and style, and I wear clothes that were carefully selected to complement my coloring and build. Without all that effort and attention to detail, I would be much more common looking."

"That's hard to believe."

"Believe me. It is far easier to look bad than it is to look good. Effort must be put into looking good, for everyone. With only one change, a bad haircut, a handsome actor can be transformed into a cold and unattractive killer, like in the movies. I considered," he said, glancing at me, "letting you see me in an unflattering light, but could not bring myself to do so."

"Vain, Dontaine?" I said, teasing softly.

"Utterly. With my suit already so untenable, I could not bring myself to willingly give up the few advantages I have."

"It's not a contest or a competition, Dontaine."

"Is it not? Of the men you have chosen, one is the ruler of Hell. The other two are Warrior Lords."

"Amber and Gryphon were not Warrior Lords when I met them," I pointed out.

He looked surprised, as if that had not occurred to him before. "I stand corrected," he said thoughtfully. "However, to return to my original point, how much effort it takes to look your best does not matter so much as the final result—what you can become. Even with the same exact treatment you just had, many women still would not be able to look the way you do now. The bone structure, flawless skin, slender build—you already possessed all that. The makeup and clothes and hair simply drew out your natural beauty, made it more visible to others."

"But I don't look like this every day."

"The important thing is that you *can*."

He parked the car and came around to open the door for me.

"Where are we going now?" I asked.

"To have dinner. I told Rosemary that we would be dining out tonight." He offered his arm and I took it. And with that one gesture, I suddenly felt nervous and self-conscious, like I was going out on a date.

We drew looks as we walked down the street. How could we not with Dontaine by my side. But this time it wasn't just women who gazed at us, it was also men. And most of the looks, not all but most of them, were for me and not my gorgeous-looking companion. For the first time in my life, I drew looks. Registered on men's radar—human men—in a way I never had before.

"They are finally seeing you the way we have always seen you," Dontaine murmured.

"I always looked this beautiful to you?"

"Yes. We can perceive you with senses other than our eyes."

"I know all Queens emit aphidy." A substance similar to pheromones. A thought occurred to me. "Do I still have that? Aphidy?" I asked, and saw the answer in his eyes.

My aphidy was gone, another Monère part of me lost. "Then why?" I asked, feeling shaken, confused, lost. "Why on God's earth do you still *want* me?"

I poised to run from him, faced with yet another devastating piece of me gone. But he was there, so fast, his hands gently grasping my arms, holding me still, not letting me turn from him. His face was tense, harsh, his eyes burning.

"Because you offer something even rarer than power or aphidy. You offer something that few other Queens offer— love. You bestow love on all you take under your care. And intimate love to only a few. I saw it once in your eyes for me, and I want to see it again. I need to, as much as I need to breathe air. Mona Lisa, this one thing—love—you have still to give. Do not deny me. Not when my soul needs you, cries out for you."

My heart was pounding in my chest, adrenaline flashing through my system. Fight or flight. Flee . . . or embrace the need I saw before me. And the man who held such yearning need.

Love, he said. The one thing I had left to give. The one thing I still denied him and what he so obviously craved. Had I been that selfish, that blind? Had I been so frightened of losing this new love, of having it ripped from me by death the same way Gryphon had been taken from me, that I pushed it away in the name of unselfishness, when all the while it had been done for the most selfish reason of all? To keep me safe, to keep me protected from loss?

I'd told Dontaine that he was too handsome and I too plain. He had transformed me into something beautiful, striking.

And when I thought I had nothing left to give a man, he told me I still had the most precious thing of all—love.

A man, handsome, loyal, and strong, with a face and body that dazzled the eye, stood before me, wanting me, needing me. And I wanted him, too, in turn but was too cowardly to grab what was being so freely offered to me— love in turn.

Are you going to be a fool and push him away from you yet again? Do you need to lose him, too, before you realize how much you should have treasured him instead?

No! I cried within. "No," I said, and watched as his face fell. "I'm through running away . . . when all this time I should have been running to you."

I murmured his name with aching need, with naked want, feeling all the adrenaline flooding my system shift down a new, more urgent path. Watched his face shift from despair into painful hope.

"What are you saying?" he asked roughly.

"I'm saying yes." And kissed him. Kissed him with love and need. Plastered myself against him and felt an answering tremor pass from that strong body to mine. Felt him stir, grow hard and firm against me.

His hands gripped me, held me away. "Yes?" he asked, his dark green eyes shining almost jewel bright. His mouth was smeared red by my lipstick, like a primitive mark of ownership.

"Yes," I answered.

He turned and pulled me down the street at a pace so quick it was almost a run.

"Where are we going?" I asked.

"To the nearest room."

I laughed. Said breathlessly, "Sounds good to me. You have my lipstick on your lips."

He smiled sharply at me, not faltering in his speedy pace. "Good. When we're through, I want it smeared all over my body." His words, the intent look in his eyes, weakened my knees.

We flew past people who turned to stare at us, and I didn't care. We whipped down two blocks, three. Turned a corner and stopped at the first doorway. Key in hand, he quickly opened the door and pulled me inside, up a flight of stairs.

"This isn't a hotel," I said.

"No, an apartment building. One of ours." Then he was opening a second door and pulling me inside a room. Before the door closed, he had my back against the wall, his body pressed to mine. He groaned at the contact, that hard, strong body shuddering as I wrapped my legs around him and adjusted our bodies so that his hardness notched against my softness.

"Condom," I gasped.

He lifted my left leg higher and pulled something out of his back pocket. "Got one," he muttered and set me back down on the floor so he could undress me.

A terrible thought came to me as he pulled off my shirt. "Maybe I'm completely human now. Maybe we're too different in chemistry to find pleasure together."

His hard body plastered me to the wall again, his hips, his hardness grinding into me. "Does this feel like no pleasure?" he growled, nipping at my lips.

A sweet feeling of need, of building pleasure rippled

through me at that lovely thrust and swivel of his talented hips. "Okay, guess you're right."

I pressed him away, and his weight shifted back, not because of my strength . . . no, I was vividly aware of how little there was of that . . . but because it was my desire and he was not yet entirely certain if I had changed my mind. He stepped back hesitantly, and I tackled his shirt, the reason I'd needed the room, unbuttoning it with swift, hasty speed, pushing it off him.

"Oh, my," I said, looking at the treasure I had unearthed. I moved my hands, my lips, over the lovely expanse of his torso, branded red kisses across the white skin of his chest, and felt his hesitancy melt away. My hands moved to the waistband of his trousers.

"Me, first," he said, and tugged down my dress pants. Easy to do with the elastic-banded waist. Underwear came off next, then my shoes, one foot then the next. Moving in a blur of speed, he draped my pants and top neatly over a chair, and returned to me, kneeling and pressing his mouth to me before I knew what he intended. A swirl of his tongue against my shaved nether lips had me crying out in shock, in weeping pleasure. Then the electric buzz of his tongue licking there over the little bud he had searched out. The sensation of him, of his touch, had me screaming and jerking in a quick, explosive climax.

"I think that answers the question of whether or not we can feel pleasure together." His smile was sharp and feral, an aggressive male intent upon the woman he was about to mate. The sight of him looking up at me like that, with his red lips, branded by me, moist with my body's most intimate fluids, rolled another shudder of gratification through me, inside me.

"Take off your pants," I panted.

He did so with a quick economy of motion, not taking his eyes off me, burning, bright, intense.

I moved my gaze over him—those brawny arms, wide shoulders, wide muscled chest tapering down to a flat abdomen, every part of him strongly cut, perfectly defined. And then lower to where he lay thick and pointed.

My gaze slid hungrily over his shaft. Watched it bob under the hot caress of my eyes. Moved down his bulging thighs, the thick muscles of his calves, the delicate arch of his feet. I moved my gaze just as slowly back up. Licked my lips, smiled. Shook my head when he started to rip open the packet.

"Not yet." Brushing his hands aside, I knelt between his legs. "My turn." My turn to run my hands down the backs of his thighs, to flex my hands there, testing the hard muscle. To sink my short nails in, just a little, into that taut, supple flesh. My turn to lick him, taste him, encircle the thick base of his male organ with my hand and take him slowly, luxuriously, into my mouth. To smear every inch of that hard rosy flesh with the red paint of my lips. To suck and draw on him, and watch that red rosy flesh begin to glow luminously bright, spread from there out to the rest of his body. I watched him glow with lunar light. Watched him glow with pleasure as his hands buried themselves in my hair, gripping tight, pressing my mouth down over him just an instant before he eased me gently back.

"No more, please, or I will go, and I don't want to yet. Not until I'm inside you for the first time."

"You were inside me before."

"But not here," he said, fingering my swollen folds. "Not touching your womb. Not facing you, kissing you, feeling your heart beating hard against mine as I take you. Don't make me wait any longer."

"No. No more waiting."

With his face etched fierce with desire, he ripped open the packet and slid on the condom like a pro. I knew he'd never used one before; I'd had to explain to him what a condom was a couple of weeks ago.

"You practiced."

"Yes," he growled, drawing me to my feet. One easy lift and he hoisted me up, so effortlessly strong, and began to sink me slowly down on his shaft. My legs wrapped tightly behind his back, his waist, and I cried out, my body dancing with little twitches and shudders as I felt him enter me, penetrate me, sink inside me as he kissed me and drank up my cries.

"Look at me," he whispered. My eyes fluttered open, locked with his. How gloriously bright and beautiful he was. A creature of light, all aglow. With his strong body, beautifully handsome face, and blond hair turned almost white in the luminescent light, he looked like a fierce warrior angel. All he needed was a pair of wings and a sword in his hands.

Then he sank into me that last final inch, and all thoughts of angels and wings disappeared and it was just Dontaine and me, this beautiful Monère man making love to me—a creature broken, unable to return his light, though my body tried for one stuttering moment. Tried and failed.

"I can't glow," I sobbed.

"I don't care." He lifted me with those strong hands, careful and aware of his strength. Lifted me up, and let my weight sink me slowly back down onto him. I felt him, every single hard sliding inch of him as my greedy sheath slowly, voluptuously swallowed him back in with fluttering wet pleasure, as his eyes bound us together in even deeper intimacy.

"I don't care," he said, jaw clenched tight. "I don't need you to glow to tell me that I'm pleasing you. I can feel your body's hot, weeping response. I can see every emotion, every feeling in your eyes."

Lift and slide. Eyes locked together. I felt enveloped by him, surrounded by his light. Bonded with him.

"Sweet Goddess," he muttered. "The way you look at me. It almost hurts how nakedly you look at me. And yet I need it, crave it like a starving man. Had to see it again in your eyes."

Another lift. Another slow, wet glide back down.

"What do you see?" I whispered.

"I see your soul—beautiful, generous, and bright. I see that when you share your body, you also share your heart."

"How can it be any other way?"

"Only with you," he said. "Only with you. Sex is not casual for you because you share yourself with so few."

"I have five lovers, Dontaine."

"As I said, few."

I smiled, nipped lightly at his low full lip. "How differently you see things."

"As do you, thank the Goddess. As do you."

A rapid lift and slide. Another, then another, his hands helping now, faster, harder, deeper, his hips lifting and thrusting in thrilling counterpoint to the fast rhythm he set with his hands. And with each deep thrust, each thick slide in, small sounds were pulled from my throat. He held me with such easy strength. Tilted my body forward so that my breasts, the hardened points of my nipples dragged across his chest with each slide down and up. So that my swollen, sensitive clit rubbed against his body with each spearing upstroke. So close together that our breaths mingled in the intimate wholeness of sharing, loving.

"Love me," he cried.

"I do!" And with that final added emotion—love—my arousal peaked, and I splintered into brilliant climax. I closed my eyes. Saw—felt—a spark flicker and die in me— my body trying to match his light, and failing still to glow.

I opened my eyes as Dontaine groaned and thrust even harder into my spasming sheath, his eyes glittering, his face wild and tight. I watched and felt my climax detonate his own. Watched him give himself over to his own heaving, pulsing pleasure, sharing that final intimate moment.

With a soft cry, he pulled me against him, holding me so tight I could feel his heart beating against mine as his light faded back into him. His lips brushed my temple in a tender kiss as tears, both his and mine, mingled together in happiness and sadness. In things both lost and found.

TWENTY-THREE

WE HAD DINNER at a charming restaurant off Bourbon Street. I didn't ask if it was mine. The fact that we didn't need to pay told me that it likely was. On the drive home, we held hands and spoke little. I drowsed, waking as we pulled in front of Belle Vista. A relaxed lethargy seemed to hold me in its grip. Inside the house, I smiled and nodded as the others complimented me on my new glamorous look. As soon as we politely could, Dontaine and I retired upstairs.

He stopped in front of my room. "You seem tired. Should I leave you alone to rest?"

"Oh, no, you don't." I opened my door and pulled him inside. "You're responsible for putting all this stuff on my face. It's up to you now to get it all off." I yawned and plopped into the chair in front of the dressing table as he brought all the things up into my room. "Do you remember what to use for what?"

Thankfully he did. My face seemed oddly naked and bare after it was cleaned. Maybe because of my hair.

Hopefully, once I washed away the salon-perfect style, it would look more like the simple me I was used to seeing in the mirror.

The bed beckoned to me and I crawled onto it.

"Do you want to go to sleep?" Dontaine asked, stretching out beside me.

"It's too early, hours yet before the sun rises." I snuggled against him on top of the bedspread. "I just want to rest here for a little bit, like this, with you holding me."

My last thought was how surprisingly comfortable it was in his arms.

I WOKE UP beneath the sheets, naked, my head resting on top of Dontaine's chest. He was wide awake, a warm smile on his lips, a tender light in those green eyes.

"What time is it?" I asked.

"Six."

"I only slept one hour? It feels longer."

"It is much longer. It's six the next morning."

My eyes popped wide in disbelief. "I slept for over twenty-four hours again?" And yet I still felt so tired.

"You needed it."

"Oh no," I groaned. "I missed dinner! Rosemary's going to kill me."

"You wake up in bed with me and your first thought is of Rosemary's wrath?" He rolled, bracing his lithe, muscular body over me, his weight balanced on his hands, feet between mine.

"I must not be doing things right," he murmured and lowered his body down to brush the lightest kiss above and below—his lips soft and tender over mine, the hard silky rub of him lower down between my legs. It pulled a hungry sound from my throat, and my lips and legs opened wider in invitation.

"Much better," he murmured, rolling away to open the bedside drawer. Grabbing a condom, he ripped it open, slid it on, then slid back on top of me. "Rosemary saved us some dinner, and she's not mad."

"Good." Lifting my head, I nipped those luscious lips hovering so close to mine. "What did you want my first thought to be?"

"Of me." His eyes heated to deep green as he lowered his mouth and kissed me thoroughly, tongue pressing in slowly, delicately. "Of this." His body followed, his full weight sinking me down into the mattress, his arousal seeking its own wet kiss down below. "Of what we are together." The hot slide of his erection in—deep, deeper, deepest. My soft moan, his deep groan.

My lips sealed around his tongue and sucked deep. Down below, inside, I clenched tight with hidden muscles around his throbbing hardness filling me so sweetly, so fully. Felt him flex inside me at the twin embrace in sweet reward.

We moved in languorous rhythm, building the heat slowly. His shimmer of light started as a gentle glow, building with each unhurried stroke, each lazy kiss, some deep, some delicate. Savoring me with contentment in his eyes and happiness. Gone was that yearning intensity, that unfulfilled need. Whatever he had searched for, he had found. Never had things been so easy, so right with us.

His light brightened above me, around me, deep inside me. I felt my body try again to match his light. Sharp rending pain from the torn part of me pulled a soft cry from me.

"Did I hurt you?" His hands cupped my neck, his thumb brushing the side of my face. The pain stopped as soon as my body stopped trying to glow—to express the pleasure he was giving me.

"No, you didn't hurt me."

It was true, he hadn't hurt me, and it came suddenly to me what was so different, what was missing between us—that electric buzzing sensation I had always felt from him whenever we touched. It was missing, gone.

"Dontaine, I don't feel you," I said in surprised realization.

He mistook my meaning and resumed the deep strokes he had stopped in his concern. Green eyes shimmered above me with sparks of energy, energy that I didn't feel from him, only the stroking, the deep push and pull of him rocking above me, inside me. He quickened the tempo, almost brilliant now with light. His hand slid down my chest, brushed over my nipple. He touched me perfectly, expertly. His hips began to plunge in and out of me with rapid weight and speed, thrusting me down into the bed, dipping the mattress with each stroke. I felt him there, only there, at those two crucial points—my beaded nipples that brushed his chest with each stroke, and my tight quivering sheath. And could only lie and take what he gave me, my limbs suffused with an odd languor as my body began to buzz with sensation, not the electrifying spark that usually flared when he touched me, but the simple buildup of heated passion, of cresting pleasure. Cresting then exploding like a bomb inside me, gripping me, arching me back in hard convulsions that spasmed my entire body.

He thrust through my clenching contractions, once, twice, a third time, then with a tight ecstatic grimace, his mouth opening in a silent cry, he gave himself up to release, his hard body shaking, shuddering above mine. His heavy weight came down to blanket me, his arms wrapped around me, holding me in close embrace. I felt his heart beating strong and fast against mine, faster than my own, which was unusual. My base heart rate, already slow by human standards, was usually double his.

As if conscious of my attention on it, my heart slowed

even further, grew even weaker. My sight hazed, my consciousness dimmed.

As if from a distance I felt Dontaine pull away from me. I heard his muffled voice spiraling down to me as if through a long corridor. "Mona Lisa, what's wrong?"

All sound faded until all I heard was the hesitant beating of my heart. *Ba-boom* . . . pause . . . *ba-boom*. A much longer pause. Then nothing, no more beats. Just echoing, empty silence, the silence of my body. The realization—*I'm dying . . . I'm dead.* And nothing with that thought, no emotion, no fear. Just nothing as death claimed me once more.

I'd always thought of death as an active thing. But it was simply a cessation . . . a ceasing.

Into this floating mass of nothingness, crackling energy— excruciating pain—struck me like a lightning bolt through the heart. Sound and sight returned, life resumed, messy and chaotic. My eyes shot open as I gasped in a breath, as my heart leaped within my chest and resumed its slow and labored beating . . . *ba-boom* . . . *ba-boom*. Sound was both loud and muffled—Dontaine's words, fierce and strong, "No! I won't let you go."

His green eyes had changed to silver, I noted distantly. Sparks of light, of energy, so much energy, crackly like tiny lightning bolts in those glittering eyes, lifting his blond hair around his face like an invisible wind. His hands, pressed down over my heart, passed another burst of electrical current through me. It felt like needle-thin knives were stabbing me.

"Ow!" I mumbled. My tongue felt thick and heavy. As were my limbs as I tried to push his hands away. But it was enough to lift Dontaine's hands off my chest. No more jolts of electricity passing like a live current through me. But it still hurt! I looked down and saw that my skin was blistered red and was actually smoking!

The door flew open and people started pouring in—
Rosemary, Chami, Aquila. Dontaine pulled the sheet over
us a second before my brother, obviously pulled from
sleep, rushed into the bedroom.

"What's happening? What's wrong?" Thaddeus demanded, his voice raised up over the others.

"She was dying. Her heart stopped beating," Dontaine
said, his eyes still wild and sparkly.

"He jump-started it, I think," I mumbled weakly, my
voice slurring. "S' tired."

"I'll get Hannah," Rosemary said, rushing out.

The only one in the room that I sensed was Dontaine,
and I likely only felt his energy because he was so close to
me and revved up so extraordinarily high. The others . . .
utterly nothing. I wondered if it was the same in return, if
they felt nothing from me. No presence.

In an amazingly short amount of time, Hannah was
there, pushing her way through to me. I saw her but didn't
feel her, and that inability to sense her was like having one
of my arms or legs amputated.

"Hannah," I slurred, "am I still here?"

"Yes, child. You're still here." She glanced at the others.
"Some privacy, please."

Everyone left the room but Dontaine. "I cannot leave
her in case her heart stops again," he said stubbornly.

"Her heart stopped?" Hannah asked.

"It slowed and then it stopped and she wasn't breathing.
I sent a surge of energy through her heart, and it started
beating again."

Hannah turned back to me, her face, her voice, serene
and gentle. "I'm just going to touch you and examine you,
milady."

She placed her hands around my head. I felt her then,
the dimmest, faintest presence. She ran her hands down

my face, my neck and shoulders, inhaled sharply when she lowered the sheet and saw the red burn marks on my chest. She did a complete head-to-toe exam, and for once I wasn't bothered by being naked in front of her. Exhaustion and worry about what she was sensing . . . or not sensing . . . fretted me more than my modesty.

She covered me with the sheet again and turned to Dontaine. "Tell me everything that happened."

He did, elaborating in far more explicit detail than I liked.

Hannah turned her gaze back to me. "Yesterday, your body did not emit light during sex."

It wasn't really a question, but I nodded anyway. "Not for lack of pleasure," I said, speaking slowly. I found that if I spoke slowly enough, I didn't slur my words. "Felt my body try, though."

"Try what?" she asked.

"To match his light . . . but couldn't."

"You were tired afterward?"

"Slept for long time . . . didn't help . . . just as tired when woke up."

"And when you made love this morning?"

"Didn't glow."

"Did you feel your body try to match his light again?"

"Yes . . . but couldn't. What did you find . . . when you touched me?"

"Your aura, your energy, is dramatically less than it was two days ago when I last examined you," Hannah said. "In the week since you returned to us, you hadn't improved but neither had you worsened much."

"Much?" I whispered.

"Your energy was a tiny bit less each day. I didn't mention it because I was hoping you would stabilize."

Only this morning, I'd had the same thought and had

felt sad that I might be like that for the rest of my life, as weak as a human. Now it seemed like a state of uncommon fitness compared to the condition I'd deteriorated into.

"I made her worse," Dontaine said grimly.

"Having sex, making love, made her worse," Hannah said gently. "It seems to have expended a great deal of her energy each time. She's no longer a closed, regenerating circuit. What energy she loses, she does not seem able to get back."

"Why didn't you tell us this sooner?" Dontaine asked, deeply anguished.

"I didn't know. She's been relatively stable up till now."

"Can you help her?"

"The energy she pulled from me last week—and it was quite a lot—didn't even make a dent then, and she was in far better condition than she is now. I, alone, cannot do much. We must take her to High Court, see if the other healers there can help her. Perhaps with several of us working on her, she might be able to regain some of her strength."

"Regain. Not heal her?" Dontaine asked.

"I do not know if that would be possible, but perhaps the other healers there have more knowledge than I."

"When do we leave?"

"Right away," Hannah said, rising. "I'll phone them, let them know we're coming."

There was a heavy, painful silence after she left.

"'S okay . . . didn't know," I said, my words slurring as I rushed to reassure him.

"It's *not* okay!"

"If not you . . . then Amber."

"But it was me. Oh, Goddess. It was me!"

I reached for his hand clumsily. Felt a faint dim spark when I touched him. "You made me . . . feel beautiful."

Tears rolled down. "I'm sorry. So sorry."

"Me, too," I rasped as strength left me, as my heart slowed and stuttered. "That I wasted . . . so much time."

My vision faded.

Sound stretched out, receded from me as I was pulled back down into a tunnel of silence, into that void of nothingness.

Then sharp pain flashed through my chest, a lightning bolt of sizzling agony. Blurred images of Dontaine's face . . . silver eyes . . . other faces gathered around. Raised voices as I flowed in and out of consciousness. Words floating to me . . . *she's dying . . . the plane . . . too late . . .* Hannah touching me, collapsing to the floor. My body straining for each breath, each laboring heartbeat.

My brother's voice, "Let me help. I have some healing ability." Rousing panic as I fought to speak, to mutter, "No!" Relief as I saw Chami hold him back—Thaddeus's protector, someone to look after him when I was gone.

But who will look after Dontaine? I wondered. *Absolve him of a guilt that should not be his to bear?* That I regretted the most.

I was dying, I realized vaguely, and found the process immensely painful. Not the physical aspects, though that was no picnic. More the mental anguish it caused the others, and how my death would hurt them, all of them— Amber, Gryphon, Halcyon. Dante—Nolan's son.

"Hannah?" I managed to whisper. A weak sound, one I barely heard myself.

"She's okay," Rosemary reassured me. "Just fainted."

The crowd around me shifted, parted, and I saw a face . . . two faces in the doorway that made me seriously wonder if I hadn't died already, passed into death without being aware of it. Either that or I was hallucinating. I blinked and saw them still—a gray gargoyle and a ghost I never expected to see again: Gordane carrying Mona Louisa in his arms, saying, "Let me through," and, "Do not touch me. Not unless you wish to be turned to stone."

Mona Louisa looked as bad as I felt—weak, faint, dying.

"You real?" I asked.

"Yes, we're real," Gordane said. He knelt next to me, Mona Louisa cradled in his arms.

"How . . . cross gate?"

"I brought her another way when she collapsed and continued to fade in substance even with my continued touch. I knew that only you could help her."

Even in my confusion and disbelief, I saw how carefully Gordane held her, with a tenderness that was surprising, and how trustingly she lay in his massive arms, her fingers, so slim and fragile in comparison, delicately holding his thick wrist. Her eyes looked at me through half-closed lids.

"You're both dying," Gordane rumbled.

I wanted to argue that Mona Louisa was already technically dead, but didn't bother wasting my energy or breath.

"You must combine together again," Gordane said.

"How?" I whispered. I felt a tug of awareness, a pull toward her, but didn't know if I could do that, merge us back into one. I looked at her, wan, waning, just like me. "You agree . . . to this?"

Her ice blue eyes glinted at me. She may have been fading in body, in strength, but her personality was yet strong. "Yes," she whispered.

The last time I did this, I had sucked her essence into me through my mouth. I tried to do that now. But I had lost my ability to do otherworldly things. All I drew in now was breath.

"Can't." I gasped. "Not . . . working."

"Move her over. Give me some room," Gordane said to someone over my head.

Dontaine slid his arms beneath me, shifting me to the center of the bed, and Gordane laid Mona Louisa gently on the bed beside me. As soon as he lifted his hands away from her, she started fading, losing substance.

"Touch her!" Gordane barked. "Touch each other."

We were already instinctively reaching for each other.

The moment our hands touched, something clicked wide in me and in her. Some force reached out and pulled her to me like a magnet. Not physically—she didn't move. But parts of her began to disappear: her hair, the side of her body that was farthest away from me. Not fading away but rather being absorbed into me. Flowing her into me through our connected hands.

"Never thought I'd be so glad to see you again," Mona Louisa whispered with a mocking smile, her usual cynical self. But the look in her eyes when she turned to look at Gordane was new, different—softness and yearning . . . filled with regret. "Farewell," she whispered. Then the rest of her flowed into me like a fine mist, like a wonderful healing balm slathered on my invisible wound, and that deep inner ache disappeared.

I was healed. I was well. I could feel everyone's presence. And I was so incredibly tired, as if my body had just run a marathon, and maybe it had, the equivalent of one, at least, in its efforts to hold me to life. Now that my body didn't have to fight so hard anymore for each breath, each heartbeat, all my strained and fatigued muscles suddenly relaxed.

"She's okay, Gordane," I said, my voice no longer weak. "We're okay . . . just really, really tired. Sleep now," I muttered. And did just that.

TWENTY-FOUR

I AWOKE THE next evening to find Amber, Dontaine, and surprisingly, Gordane seated in three chairs arrayed around the bed. I found them a most lovely sight.

I was alive and well, and spent the next ten minutes re-assuring Dontaine and Amber of that. Someone, probably Dontaine, had dressed me in one of the comfortable T-shirts I usually wore to bed, for which I was immensely grateful. My modest tendencies were back in full force, it seemed.

The men were fine until I held out my hand to Gordane, who had been sitting quietly, watching us. He stood and walked to me, or tried to. Dontaine and Amber were suddenly in front of me, two solid barriers of flesh, barring his way. They both jumped when I slid out of the bed and pinched them. "Stop it, you guys. He won't hurt me. He saved my life, remember."

They grudgingly moved aside and let Gordane through. Tensed when I reached out and grasped his hand. Relaxed when nothing bad happened.

"Why did you stay?" I asked.

"To make sure you were well," Gordane replied.

"I'm well." I waited expectantly, a slight smile on my face.

"And Mona Louisa?" he finally asked.

"She's well, too. You care about her."

"She was the only one who never truly feared my touch," he said sadly.

My fingers wrapped around his wrist in a familiar-unfamiliar way. "You haven't lost her. Not completely. She's still here, inside me, a part of me." I'd come to peace with that. It was much better than being dead.

Gordane never did tell me how he'd bypassed the gate and made his way to this realm.

"It's a secret," he said, with a roguish gargoyle grin.

I told him not to be a stranger, to visit me, since he so obviously could. And to watch over Miles for us.

"Us?" Dontaine asked, after Amber escorted Gordane out of the room.

"Yes. Both Mona Louisa and I. We intermingled. Even after her demon essence was ripped out of me, there were still bits and pieces of our personality left in each other. She was softer, did you see?"

"And what did you gain from her?"

"You. When I was the most broken, the most weak, the most undeserving of you, my heart said *I want you,* and I reached out and grabbed you instead of pushing you away. I acted selfishly."

His hands reached out, cradled my face. "It's not selfish to reach out for love. It's more selfish to push it away because of fear of getting hurt again."

"You know me so well," I whispered.

"As you do I. You're the only one who ever looked deeper beyond the surface beauty. The only one who gave me a chance to show you who I truly am—not just a pretty face, or the possessor of a rare talent and fertile bloodline.

You expected more of me, and because you did, you made me more." He suddenly faltered. "But perhaps you're right. Perhaps it was selfish . . . me wanting you, pursuing you like that. I almost killed you."

"Odd circumstances," I said dismissively. "We usually gain strength from sex, not lose it."

"It was never just sex for you," Dontaine murmured tenderly. "It was making love. Your heart was fully engaged."

"I love you," I said. No longer did I feel undeserving of him, or fear the pain of his loss. No longer would I try to skim lightly on the surface of life, withholding my feelings, walled up by fear. Life and love were precious, to be grabbed by both hands and a glad heart.

"If you run from me now," I told him, "you won't get far. I'll chase after you."

"Would you?" Dontaine smiled.

"Count on it. I died three times, if you count life by the definition of a beating heart. Two of those times, you brought me back, you wouldn't let me go. You're stuck with me now."

He crushed me to him, and I held him just as tight. I had died three times—I was through running away from love.

I wrapped my mind around the idea of being more selfish, and thought, *I can live with that.*

Yes. I could most definitely live with that.

Turn the page for
a preview of Eileen Wilks's
new paranormal romance

MORTAL SINS

Available February 2009 from Berkley!

ONE

SOUTHERN AIR HOLDS on to scent. Scent is vapor, after all, a chemical mist freed by heat to hang, trapped, in moist air. In his other form, Rule knew this.

In this form he knew only the richness. His world was more scent than sight as he raced through silver-shadow woods, through air heavy with moisture and fragrance. Layers and layers of green overlaid the complex stew of water from a nearby stream with its notes of kudzu, rock, and fish. Rhododendron's subtle vanilla scent jumbled with moss, with dogwood and buckeye and the sugary scent of maple, punctuated by the cool tang of pine.

But it was the musk, blood, and fur scent of raccoon he chased.

A three-quarter moon hung high overhead as he leaped the stream, muscles reaching in exhilarated approximation of flight. He landed almost on top of the prey—but his hind feet skidded in slick red clay. A second later, the raccoon shot up a tree.

He shook his head. Damned raccoons always climbed if they got a chance. He didn't begrudge the animal its escape, but wished he'd had more of a chase first.

Deer do not climb trees. He decided to course for that scent.

Coursing was as much excuse as action. He'd eaten well before Changing, so hunger was distant; the real delight was simply being in motion, reading the world through nose, ears, the pads of his feet.

The human part of him remained, a familiar slice of "I" that was not wolf. He remembered his two-legged thoughts and experiences; they simply ceased to matter as much. Not when air slid through him like hot silk, pregnant with a thousand flavors. It was probably the human part that felt a pang for the wonders of these southern woods, remembering the hotter, drier land claimed by his clan in southern California. His grandfather had made the decision to buy land there for Nokolai's clanhome. In that place and time, the land had been cheap.

It had been a sound decision. The clan had prospered in California. But at Nokolai's clanhome, wolves ran on rocks scattered over hard-baked ground, not on a thick bed of pine needles and moss, through tree shadows surprised here and there by the tumble of a stream.

Rule had run as wolf in many places, yet there was something special about this night, these woods. Something new. He'd never run here as wolf before. Not with Leidolf's clanhome so near.

The spike of worry was real, but fleeting. Wolves understand fear. Worry is too mental, too predicated on the future, to hold their attention. The slice of him that remained man wanted to hold on to that worry, gnawing it like a bone that refused to crack. The wolf was more interested in the day-old spoor of an opossum.

This was why he ran tonight: too many worries, too

much gnawing at problems that refused to crack open and release their marrow. He'd learned the hard way that the man needed the wolf at least as much as the wolf needed the man. These woods were sweet. He'd find no answers in them, but tonight he wasn't seeking answers.

Lily said they hadn't come up with the right questions yet.

Rule paused, head lifted. Thought of her was sweet to both man and wolf. If only she could . . .

He twitched his ear as if a fly had bitten it. Foolishness. Both his natures agreed on that. Things were as they were, not as he might wish them to be. Females did not Change.

An hour later he'd found no deer, though he'd crossed their trails often enough, along with many others—a pack of feral dogs, a copperhead, another raccoon. Perhaps he'd been more interested in the distractions than in the hunt when there were no clanmates to join the chase. He wished Benedict was here, or Cullen . . . wished, though he tried not to, for Lily. Who could never share this with him.

His son would. Not yet, but in a few years. His son, who slept in a nearby town tonight—a town that would not be Toby's home much longer. In four days they would meet with the judge for the custody hearing, and as long as Toby's grandmother didn't change her mind . . .

She wouldn't. She *couldn't*.

Feelings thundered through him, a primal cacophony of bliss, fear, jubilation. Rule lifted his nose to the moon and joined in Her song. Then he flicked his tail and took off at a lope, tongue lolling in the heat.

At the base of a low hill he found another scent. The chemical message was old but unmistakable. At some point in the last few months, a Leidolf wolf had marked the spot with urine. Something more visceral than recognition stirred as the portion of new mantle he carried rose, *knowing* the scent. Welcoming it.

Briefly, he was confused. But the message of the power curled within him was clear: this wolf was *his*.

The man understood this change, had expected it, and memory supplied the reasons, so the wolf acknowledged the change and moved on. He wound up the little hill, bathed in the aural ocean of cricket song, anticipating grass. His nose informed him of a grassy place nearby, a spot where some alteration in soil had discouraged trees.

He liked grass. Perhaps it would be tall and home to mice. Mice were small and tricky, but they crunched nicely.

A thought sifted through him, arising from both ways of being: A few months ago he wouldn't have noticed a scent trace as old as that left by the Leidolf wolf. Had the new mantle coiled in his belly made it possible to sort that scent? Or was it because there were two mantles now? Perhaps this night, these woods were unusually magic because he carried more magic within him.

He would consider that in his other form, which was better suited to thinking. For now . . . at the crest of the hill he checked the moon, aware of time passing and a woman who waited in the small town nearby . . . asleep? Probably. He'd told her he would be gone most of the night.

Part of him thought this was a poor way to spend the night when he could have been in her bed, but there was grass ahead, the chance of a mouse or three. He was here, not there, and it was impossible to regret the night.

It was growing late, though. The fireflies had turned off their glow-sticks and the moon was descending. He would investigate the tall grass, he decided. Then he'd return to the place he'd left his clothing and to the shape that fit those clothes.

The grass was indeed tall, and the pungent smell of mice greeted him as he approached the tiny meadow. Rabbits, too, but rabbits were for days, since they seldom venture out of their burrows in the dark.

A breeze rose, whispering in the grass and carrying a host of smells. He paused, curious, and tested the air.

Was that . . . ? Corruption, yes; the stench of rot was unmistakable, though faint and distant. It meant little. Animals died in the woods. Besides, the smell came from the general direction of the highway. Animals were hit by cars even more often than they died naturally. But was it an animal?

The mantles might help him find out.

They slept now. He wouldn't call them up, not even just the one he considered truly his—that portion of the Nokolai mantle his father had given him years ago. To call one meant both answered, and he'd been warned. Drawing strongly on the portion he held of the other clan's mantle could kill the mantle's true holder, who clung so narrowly to life.

Not that Rule objected to Victor Frey's death. In other circumstances he'd celebrate it, but he didn't want the clan that would come to him with Victor's dying. And neither he nor Nokolai needed the ruckus that would follow.

Could he use the mantles without actually calling them up?

The wolf thought so. The man, troubled by instinct or too much thinking, wanted to try.

With a wisp of attention, Rule woke the twin powers in his gut. He focused again on the trace of scent carried by the breeze, not so much using the mantles as including them in his intention.

That scent sharpened in his nostrils immediately. Not a dog hit by a car, no. Nor a deer brought down by disease. Though the rot-stench overpowered the rest, he was almost sure the body he smelled had never walked four-footed.

Go. The breeze might die, or this new acuity fade. *Go. Find out.*

He launched himself into a run.

Wolves are largely indifferent to death as long as it doesn't threaten them or theirs. The body he chased was certainly dead, so the wolf felt no urgency. But the man did. Rule ran for over a mile—not full-out, not over unfamiliar terrain with no immediate danger or prey. But he was fast in this form, faster than a born-wolf.

By the time he slowed, he knew he'd been right about the highway. He heard cars cruising perhaps half a mile ahead . . . not many. It wasn't a major highway.

But what he sought lay within the woods. The rankness made his lip curl back from his teeth as he approached. Some other scent hid beneath the stench, but even with the mantles' help he couldn't sort it clearly, smothered as it was by putrefaction. Whatever it was, it brought up his hackles and started a growl in his throat.

Unlike some predators, wolves don't sideline as scavengers; only one on the brink of starvation would consider eating meat this rotten. And Rule was too much man even now to feel anything but a sad sort of horror at what lay in a shallow ditch between a pair of oaks.

Not all beasts are so picky, however. And he hadn't been the first to find them.

Two

I N A SMALL, upstairs room in large frame house, Lily Yu was sleeping. She didn't know this.

She knew pain, grief, despair. A sky overhead that wasn't proper sky, but a storm-colored dome, dimly glowing. In that surreal sky, legend battled nightmare—a dragon, dark and immense, grappled with a flying worm-thing whose gaping jaws could have swallowed a small car. The ground Lily knelt on was stone and dirt without a trace of green.

In front of her, unconscious and bleeding, lay a huge silver-and-black wolf.

So much blood. She couldn't see how badly Rule was hurt, but it was bad. She knew it. The demon had ripped him open so thoroughly even he couldn't heal it in time. Rule needed a doctor, a hospital, but there were no hospitals in Hell.

She knew what she had to do. It was a hard knowing, as hard as the stones of this place—and as certain as spring in that other place, the Earth she remembered. The Earth she would never see again.

Another woman knelt across the wolf's ripped and bloody body, a woman bound to Rule as she was bound because she, too, was Lily. Another Lily, the one who could take Rule home.

She looked up now and met her own eyes. "Leave now. You have to go right away and take him where he can heal. To a hospital. He'll die here."

The other-her swallowed. "The gate—"

"Sam told me how to fix it." That's what the dragon had told them to call him. Sam. Was that a bit of desert-dry dragon humor? She'd never know.

So much she'd never know. Never have the chance to learn.

Other-Lily's eyes widened, and Lily saw her own dread knowledge reflected back at her—a certainty the other tried to deny. "There has to be another way."

"Funny." Her lips quirked up, but her eyes burned. "That's what I said." She reached up and ripped the chain with its dangling charm from her neck, the emblem of her bond with Rule. "There isn't, though. You're the gate."

Slowly the other-her held out a hand.

Lily dropped the toltoi charm into it. "Tell him . . ." Feelings smacked into her, a torrent too churned and powerful to sort. She looked down, blinking quickly, and stroked Rule's head. She didn't care that her voice shook. "Tell him how glad I was about him. How very glad."

Other-Lily's fingers closed around the necklace. She nodded, her face stark.

Lily pushed to her feet. She tugged at the top of her sarong, and it came open. "Bind him with this. He's bleeding badly." She tossed it to her other self and took off running. Naked, barefoot, she ran full out.

There were others nearby, too. Rule's friends—a sorcerer, a gnome, a woman he'd once cared for. And there were demons, the demons they fought. Not so many of them yet, but more were coming. Hundreds, maybe thousands more. And there was one demon, one small and insignificant demon, who was something like a friend. A little orange demon named Gan, who wasn't fighting as were the others, and so saw Lily race for the cliff. And understood.

"No!" Gan howled, and started after her. "No, Lily Yu! Lily Yu, I do like you! I do! Don't—"

She reached the edge of the cliff. And leaped.

And as the air rushed past, heavy with the scent of ocean, whistling of terror and death, the dragon who called himself Sam whispered in her mind, *Remember.*

The opening bars of Beethoven's *Fifth* cut through the whistling wind, snatching Lily away from the impact just in time. Her eyes popped open on darkness, her heart pounding in soul-sickening fear. Automatically her hand stretched out for her phone on the bedside table. And bumped into a wall.

That simple, unexpected collision with reality jolted her back the rest of the way, though it took her a second to figure out why her bedside table wasn't where it should be. No, why *she* wasn't where she should be.

Lily had slept in too many beds in too many places lately. Home was San Diego, but she'd recently spent several months in Washington, D.C., getting special training at Quantico . . . among other things. But she and Rule were back in San Diego now, staying at his place. Only this wasn't Rule's apartment.

She was in Halo, North Carolina. This was Toby's home, Rule's son, where he lived with his grandmother, Ruby Asteglio. It was 3:42 A.M., and Beethoven's *Fifth* was Rule's ringtone. She crawled across tumbled sheets to retrieve her phone from atop the chest of drawers. "What's wrong?"

Rule's voice was steady, but grim. "I found bodies. Three of them. Humans. They're in a shallow grave, stacked on top of each other. The adult is on top."

"Shit. Shit. The adult? Then . . . you're sure? Stupid question," she corrected herself, juggling the phone so she could yank off the oversize tee she'd slept in. "I hate it when it's kids, that's all." She paused. Suitcase. Where was her . . . oh, yeah, in the closet. They'd arrived late enough that she hadn't unpacked, so she'd tucked it in the closet.

Lily yanked open the closet door open and dragged out her suitcase. "They're in the woods?"

"About half a mile east of Highway 159, north of town. I'll wait for you at the highway."

"I'll find you." That part would be easy. Like a compass needle knows north, Lily knew where Rule was. That aspect of the mate bond came in handy.

Chosen, the lupi called her—and so did Rule, but not often. Mostly he called her *nadia,* which she'd learned came from a word meaning tie, girdle, or knot. But the lupi meant well when they called her Chosen, believing she'd been selected for Rule by their Lady—a being they insisted was neither mythical nor a goddess, though she seemed to play in the that league.

Nine months ago Lily had met Rule's eyes, the two of them chosen for each other, knotted up together by the mate bond. Nothing had been the same since.

Good thing she'd also fallen in love with him.

Lily wedged the phone between her chin and her shoulder while he gave her more details as she dug out jeans, socks, a tee. Clothes to tramp the woods in. She'd want a jacket to hide the shoulder harness.

When he finished she said, "Sounds like you've found the vics of that murder Mrs. Asteglio told us about. The local cops ought to be grateful, but I wouldn't count on it. Ah . . . it's okay for them to know you found them, isn't it?"

"I didn't call you instead of the local authorities to avoid involvement. I'd have kept you out of this if I could. No, don't argue," he said before she had a chance. "I know you've seen bodies. That's not the point. These bodies . . . there's a small pack of feral dogs in the area."

Oh, ugh. "The dogs dug them up."

"So it looks. Smells that way, too."

"You're sure it was dogs? I'll be asked," she added hastily. He knew she wouldn't accuse him of anything so vile, but others might. "And there are other carnivores around, aren't there? Bears."

"Bears are unlikely at this elevation, and the scent is quite clear. Five distinct canine scents near the grave, though only three are actually on the body. "

"Dogs, then." Lily frowned. Why *had* Rule called her? He could have phoned in a tip anonymously. "What haven't you told me? There's something important you aren't saying. What is it?"

"A smell. In addiction to dogs and decay, there's a smell that . . . but I could be wrong. It's faint, and so smothered by normal putrefaction I can't be sure. You'll be able to tell."

Tell what? Not the nature of the scent, because she'd never notice it. Compared to lupi, humans were all but scent-blind.

All at once she keyed into the phrase he'd used: *normal putrefaction*. "Shit. Oh, shit. Tell me the rest of it."

"Death magic. I'm not sure, but . . . I think the bodies smell of death magic."

ABOUT THE AUTHOR

A family practice physician and Vassar graduate, Sunny was finally pushed into picking up her pen by the success of the rest of her family. Much to her amazement, she found that, by golly, she actually *could* write a book. And that it was much more fun than being a doctor. As an award-winning author, Sunny has been featured on *Geraldo at Large* and CNBC. When she is not busy reading and writing, Sunny is editing her husband's books, literary novelist Da Chen, and being a happy stage mom for her two talented kids.

For excerpts and other news, please visit her website at www.sunnyauthor.com.

The darkly sensual Monère novels
by national bestselling author

SUNNY

"A refreshing, contemporary urban
erotic horror thriller."
—*The Best Reviews*

MONA LISA AWAKENING

MONA LISA BLOSSOMING

MONA LISA CRAVING

"Sizzling . . . [An] intrigue-filled
erotic paranormal."
—*Publishers Weekly*